WHIRLWIND COURTSHIP

"How can you say that?" Amy asked. "We're not ready to have a baby. We've hardly begun seeing each other."

"I didn't say my reaction was logical, Amy. You asked me how I felt and I told you. I wouldn't have minded if you were going to have my baby."

"Oh, Seth!"

"Don't sweat it. You're not pregnant."

"That's not the point. You're thinking way too fast, here."

"It can't be helped. I've never made a secret of how I feel about you."

Her expression incredulous, she returned, "You've never made any secret of the fact that you want me sexually, but we haven't discussed feelings, yours or mine."

"I didn't think I could have been any more clear in how I felt. Why do you think I've been in such a rush with you?"

"It's part of your nature."

"A part I can control if I want. With you I don't want to slow down. I don't see the need because my feelings have been enagaged from the start." He gazed into her eyes. "I love you, Amy. . . ."

BOOK YOUR PLACE ON OUR WEBSITE AND MAKE THE READING CONNECTION!

We've created a customized website just for our very special readers, where you can get the inside scoop on everything that's going on with Zebra, Pinnacle and Kensington books.

When you come online, you'll have the exciting opportunity to:

- View covers of upcoming books
- Read sample chapters
- Learn about our future publishing schedule (listed by publication month *and author*)
- Find out when your favorite authors will be visiting a city near you
- Search for and order backlist books from our online catalog
- Check out author bios and background information
- Send e-mail to your favorite authors
- Meet the Kensington staff online
- Join us in weekly chats with authors, readers and other guests
- Get writing guidelines
- AND MUCH MORE!

Visit our website at
http://www.zebrabooks.com

EVERY DAY

Marie Mosley

ZEBRA BOOKS
KENSINGTON PUBLISHING CORP.

http://www.zebrabooks.com

ZEBRA BOOKS are published by

Kensington Publishing Corp.
850 Third Avenue
New York, NY 10022

All Kensington titles, imprints and distributed lines are available at special quantity discounts for bulk purchases for
sales promotion, premiums, fund-raising, educational or in-
stitutional use.

Special book excerpts or customized printings can also be
created to fit specific needs. For details, write or phone the
office of the Kensington Special Sales Manager: Kensington
Publishing Corp., 850 Third Avenue, New York, NY 10022.
Attn. Special Sales Department. Phone: 1-800-221-2647.

First Printing: November 2001
10 9 8 7 6 5 4 3 2 1

Printed in the United States of America

For Vic
with love
This book was waiting for you.

Thank you, John Scognamiglio, for continuing to believe, and Joyce Flaherty, whose friendship and support I will cherish forever.

To my new family, Lisa and Tricia, and my ever-constant family, Josh, I love you.

Chapter One

There were days, and then, Amy Chandler rued, there were days. This particular Wednesday was definitely one of the latter. The morning had not gone well, and she'd had such high hopes.

But then, she always had high hopes. Ducking her dark blue compact in and out of traffic, she reminded herself that *that* was what she loved most about morning. It was proof positive of the new and the fresh. Anything was possible, including making it from one end of Jefferson Avenue to the other in under ten minutes.

With a flick of a glance into her rearview mirror, she executed one of those maneuvers that would have had her mother gasping. She could just hear the intake of breath followed by the strained admonition: *Amy Elizabeth Chandler, you scare the daylights out of me when you do things like that.*

Amy Elizabeth Chandler had to smile. Her driving had been a source of fright and irritation to her mother—and her father, for that matter—ever since she had been old enough to raise their car insurance rates. Now, at twenty-nine, she paid her own insurance, thank you very much, but her mother still worried. Her father had up until the day he died. He'd be shaking his head at her this morning.

"Bear with me, Dad," she muttered, zipping through the intersection on the tale end of a yellow light. Another blue-eyed glance to the rearview mirror showed no signs of a police car anywhere, and she relaxed her grip on the wheel. The last thing she needed was one more ticket for speeding. She had collected an embarrassing number of them over the years, the most recent just a few months ago. That particular incident had resulted in her being held in contempt of court because, in the rush that was her life, she'd forgotten to mail in her fine. What should have been a thirty-eight-dollar penalty had jumped to a painful seventy-five in the blink of a judge's eye.

Sighing in resignation, she resolutely eased off the accelerator. When was she going to learn to slow down—both literally and figuratively? It seemed that all her life she'd been hurrying from one place to the next, one project to the next, one idea to the next. As a child, she had been deemed a whirlwind bundle of energy. As an adult, the trait was less cute. It was something with which she had struggled for some time.

Reminding herself of all this should have alleviated her anxiety, but she truly hated being late for work, and she normally wasn't. More times than not, she was the first person into work at Chandler Graphics. Today she was the last, as the office manager, Cicily Taylor, subtly pointed out.

"I know, I know," Amy announced, holding up a slender hand as she rushed through the showroom and down the hall. "Mr. Kazlowsky is waiting for his proof on that program cover."

"He's already called in," Cicily informed her.

"I'll bet he has."

"Everything all right with you?" This directed to Amy's back.

"Clocks, Exxon, and ducks."

That said it all. She'd forgotten to set her alarm last night, the car had needed gas first thing, and the flock of mallards that had adopted her and lived in her backyard had insisted on being fed. Twice.

She had Mr. Kazlowsky's program cover off the printer and through the fax within ten minutes. Then she played catch-up, or tried to, at least. Sitting in front of her computer, mouse in one hand, cup of hot tea in the other, she managed to typeset three lines of copy on a promotions layout before she was interrupted.

"Ducks?" came the voice of Barbara Chan from the doorway.

Amy threw her a droll look.

"Couldn't you think of a better one than that?"

"No, because there wasn't one, because it was the truth."

"Must be nice being the boss's sister," Barbara teased.

And it was teasing. Barbara was one of three other graphic designers at Chandler Graphics, and Amy's best friend. Since their college days together, they'd been very tight.

"Don't you have anything better to do than harass me?" Amy asked, turning her attention back to her screen.

"As a matter of fact, I do. Tom and I have plans for dinner tonight, but his cousin's in town and I was sort of wondering—actually Tom was wondering—"

"Oh, no." Amy cut her off in mid-ramble. "I'm not going out on a blind date."

"Why not? It would be fun."

"We've been through this before, Barb."

"Not with Tom's cousin."

"That doesn't make any difference."

"Sure it does. The guy is great."

That earned Barbara another droll look, this one edged with pain. "According to Tom. He'd say anything it took to arrange a date for this guy. For all I know, he could have an ego a mile wide."

"He doesn't, I don't think. But even if he did, Tom and I would be there to deflect the worst of it." Barbara lowered her chin. "Please, Ame. Tom just got back from Chicago. I haven't seen him in two weeks."

Amy set her cup down and swiveled in her chair to face Barbara fully. "Which means that after dinner you two are going to want to be alone. What am I and 'cousin' supposed to do then?"

"Nothing. He can go back to Tom's apartment. Tom and I will go to mine. You go home. I promise. It's just dinner, for a couple of hours—just enough time to show 'cousin' a nice time, and that's it."

Amy clicked her back teeth together in a quick staccato. Damn, she hated this. Dating was iffy at best, the pits when it was something as pressured as a blind date. She hadn't been on one in years, not since the last time Barbara had pleaded in the same beseeching voice she used now.

Eyeing Barbara with a blatant show of irritation, she tried to collect the necessary strength to refuse. All she got for her effort was a visual reminder that Barbara was her best friend. They had a history that spanned the apprehensions and joys of college, the deaths of both their fathers, a failed marriage for Barbara, the stress of their jobs. There wasn't much that either wouldn't do for the other.

"It's a good thing I like you," Amy muttered, threading both hands through the sleek, short cap of her dark hair.

"Thanks, Ame." Barbara beamed. "I'll get with you later on the details."

"You owe me," Amy complained, but Barbara was already out the door and down the hall to her own office.

The layout on Amy's screen was suddenly uninspiring.

She leaned back in her chair, thoughts of the night to come souring rapidly. It wasn't that she had an aversion to going out; she truly enjoyed being with interesting people. She *didn't* enjoy having to wade through the scores of apathetic, selfish, irresponsible, humorless egotists to find those interesting people.

For that reason, she'd given up on dating as most would define it. She could do without the entire process of awkward smiles, the lapses in conversation, the inevitable question of whether the date would end in her bedroom or not. The tension of it all precluded enjoyment of any kind on her part. With the exception of Greg, the same couldn't be said of most of the men she had dated.

Dear, sweet Greg. Dating him had been nice. Being engaged to him had been nice. Not splendid or passionate or intense, but nice. She often wondered what life would have been like had they married. *Comfortable* came to mind. Pleasant.

Further words failed her, so she resorted to her forte, colors. Marriage to Greg would have been tan, any of the pastels, perhaps a shade of silvery gray. All acceptable, if *acceptable* was what she wanted in life. It wasn't. She was after scarlet and navy blue and emerald, with just a touch of neon gold for the exciting accents life had to offer.

That's what she thought of when she thought of the kind of marriage she wished for. A relationship as deep and rich as her internal pallet. Such was the stuff of her parents' marriage, a vibrant blending of commitment and devotion and an ever-constant love that had bound Ellen and Sam Chandler to each other and the two of them to their children. The end result had been a family in the truest sense of the word.

Without a second thought, she picked up her phone and dialed her mother's number. After seven rings, she hung up, disappointed but realistic. Ellen Chandler wasn't one to sit around. Between her garden and her grandchildren and the church auxiliary clubs to which she belonged, the woman stayed busy.

Amy knew it was for the best. At her husband's death, Ellen had had to do something to fill the void. For thirty-five years, Sam Chandler had been the other half of his wife's existence. Amy couldn't think of a time when she hadn't thought of her parents as extensions of each other. They had been that finely tuned to each other, that attached and in love.

The signs of that love had abounded through her childhood. A tender touch, an understanding smile, the hugs that were given freely and frequently to her and her brother and sister. Growing up, the Chandler kids had been secure for those outward displays, secure enough to develop and grow, and not necessarily in the same directions.

In interests and opinions, Amy was not a carbon of her brother, Mark, and they both were only vaguely similar to Claire. That had certainly made life interesting. The inevitable squabbles had been a very real part of their childhood fabric.

Amy smiled in wistful, if not rueful, memory. No one could ever accuse the Chandlers of not being opinionated, and different opinions had led—and still did lead—to arguments. She had to marvel at her mother's ability to cope with the variety in personalities—had to marvel at her genius to cope, day after day, with the sheer energy and vibrancy that had existed in her household.

Buoyed by that sense of wonder, Amy crossed the hall to the closetlike kitchen and made herself another cup of tea. Mark entered five steps behind.

"What's so funny?" he asked.

She raised her brows at him. "Nothing. Why?"

"You're smiling."

She was and she hadn't been aware of it. "I was thinking about Mom and what it was like for us growing up."

In his charcoal suit and wine striped tie, Mark was the consummate successful businessman: fit, tanned, polished in a way that only a middle-aged man could be—and obviously on his way out. Still, he paused to lean a shoulder against the door and give in to a crooked smile. "We were loud and wild."

"Mom held it all together somehow."

"She was too stubborn to ever let her kids get the best of her."

"We weren't that bad."

"We were brats."

"Speak for yourself. I was a perfect angel."

Mark shook his head in good-natured disagreement. "You were spoiled."

"I was not."

"Sure you were. All babies of the family are spoiled."

"I could say the same about you. The oldest and the only boy in the family? Don't tell me Dad and the grandparents didn't think you were God's gift."

Instead of debating that, Mark shoved away from the door. "Dad called you his 'peanut.' "

"So?"

"Claire and I didn't have nicknames. It was always Mark and Claire. You were 'Peanut.' "

Amy missed the endearment, so much so that in the wake of Mark's departure, she stood at her office window instead of returning to her screen.

Peanut. As far back as she could remember, her dad had called her that. He'd said it was because she was a little peanut of a thing. She supposed she had been—still was in comparison to Mark's six feet and Claire's five-eight. At an average five-five, Amy was the peanut of the family.

The stature had never impeded her in any way. In fact, it might even have helped. Not for a minute had she tolerated the obstacles inherent in being the youngest and the smallest.

You can't come with us, Amy; you're too young.

You can't go on that roller coaster; you're too small.

Even at the age of five, she hadn't put up with that mentality. She'd ridden her bike down the steepest hills, climbed higher than anyone in the Olsons' dead tree, run as fast as she possibly could, and dared anyone to say that she was too small or too young.

By the time she'd settled into school, the pattern to overachieve had become part of her nature. Average grades hadn't satisfied her. She got her A's, although a good portion of that could be attrib-

uted to sheer grit. To this day, she detested math
to the point that she'd willingly pay someone to
balance her checkbook. And she'd rather empty
the dishwasher three times a day than sit down and
write a letter. Thank God for the phone.

No, art was her strong point. She'd been blessed
with the talent to draw right from the start. It was
a talent to which no one else in the family could
lay claim, one from which she had derived as much
pleasure as her parents and siblings had.

Attending student art shows had been one of
those special Chandler events. Claire had had her
piano recitals, Mark his soccer tournaments, but
Amy had had her art shows. The whole family
would pile into the minivan and head off to the
school or the town hall or Fourth of July craft
shows.

Blue ribbons had always elicited praise and hugs;
honorable mentions brought loyal denouncements
of the judge's abilities to see the true value of her
work, even in a field as subjective as art. The love
and loyalty were what had gotten her through those
times when joy had been rampant and when disappointment had reigned.

She'd had her share of the latter, and although
she wasn't prone to getting mired in depressing
sentiments, she thought back to her father's passing with telling ease. Losing him had been like
losing a part of herself. Amy defined herself as
many things, not the least of which was a member
of a family. For the first twenty-five years of her
life, that family had included Sam Chandler.

His presence had been everywhere, from the
familiarity and comfort with which he sat at the
head of the table each night to the heat of his
irritation when he'd had to scold her, to the way

he would catch his wife up against his side for no other reason than that he wanted to have her near. Sam Chandler, in all his facets, had been intertwined with his children and his wife.

It was no surprise, then, that his death had forced a change in the very nature and spirit of the family, and in so doing, in Amy herself. That was the essence of mourning, though: remembering, rethinking, accepting, and finally adjusting the inner sense of self. Through it all, the Chandlers had clung to each other emotionally and, many times, physically. They'd come to one another's aid with a complete sense of sharing.

There was no doubt in Amy's mind that sharing was what they did best. It was second nature for her to buy a dozen apples and take six to Claire and the kids. For Mark, cutting the lawn meant cutting Ellen's lawn as well. Claire gladly house-sat for Amy and baby-sat for Mark and Peggy.

Amy couldn't imagine life being any different. It was, she surmised while tucking childhood heirlooms away in favor of the computer screen, simply how things were.

From that, she derived a sense of contentment. The morning that had seen her late start fell away to an afternoon of peaceful, steady work.

"Amy, pick up line one," Cicily's intercom voice announced shortly before two.

Annoyed at the interruption, Amy pressed the interoffice key instead. She was designing the most interesting part of the layout. Talk would interfere with her concentration. "Who is it?"

"Commonwealth Hospital."

She frowned at the receiver. No one had told her a thing about a possible account with Commonwealth. "Amy Chandler," she said.

"Ms. Chandler, this is Mrs. Ferguson, the charge nurse at Commonwealth Hospital emergency room. Your mother was brought in a little while ago and she wanted us to contact you or your brother."

Emergency room . . . your mother . . . Out of everything else the woman had said, that was all Amy heard. "What happened?" she asked, feeling her entire being shift off-kilter, feeling desperation and fear rise up to swallow her whole.

"It appears to be a stroke."

"Oh, God." *A stroke.* Images of paralysis and coma and death stole most of her strength. Anticipations of a funeral and a hideous, horrible emptiness where her mother should be left her numb. "How bad is it?"

"Dr. Donovan will be able to tell you better. Can you hold?"

"Yes, yes." She didn't want to, didn't think she could wait the agonizing minutes it took for the nurse to put the phone down and summon the doctor.

Mark. She had to find Mark. And Claire.

"Cicily," she yelled. Two seconds became five became ten. *"Cicily!"*

Her round face appeared in the doorway. "What are you yelling about?"

"Find Mark. Where's Mark?" And still no doctor on the other end to tell her if her mother was alive or not.

"He's gone over to Virginia Beach."

"Page him. Get him on his cell. Mom's had a stroke. She's been taken to Commonwealth."

"Ms. Chandler?"

At the sound of the deep male voice in her ear, Amy gripped the phone as if the instrument were the only direct link to her mother. "Yes . . . yes, this is Amy Chandler.'' Eyes darting around the office, she saw nothing, nothing at all.

"This is Dr. Donovan. I'm the emergency physician at Commonwealth. Your mother was brought in via rescue squad—''

"The nurse said it was a stroke.''

"So it appears.''

"How bad?''

"We're assessing her now. She seems to be stable, but I've ordered a series of tests. We'll check her out and decide what needs to be done.''

"Is she in pain? How *bad* is it?''

"She's lucid enough to have given us your number, but you might want to get over here.''

"Of course, yes, I'll be right there.'' She hung up without even thanking the man, or asking anything more. She automatically dialed Claire's work number.

"Claire O'Riley.''

"It's me. I just had a call from the emergency room at Commonwealth. Mom's had a stroke.''

"What?''

"Mom's—''

"Oh, my God. What happened?''

"I don't know.''

"How bad is it?''

"*I don't know!* I'm going over there now.''

"Is Mark going with you?''

"He's not here. I had him paged.''

She would never be able to remember the rest of the conversation, or running out of the office, getting into her car, and making the longest drive of her life.

Chapter Two

Claire Chandler O'Riley rarely used the word *stupid*. She didn't allow her children to use it. Her own parents had been so adamant that she not throw the term about that, as a defiant preteen of twelve, she'd pulled out the family dictionary and checked to see if there was some hidden sexual meaning that only adults understood.

Noah Webster had disappointed her not only with the lack of a sordid meaning, but also with the definition she'd found inherently cruel. She'd hated to think that anyone was actually dumb or worthless.

But now, as she leaned across her desk, a synthetic smile fixed to her face, she had to admit to herself that the man sitting opposite her was quite possibly the *stupidest* person she had ever met.

"Let me explain it again, Mr. Walker. Just because you have checks in your checkbook doesn't mean you have money left in your checking account."

Mr. Walker grimaced, his Pillsbury-DoughBoy

face creasing in blatant confusion. "It just doesn't make sense, ma'am."

For the third time, Claire corralled her waning patience and tried to explain. "You see, you have to deposit money into the account." *Stupid, stupid, stupid.* "Think of the checks as a replacement for actual cash."

Ten minutes later, to Claire's everlasting relief, Mr. Walker got to his feet and made straight for the teller line with several slips transferring funds from his savings account to his checking account. Claire wasted no time in heading for the employees' lounge.

Bottle of Tylenol in hand, she mentally reviewed the exact wording of her job description. The last time she'd checked, there had been no mention that new-accounts secretaries of the York River Bank and Trust were supposed to be subjected to idiots whose elevators didn't go all the way to the top. That had been happening more frequently lately, and she resented the fact that it was she who always seemed to be stuck dealing with the bank's less cerebral customers.

Lowering herself to the sofa, she jammed her elbows on her knees, planted her forehead firmly on her fingertips, and waited for the Tylenol to take effect. With the headache she had, thirty minutes was going to be twenty-nine minutes too long. What she really needed was to go home and curl up with her comforter.

It was, of course, out of the question. The stack of files on her desk was growing even as she sat there. And besides, people didn't go home every time they had a headache—at least hardworking, thirty-eight-year-old, underpaid people like herself did not.

Easing her shoes off, she tucked her legs under her and slid back into the corner of the sofa. It was a far cry from perfect, but it would have to do. And if not? Well, she'd buy more Tylenol and send the damned bill to the corporate chiefs in Richmond who didn't have the slightest idea what it was like to deal with the public. Vice presidents et al. sat up in their executive offices and handed down policy while it was left to people like her to see that profits were maintained.

She was not capable of thinking about profits just then. The best she could summon was a mental list of what she had to do after work. She was scheduled for a mammogram at 2:15. Caustically she wondered what sick Nazi mind had devised that little test. She was also out of milk and toothpaste. And her dry cleaning was ready, and the cat might have an ear infection.

Scratch the mammogram, but could she still squeeze in a trip to the store, the cleaners, and the vet before the kids got home from school? Her heavy sigh of resignation was a cheerless testimony to the fact that, whether she like it or not, she was going to have to try.

That conviction saw her back to her desk. Headache tamed to a tolerable degree, she made a point of keeping her expression pleasant. She was, if nothing else, a professional.

In a subconscious reminder that she was more, her gaze automatically dropped to the framed picture of her children, and her smile became genuine. Bethany and Michael. They were the joys of her life, even though Bethany was at that age when she had to have everything her girlfriends had, and Michael tended to overdose on Nintendo. At ten and eight, they were good kids, bright, happy, and as well adjusted as any children whose father had died prematurely could possibly be.

Without meaning to, she gazed at her left hand and a hollow sensation settled about her heart. No matter how hard she tried, she could not get used to seeing her ring finger bare. Even after three years, there were still times when she worked her thumb over the spot where her wedding band had resided for thirteen years—times when she missed Dan with a yearning that, in her more vulnerable moments, had the power to strip her down to a bunch of raw nerves.

Those moments were the worst. Poise was slaughtered by insecurity, happiness by rancor. For her children's sake, she tried to maintain and not make them victims of her emotional frailties, but she didn't always succeed. On good days, she had only so much patience and understanding. On bad days, she spent a lot of time resenting Dan's premature death, feeling like a fraudulent mother and daughter and sister. During those moments, she could not remember what it felt like to be a woman.

"Claire, could I see you in my office?"

She nearly flinched at John's voice and glanced back over her shoulder to see the branch manager returning her gaze from his office door. "Sure, John."

How cool she sounded—how direct and perfectly put together. Capable, efficient Claire. No one knew that there were days when the only thing holding her together was sheer determination and the support of her mother and Amy and Mark. Quite literally, she thanked God for them.

And, she silently confessed in something close to defeat, she thanked God for her job, aggravating though it could be at times. Work came to her rescue. Here she was forced to concentrate on impersonal matters. There was little time for cringing at inner weaknesses or wallowing in self-pity. Seeing where her reflections had been going minutes ago, she seized this opportunity with both hands.

Out of habit, she checked her hair, secured in its neat brown twist at the back of her head. It was her work look, right along with her tailored blue suit and her two-inch heels—the look that smacked of poise and skill and experience. She drew on all three as she sat to face John on the other side of his desk.

"I've been going over these reports you turned in last week," he began, his attention focused on the folder before him, his sandy brows angled sharply over mellow gray eyes.

It was typical John, Claire knew . . . now. Last year, when he'd been transferred in from the Portsmouth office, she'd found his intensity unsettling. After the laid-back affability of Mr. Andrews, the previous manager, John Spencer's honed nature had taken some getting used to. She had had to adapt to his manner just as she had had to adapt to all changes that came her way, with self-control, dignity, and a certain amount of private bitching.

"I think you'll be pleased with the numbers," she said.

"I am. Sales of MasterCards are up by ten percent from last year." He substituted one report for another. "And you exceeded our projected goal of two million-five in savings by a nice half a mil." Lifting his head, John looked straight at her for the first time since she'd sat down, and smiled a slow, satisfied, masculine smile, the kind that men normally saved for their teammates when they'd won a game. "Nice job."

Claire *was* rather pleased with herself. She'd worked hard—no, she'd busted her buns this past year. "Thank you."

"No, I mean it. You've done a great job."

This was another aspect of John that had taken some getting used to, his readiness to praise when praise was warranted. Mr. Andrews, for all of his laughter, had only ever thought to point out a person's shortcomings or mistakes. It had taken her close to six months to learn how to accept John Spencer's honest compliments.

Sitting back, she crossed her legs, one side of her mouth curling subtly. "Thanks, John."

"We're going to look pretty damn good on paper this year."

More to the point, *John* would look good on paper. What she and everyone else in the branch did reflected on him. Bottom lines and ultimate responsibility were part of the fallout of his position. For John's sake, as well as her own sense of pride in achievement, she was glad for her accomplishments. John was a nice man. He deserved some recognition for doing his job as well as he did.

He was also a fair man. John would not fail to recognize her hard work when appraisal time came along. If he held true to form again this year, she would garner another increase in salary.

The nice, fair man with the thinning blond hair and crow's-feet bracketing his eyes leaned back in his own chair. "So what are you going to do for an encore?"

"What are we shooting for?"

"More of your same great work."

At John's continued praise, her heart rate sped

up. And her brain had to have released a huge dose of endorphins, because she was suddenly feeling pretty good. Tipping her head to one side, she gave him one of her jauntier grins. "I think I can handle that."

With his elbows on the chair's arms, John steepled his fingers in front of his chin, his expression teasingly speculative. "Remind me never to come within a hundred yards of you if you've got that infamous land in Florida to sell."

"What can I say? Some people are born to shop. I guess I was born to sell."

"It's a rare talent."

"So is walking backwards on one's hands," came her good-natured, self-effacing quip.

His man-to-man smile softened a bit around the edges and she laughed, not adverse to the switch from undiluted business to urbane pleasantries. John might be her boss, but he was also that indistinct anomaly that fell into the category of not quite a friend but more than an acquaintance.

How that had come to be, she wasn't sure. His keen intelligence, her dedication, his business savvy, her competence, his sense of humor, her need to laugh: all the pieces had meshed together somehow for a unique working relationship.

Neither ever forgot where the lines were drawn—that he was an officer of the bank and she was a secretary, that it was against corporate policy for them to be more than coworkers. But sometimes, like right then, she had the distinct impression that there was a sexual awareness between them, the kind that exists between a reasonably handsome man and an almost-attractive woman simply because they are of opposite sexes. The awareness was sensitizing and harmless. And she was just human enough, just needy enough, to enjoy it.

The phone on her desk rang, the sound jerking at her internally. Outwardly, she came smoothly to her feet. "Are we done here?"

"For now."

At her desk once more, she spoke into her phone. "Claire O'Riley."

"It's me."

Short as the greeting was, she recognized Amy's voice at once. Her good humor increased, only to plummet with Amy's next words. "I just had a call from the emergency room at Commonwealth. Mom's had a stroke."

Claire felt as if her mind divided itself into a dozen different parts. It was the most absurd sensation, one that she recognized on a peripheral level, one she knew she'd felt only twice before—at the deaths of her father and her husband.

Thoughts flashed with remarkable speed, all the whats and hows and whys. Into that mélange came devastating memories and a sickening sense of déjà vu: first Dad, then Dan. She couldn't go through this again. She simply could not. And all the while, she was ridiculously and illogically aware that her brain continued to function on a basic level, sending messages to a body that refused to listen.

Adrenaline pumped furiously; muscles quaked; her stomach heaved right up against her heart. "What?"

"Mom's—"

"Oh, my God." No conscious thought there. She was reacting solely on innate reflexes. "What happened?"

"I don't know."

"How bad is it?" The urge to cry struck hard.

"I don't know. I'm going over there now."

"Is Mark going with you?"

"He's not here. I had him paged."

"I'll . . . meet you there. I'll get there as soon as I can."

Not even aware that she did so, she hung up the phone and walked into John's office. He rose the second he saw her face.

"Claire, what's wrong?"

Eyes wide, she stared at him for no other reason than that she couldn't form any words.

"Claire." He rounded his desk and took hold of her by her arms. "What happened?"

"My mom's had a stroke." As if saying the words aloud could free her from her daze, she came alive suddenly, clearheaded for the first time in minutes. "I have to go. I . . . I'm sorry, but I have to go."

"Of course." Following her back out to her desk, John warned, "But I don't think it's a good idea that you drive."

"I'm fine."

"Not according to the size of your pupils or the lack of color in your lips."

She couldn't even think about debating the issue with him. "I have to call my mother-in-law so she can meet Mike and Beth at home."

"Fine. While you're doing that, I'll arrange things here. Then I'll drive you over. Where is she?"

"Commonwealth."

She didn't say too much more after that. As John maneuvered through traffic on I-64, she stared out through her sunglasses, watching familiar land-scapes flash past her.

Coliseum Mall . . . and Christmas shopping with Mom. Every year, they'd taken Mike and Bethany to sit on Santa's lap, and Mom had been right there, listening to secret lists, assuring Santa that her grandchildren had indeed been very good that year. It was Mom who bought the traditional pictures of the kids with Santa, insisting on getting the family package so everyone who wanted snapshots would have one.

The community college. As though it were yesterday, Claire could remember standing in line to register for her freshman classes. Mom had been beside her, assuaging her seventeen-year-old daughter's insecurities without making Claire feel as if she were a little kid needing to hold her Mommy's hand.

The sign ahead read "Newport News, Next Five Exits." An embarrassing sweetness stole through Claire. At the age of eight, she'd thrown up in the backseat of her mother's brand new car, her squeaky, high-pitched warning that she was going to be sick coming far too late. By the time Mom had pulled the car off the road, just past that big, green road sign, the damage had been done.

Claire could still remember standing on the roadside, her jeans and Keds a mess, tears in her eyes and that awful vomit taste in her mouth. In her eight-year-old mind, all she had been able to think was that she had really done it this time. Puking in a car was bad enough, but to do it in a car that her parents had only had for five days was cause for real fear.

Mom had heaved a sigh, shaken her head, and then grabbed several bottles of club soda from the groceries in the trunk. Right there, in the shadows of that big, green road sign, Mom had flushed down Claire's clothes and the backseat of the car. When she'd done all she could, she had given Claire a comforting smile and a tender pat on the shoulder, then driven them home with all the windows rolled down. Sitting in the front seat, Claire had thought her mother was the best mom in the whole world.

The Ramada Inn just off the northbound exit . . . and Claire shut her eyes. A senior graduation party she wasn't supposed to attend had taken place in that motel. A party that had gotten out of hand with ear-splitting music and illegal alcohol. The management had complained, the cops had arrived, and three dozen newly graduated seniors of York High School had scrambled for cover.

She had raced for her car, parked out behind the pool. With most of the action out front, she had believed herself safe, until she had nearly run right into her father. Then *safe* had become a very relative term.

It had been Mom who had talked Dad into postponing the inevitable reprimands until the morning, Mom who calmed Dad down when his temper reached critical mass, Mom who agreed with all Dad had to say and yet still managed to offer sympathy.

"Oh, God," she whispered, her throat so tight it actually hurt.

"Are you all right?" John asked, giving her a quick glance.

"I don't know."

"The worst thing you can do is anticipate."

"I wasn't. I was thinking back, remembering." As in some morbid kind of eulogy. A lifetime of memories gushed into her consciousness: baptizing the kids, her father's funeral, family vacations, watching Dan slip into death. Mom had been there through all of that and so much more, the nucleus around which the rest of the family rallied. "This is so sudden."

"Most strokes are."

"Are they?" She snapped her head about, latching on to the sight of him. "How do you know?"

"There's a history of strokes in my family. Two grandparents and my own father had strokes."

"And?" She waited for him to tell her that they had all survived, that none had been overly debilitated.

"And," he replied on a long exhale, "my grandfather died, my grandmother ended up in a nursing home, and my father recovered with minimal damage. The point is, don't try to second-guess this. You'll only make yourself crazy."

Kind words, offered with the best of intentions, but she wanted—needed—assurances and promises that her mother was well.

Moments later, the beige structure of the medical center came into view, and Claire pressed a hand to her stomach where fear was tightly coiled. Her husband had died here. She hadn't allowed herself to think about walking through the emergency room doors again for anything more significant than a few stitches to a cut knee or an X ray for a broken finger. Yet here she sat, her hopes and intentions counting for nothing.

The few minutes it took for John to reach the receiving area were surreal, with time stretching out and slowing down and, if it were possible, going sideways. She kept telling herself that this wasn't real; it wasn't real; *it was not real.* Someone else's mother lay inside; someone else's confidante and best friend and teacher and lifesaver was hooked up to monitors while a bunch of passionless doctors did their thing.

How she kept from crying, she didn't know.

Where she found the presence of mind to thank John was another mystery. "I really appreciate this," she blurted out as she opened the car door. I'm not sure I would have made it here in one piece."

"You go on in and I'll park the car," John said.

"You don't have to stay, John."

"I know. Just for a while, until I know you're all right."

"Amy's inside. Mark will be here soon." They would take her as close to "all right" as she was going to get.

"Go on," he ordered, lifting his chin toward the hospital doors. "Your mom is waiting."

The tears she had controlled so well to that point rose up swiftly. Empty inside except for the dread, she bit her lower lip, nodded, and then got out on visibly shaking legs. John drove off and she was suddenly alone, the sensation of absolute isolation saturating her entire being.

She hung back, not wanting to go inside and learn what she had to learn. At least standing where she was, she could pretend that nothing was wrong, that Mom was fine, that the family was still relatively intact. Knowing that such reluctance was useless and cowardly didn't make her feel any better. At that moment, she knew she *was* useless and cowardly.

And stupid—dumb for floundering in self-pity and worthless for not hurrying inside to offer Amy her support. "Peanut-pie" Amy with her optimistic élan and her gritty determination. She might be the baby of the family, but she was incredibly strong.

Determined to be as tough, Claire made a swipe at her tears and then left *useless* and *cowardly* and *stupid* behind.

Chapter Three

Life was great. Mark Chandler made a point of reminding himself of that several times a day. He did so now as he was shown to a window table in one of Virginia Beach's ocean front restaurants. He'd paid extra for this table, for the privilege of the view. Being able to afford that perk filled him with a sense of satisfaction that normally would have been very pleasant. Today the gratification was there, but in abbreviated form.

Settling himself comfortably, he didn't allow himself to dwell on his lack of appreciation. He'd been suffering from the slight apathy for some time. Like a lingering case of the flu, it would eventually wear itself out. Until then, he would ignore it the same way he would a mild sore throat, reminding himself instead to be grateful for what he had in life.

There was much. At forty-two, he had attained most of the goals he had set for himself. Chandler Graphics was the premier graphics company in the area, growing from a small two-room office venture with one computer and one copying machine to the multimillion-dollar operation it was today. His client list was the envy of more than a few of his business associates. The money that had been so scarce ten years earlier was now enough that few of his employees complained about salaries.

On a personal level, he had all a man could want: a wife who loved him, and three kids who thought he ranked right up there with 'NSYNC and WCW Wrestling, and that included Goldberg. His relationship with his sisters and his mother was intact, and added to all that, he was healthy.

But slowly slipping past his prime.

The thought invaded at the same time as the waiter.

"Chivas, straight up." He placed his order with an undercurrent of tension in his voice, and he didn't give a damn if the waiter noticed or not. He strongly suspected he had stumbled on part of the underlying cause for his recent discontent.

With his gaze fixed on the waves, he heaved a sigh that came straight from his gut—washboard abs he worked hard to maintain. One hundred sit-ups a day, plus push-ups, plus weights, plus racquetball at the club three times a week. He accomplished all of that and more; he had for years. The only difference was that now it took him seven minutes instead of four to cram those sit-ups in before his morning shower, and those racquetball games had begun to leave his knees and shoulders aching.

Welcome to middle age. Whoever had said life began at forty didn't know jack-shit about a receding hairline or the sudden discovery that he needed bifocals. Bifocals—old fart glasses, for Christ's sake. It was enough to make him puke.

Thank God sex was still good. He could get it up as easily now as he had when he had been in his twenties. He took a real male pride in that. Peggy, sweet wife that she was, said it didn't matter, but like most women, she didn't understand. She tried to, but the bottom line was, women were never going to fully comprehend the intrinsic connection between a guy and his cock any more than a man could understand what it was like to have a period.

It was that simple or complicated, depending on one's point of view. He'd settle for simple; he always did. Why take an already complex world and make it worse? That philosophy had been his ever since he could remember. Some considered the common-sense attitude passé for today's business world, but it was how he preferred things to run.

To that end, he checked his watch. He hadn't gotten where he was today by sitting around on his ass, contemplating his philosophies. Nor had he attained his success by waiting for potential clients who didn't know how to tell time. At quarter after the hour, Frank Bellieux was fifteen minutes late. If the old bastard didn't represent a possible seventy-five-thousand-dollar account, Mark would have been in his Mercedes and headed back to the office.

Trouble was, he and Bellieux went back a long way. Bellieux had been a crony of Sam Chandler, Mark's father. That put a different slant on the issue even though, as a rule, Mark didn't adhere to any good-old-boy network. Frank Bellieux did, and if Mark didn't miss his guess, Bellieux was going to try to use his past friendship with Sam to wrangle on the cost of doing business.

Swallowing a scoff right along with his Scotch, Mark mentally kicked himself for agreeing to meet with Bellieux, but seventy-five thousand dollars was too sizable a chunk of money to be overlooked. If the old bastard was going to take his advertising money somewhere, Mark intended for him to take it to Chandler Graphics.

So he waited, patience waning, irritation escalating as he mentally dismembered Bellieux, stuffing body parts in unlikely places. It came as an unexpected shock when he spotted Frank's daughter heading his way instead of the old bastard himself.

"Rene," he found himself saying as he came quickly to his feet, his smile as genuine as his surprise.

"Hello, Mark. Sorry I'm late."

"That's all right." Where only seconds ago he'd been seething with resentment for Frank's tardiness, he was now more than willing to be accommodating, perhaps because Rene Bellieux had thought to apologize as her father never would have. Or perhaps because in his limited dealings thus far with Rene, he'd found her to be fair, direct, and savvy. "I think I may have gotten my wires crossed. I was expecting your father."

"No, no mix-up," she returned with a breeziness that was part of her nature. "Dad and I came to an understanding last night that I'd be handling all of the advertising for Bell Electronic Systems from now on." Slipping into the seat he held for her, she added on a hint of a grunt, "Actually, I had to threaten him with walking out on the company in order to get him to see reason. He suddenly found himself without his vice president." With an acidly sweet smile she purred, "The man defines the word *stubborn*, but then I'm sure you're well aware of that."

Mark was, to the point that his mood lightened

considerably just knowing he wouldn't have to put up with Frank's unreasonable obstinancy. His mood hiked up another notch at the realization that he would be spared the bullshitting to which Frank was so partial. Mark had grown sick of it through the years, but he'd tolerated the old bastard's ways—all for the sake of Chandler Graphics. The responsibility inherent in that had at times had him feeling like a whore.

The sensation was repugnant, even now capable of churning in his stomach like vomit that refused to come up. He sent a bit of Scotch down to help alleviate the feeling, telling himself that every business dealing with which he'd ever been involved had been necessary. His livelihood as well as those whom he employed depended on the continued influx of accounts, and that meant that occasionally he'd sacrificed a few of his standards and, detestably enough, slices of his pride.

"Father sends his regards." Rene broke into his thoughts, her expression drolly humorous. "He also gave me a list of things to tell you, but don't worry; I've already trashed half of what he said and forgotten the rest."

Mark laughed. Rene was definitely her own woman. He liked that. He liked her. She was ten times the businessperson her father was, and a hundred times better to look at. Willowy with a dark cap of chin-length hair, she had legs that went on forever and eyes as brown and liquid as melted chocolate. Mark was honest enough to admit that the elemental female beneath her tailored business suit was extremely appealing.

"I'm sure your father means well."

She raised one dark brow in a scoffing arc. "Don't stick up for him, Mark. He should have retired long ago. Actually, I'm amazed he's hung on this long, but he built the company up from nothing. For thirty-eight years, it's been his baby, his life.''

How well Mark understood the feeling. To varying degrees, he involved himself in every aspect of Chandler Graphics. As owner of the company, he knew it better than anyone else; he was his own best salesman, and that kind of commitment resulted in his bringing in a good portion of the sales revenue.

That kind of commitment was his responsibility, and responsibility was at the core of his life. He was a father, a husband, a brother and son, and a successful businessman. As such, the list of people dependent on him was lengthy. Peggy and the kids, his sisters, even his mother. And, of course, the staff and their families. They each viewed him in their own respective ways.

To his clients, he was the source of a vital service. To his employees, he was the guy who signed their checks. To his wife, he was lover, best friend, and lifelong partner. His kids saw him as everything from little-league coach to the ultimate authority, with a good deal of security thrown in.

With Amy and Claire and his mother, things were a little different. Not only was he Amy's brother he was also her employer. He was Claire's brother, and her shoulder to cry on. He was his mother's son, but also the "man around the house," a spot left vacant when Sam Chandler had passed away.

As definitions went, Mark understood that all were accurate and, despite the variety, connected by a common thread. He was in every case the man to whom people looked for one reason or another.

This wasn't a revelation. He had been aware of his unique position for several years, and it was something with which he was very comfortable. To be honest, he took a certain pride in the position. He wouldn't go so far as to say it stroked his ego, but it did satisfy something within him, perhaps the need to be in charge or appreciated. Maybe his being so central in people's lives validated his own life. Whatever it was, he enjoyed the sense of strength he derived from being a pivotal figure.

Sitting opposite the infinitely feminine Rene Bellieux intensified that sense of strength, making him feel invincible, and powerful enough to cram those morning sit-ups into two minutes.

He felt a spurt of laughter rumble up from his chest.

Yeah, life was good.

Until the cell phone at his waist beeped.

He spotted Amy first, sitting in one of the chairs against the wall, her face white and worried under the hospital's fluorescent lights. With her arms wrapped about her middle and her legs crossed tightly, she looked tense, her nerves stretched.

Automatically, he searched for Claire and instantly felt better to find her there in one piece, standing at the far end of the emergency room waiting area. Of the two sisters, Claire was the more vulnerable, the one who would have been more likely to have panicked and driven her car up a tree in trying to get there.

"Hi," was all he said. It was enough. Amy saw him as soon as he came through the doorway. She was off her chair and in his arms, oblivious to others in the room who might have stared. He held her, absorbing some of her tension while his gaze trav-

eled to Claire. He could see her tears. In silent
invitation, he lifted an arm.

Not until he held both did he ask, "How is she?"

As expected, it was Amy who collected herself
first and stepped back. "They're doing some tests
on her. A CAT scan, I think."

More stridently, Claire added, "No one will tell
us anything."

He kept his arm about her shoulders. She hadn't
moved away. From past experience, Mark knew she
needed the comfort his physical presence pro-
vided. "I'm sure when they do know something,
they'll tell us." To Amy he asked, "Have you seen
her?"

Amy nodded, scrubbing her hands through the
short layers of her hair in a habit that went back
to her childhood. It was a sure sign that she was
stressed. "Yeah, for a bit. She was hooked up to
all kinds of monitors."

"How was she?"

She struggled with this. "A little confused. She
knew who I was, but . . ."

Claire jumped onto her sister's fading words.
"Well, they wouldn't let me see her. By the time
I got here, they were carting her off."

"Only because it was necessary," he advised.
"Don't assume the worst."

"How can you say that?" Claire flung a hand
toward the nearby triage desk, its pristine efficiency
obviously not humane enough for her. "The
nurses have all the compassion of cinder blocks."

"Please, don't start," Amy entreated before Mark
could.

"Don't start what?" Claire snapped.

"Spiraling out of control. It isn't going to help.

The doctors and nurses are doing everything they can."

"Why don't you sit down, Claire," Mark suggested, already leading her to the chair Amy had vacated. The last thing anyone needed was for Claire to instigate a verbal thrust and parry now. It might have been an outlet for her tension, but this was neither the time nor the place. "Let me see if I can find out anything."

That was as much for his own benefit as for Claire's and Amy's. The shock of hearing that his mother might have had a stroke still vibrated through him. Stepping up to the desk, he went through the ritual of explaining why he was there.

The nurse told him as much as she could. It wasn't much. At his sisters' side again, he rubbed a hand across the back of his neck. "They're bringing her up now."

"Will we be able to see her?" Claire demanded.

"The nurse thinks so."

"What about the results of the CAT scan? How long before we know the results?"

"I don't know. The doctor has to go over all of that first."

She pinched the bridge of her nose, squeezing her eyes shut as though in pain. "What's his name?"

"Donovan," Amy supplied. "I spoke to him on the phone."

There didn't seem to be much more to say after that. The process of sitting and waiting stretched out into eon-long minutes that skewed time. A sensation of being hyperaware claimed him. Every sound, every odor, the comings and goings of the hospital staff all scraped over his senses. It was as though every receptor in his body was wide open. He was bombarded with impressions.

Out of self-preservation, he stood and wandered down the hall past the registration desk, acutely aware of others around him. As never before, he was conscious of the frail humanity in all of them, and in that, he felt absurdly bonded to these other people. People he didn't know, people he would never know. For the time they were there, they were all linked.

He cursed at the course of his thoughts, deciding that forty minutes of waiting had finally taken its toll. He pulled out his cell phone and called home. The sound of Peggy's voice was a balm.

"Hey," he muttered.

"Hey, yourself. Cicily called me from the office. Are you at the hospital?"

"Yeah."

"How's your mom?"

He leaned a shoulder against the wall and exhaled deeply. "No news yet. They ran some tests. We're waiting now for the results, to see her, to talk to the doctor."

"Do you want me to come out? I can get a sitter."

The concern in Peggy's voice was part of who she was. He soaked it up. "No, stay home. There's no need to disrupt the kids. Besides, we don't know how serious things are."

"Cicily said something about a stroke."

"We're not sure yet. Amy talked to the doctor. That was his initial opinion."

Whether Peggy heard the frustration in his voice or whether she was catching some hidden insight on her wife-radar, he didn't know. Either way, her voice took on that soft, supportive tone he'd come to value through the years. "Are you okay?"

"Hangin' in there."

"Are you?"

"Yeah. Keeping Claire from going off the deep end gives me something to focus on."

"She must be a basket case."

"Close."

"And Amy?"

"You know Amy. She's a tough nut."

"Tell them I'm thinking about them."

"I will. How are the kids?"

"The usual. Homework, playing, teasing each other mercilessly."

He longed for that very ordinariness right now. "Look, I don't know how long I'm going to be."

"Whenever. We're having Italian for dinner. Easy to microwave. I'll make up a plate for you."

"Thanks, hon."

A hint of a smile tinged her voice. "No sweat. Just do what you have to do there and call if something comes up."

"I will. Talk to you later."

"I love you."

"Same here." He hung up feeling better, realizing only then just how deeply his composure had plummeted. He returned to his sisters, mentally kicking himself in the ass. He was supposed to be the strong one here. He was the head of the family. He wasn't supposed to fall victim to emotional weakness.

By the time he entered the waiting room again, he had it together. A good thing, too, since Claire had progressed past tears and was biting her nails. Thankfully, a nurse approached and told them they could go on back and see their mother.

She was hooked up to an IV. And a monitor. In a tiled, curtained-off cubical. Surrounded by all kinds of paraphernalia, she looked all of her sixty-two years. Only her eyes, bright in spite of the telling signs of recent strain, were vividly young, alive, warm. She smiled at the three of them.

"Gee, Mom," he teased, a surge of relief sending adrenaline through his veins in a crazy rush, "if you had wanted to get us all together, you could have invited the family over for Sunday dinner."

Amy crowded in on one side of the bed, Claire on the other. Like two avenging angels, they took up their posts, Amy smiling hugely, Claire blinking back tears.

"How do you feel, Mom?" Amy whispered.

"Embarrassed," Ellen whispered back with more force. She fingered the tape securing the IV to her hand. "All this fuss."

Claire carefully gathered that hand between her own. "Do you hurt?"

"No."

"You sound better than you did earlier," Amy noted.

Mark had no idea how his mother had sounded, if her words had been slurred or sensible. The proof before him now was that she was lucid and coherent, sounding exactly like her old self. He took great comfort from that.

"What happened?" he asked.

Ellen related the events of the morning, imbuing each word with a touch of acid. "It's all so ridiculous. I was at the mall with Laura Morris, and the next thing I knew I was in the ambulance."

Amy frowned in earnest. "Did you feel funny or have any pain?"

"A little dizzy, I suppose. Nothing unusual for an old woman my age."

"You're not old," Claire insisted.

"I'm not young, either."

But she was herself, Mark thought. Even lying there on a hospital bed, surrounded by thousands of dollars' worth of equipment, even after having been run through God only knew how many tests, she was still, quite simply, Ellen Chandler. Sensible, steadfast, slightly self-effacing. He'd never known her to be anything else.

Mentally leaning back, he marveled at her strength. How did she come by it? Such fortitude wasn't a byproduct of her age. She'd always been a rock for the whole family. In times of crises as well as joy, Ellen Chandler was the cog around which all the Chandler wheels turned.

And nothing could have shoved her mortality in his face like that one realization.

His gut clenched in contradiction to the optimistic evidence before him. An asinine reaction considering he'd already lost one parent, but there it was. Somehow he'd let himself assume Mom would go on indefinitely. He hadn't let himself think that she was mortal.

The knot in his gut rose and clenched itself about his throat. Immediately, he reached out and laid a hand along his mother's shin beneath the covers. Telling himself that he was finally reacting to the stress of the day didn't ease his discomfort. The need to touch her, however slightly, however briefly, was too overpowering to deny.

And for a few seconds, he was five years old again.

It was the man, however, who turned at the parting of the privacy curtain, the man who nodded in both courtesy and curiosity to the doctor who entered.

He introduced himself as Dr. Seth Donovan. The introductions were completed in polite, if strained, haste before Donovan focused his attentions on his patient.

"How are you feeling, Mrs. Chandler?"

"Better." Ellen's gaze was direct.

Donovan's gaze behind his gold wire-rimmed glasses was even more so. "Any discomfort, confusion?"

She emphatically shook her head to the negative. He simply offered a sketch of a grin. Mark had the distinct impression that somewhere along the line the two had mentally squared off with each other and were now engaged in some kind of test of wills. They considered each other with open, good-natured challenge before the doctor flipped open a file and consulted his notes.

"I have the results of the CAT scan." One dark brow pulled ever so slightly inward toward the bridge of his nose. "You have had what we call a TIA, a transient ischemic attack. Technically, that means you have had a RIND." He clarified the term by spelling it out. "R-I-N-D. Reversible ischemic neurological deficit."

"What does that mean?" Claire breathed, her voice chopped into little bits of confusion and dread.

Donovan gave her his sympathetic gaze, then patiently explained to the entire group. "That means that something's happened to the blood circulation to the brain to cause other symptoms, symptoms that reverse themselves."

"Has Mom had a stroke?" Amy asked.

"Yes."

There it was, Mark thought. The truth with no varnish. What had only been a possibility was now a definite, sobering fact of bigger-than-life proportions. He exchanged glances with Amy and Claire, telling himself that knowing was better than not. At least now, something could be done.

"There are all sorts of varieties of strokes," Donovan clarified. "Stroke means that blood did not go properly to the brain for any number of reasons. It could mean there wasn't enough oxygen in the blood; it could mean there wasn't enough glucose or blood sugar; or it could mean there was a blockage in an artery and the blood couldn't get through that blockage. When you have any of those events, you have a stroke."

"Which one applies to me?"

With the same calm, reassuring directness he'd shown so far, Dr. Donovan answered Ellen's query. "The last. The tests show a small blockage in one of the arteries going to the brain."

Claire wrapped up in her arms and swallowed hard. "Is she going to be all right?"

"I can't give you any guarantees, Mrs. O'Riley, but many times in cases like your mother's, it's common to have complete recovery from a TIA."

"I really do feel fine," Ellen insisted.

"That can be typical," Donovan assured her.

"So what now?" This time the question came from Amy.

"I'd like to admit your mother for observation."

Ellen puffed up like the proverbial insulted, outraged, thoroughly wet hen. "Is that necessary?"

"In my professional opinion, yes. You need to be monitored for twenty-four hours to see what's going on. And we'll want to determine what should be done about that blockage."

Amy rubbed at her mother's shoulder. "Take it easy, Mom. It's only overnight."

"I've never liked hospitals," Ellen groused.

"We know, Mom," Mark sighed, thinking back to all the times she had balked at having a physical.

Donovan flipped his chart closed, the hint of a smile back again. "Mrs. Chandler and I have already had this discussion. I understand that doctors and hospitals rank right down there with sludge."

"Try not to take that personally," Amy suggested.

"Oh, I don't. Lots of people have aversions to anything or anyone even remotely connected to medicine." Turning for the curtain, he smoothly shifted back to the business at hand. "I'm going to make arrangements for your mother to be admitted and have her assigned to one of the specialists on call."

"But she will be all right," Claire persisted. "Won't she?"

Donovan paused, swept them all with a penetrating stare, then finally nodded. "Right now, everything looks hopeful. That's the best I can do for you."

It was enough for Mark. The sigh he released was laden with tension. He felt it drop off him like huge, weighty clumps that had suddenly been severed from invisible bonds. Everything looked hopeful.

He smiled and took a fortifying breath. Damn, but life was great. A little rocky around the edges at times, but all in all, great.

Chapter Four

As hospital food went, the sandwich wasn't bad. Amy figured that was because she hadn't slept well last night. She was running on fumes this morning. Anything would taste good, especially bacon, lettuce, and tomato, with an extra helping of mayo. Cholesterol city.

Why did the things that were so bad for you have to taste the best? And why would a hospital lunch counter have such a "medically incorrect" offering on their menu? A punchy voice in the back of her head whispered, "Maybe to drum up business for the cardiac unit." Another voice asked, "Is there such a thing as 'medically incorrect'?" If politically incorrect existed, it stood to reason that medicine could follow suit.

She didn't even bother to take her thoughts seriously. Instead, she leaned back in the booth and cupped her hands about her mug of hot tea. Decaffeinated. That was as much of a concession as her conscience could scrape up today. Yesterday had been one of the longest days of her life. It had wiped her **out completely**. Today she was paying the price.

That was okay. When she'd left here just before eleven last night, Mom had been sleepy but perfectly fine, even managing to reassure her sisters, who had flocked to her bedside. No one looking at her or talking to her would have known she'd had any kind of problem. The specialist assigned to her, Dr. Rosa Jamal, had been buoyant without being frivolous, caring without crossing any professional lines. She'd been extremely competent while still managing to be human. She'd made Mom feel better about having to stay the night. And she'd made it easier for Amy to walk out and leave her mother behind.

Leaving had been tough. An empty, incomplete sensation had accompanied her all the way home to Poquoson. Time hadn't helped alleviate the feeling, which was why, she supposed, she was back here again and it was only eight o'clock. After a night of trying to figure it out, she'd finally concluded that her restlessness stemmed from one simple reason: it felt awkward for Mom to be in the hospital. More to the point, it felt wrong for Mom to be anywhere other than in her usual domain, carrying on with her life.

The particulars of that life made Amy smile. Mom wasn't going to let this little episode set her back. She'd be in full gear again, or as close to it as she could get. Amy's smile broadened as she anticipated what Dr. Jamal would have to say about that. Mom had pretty definite ideas about her health, physicians, and how the two should or should not be related. Dr. Jamal hadn't let that faze her, though. Neither had Dr. Donovan.

His image entered her head at nearly the same

time that she noticed him standing in line at the counter. Her first thought was to wonder if he ever left the place. Then she noticed that he was wearing different clothes this morning. When he turned her way, she saw that he looked newly shaved, his eyes behind his glasses just a touch sleepy as if they, and he, needed a dose of caffeine.

Not meaning to, she continued to stare at him, undecided as to whether to acknowledge him or let him pass by. He had become an extremely important person in her life, even though they were practically strangers. For all of their brief acquaintanceship, it had been intense. In that, she felt a convoluted connection to the man.

"Dr. Donovan," she spoke up as he was about to pass her table. He paused and gave her an inquiring look. "I'm Amy Chandler. You treated my mother yesterday in the emergency room for a stroke."

"I know who you are," he returned easily, his blue eyes becoming as alert as his voice.

"I didn't know if you would or not. With so many people coming and going so quickly yesterday, I thought you might not remember me."

"How is your mother?"

"Better."

"Good. Dr. Jamal is one of the best."

"Thank you for recommending her. She made Mom feel more comfortable about being here."

He replied with a slight nod, the gesture seeming to Amy as if he were impatient to be about his business. Quickly she lifted a hand in a gesture of farewell. "I won't keep you. I just wanted to thank you for what you did for my mother. You probably get thanks all the time from grateful patients and their families. Still, I wanted to tell you how much I appreciate your expertise and your bedside man-

ner. That meant a lot to me and my brother and
sister, not to mention Mom.''

His dark brows met above his nose, the move
shifting his glasses slightly askew. Somewhere in
that frown, Amy detected an instant flash of surprise. Once his features resumed a normal expression, the surprise was gone, open speculation
taking its place.

His gaze flicked to her tray. ''Lunch or breakfast?''

The shift in topic threw her for a second. ''Uh,
both, I think. Actually, it could be last night's dinner. I'm a little muzzy this morning and trying to
catch up.''

''How late were you here last night?''

He asked as if her staying upstairs with Mom had
been a foregone conclusion. ''Eleven. How did you
know?''

The tilting of his head to one side could have
meant anything. She interpreted it to mean that
he was amazingly astute, knowing as only a keenly
perceptive physician would just how close-knit families would react in these matters. He was that kind
of man. She'd decided that yesterday.

''What about you?'' she asked, eyeing the lone
cup of coffee on his tray. ''No breakfast this
morning?''

''Afraid not.''

''Your doctor might have something to say about
that,'' she teased. ''Breakfast is the most important
meal of the day.''

One side of his mouth quirked as he pointedly
lowered his eyes to her sandwich and the little
paper cup with its remnants of mayonnaise—
damning evidence that, as breakfasts went, hers was

pitiful. The look he returned to her was mockingly humorous.

"All right, you caught me," she laughed. It felt good. Hospitals could be depressing. Sitting there alone waiting to go up to see her mother had been nerve-racking. To laugh eased her spirit tremendously and made her suddenly aware that, while she had been sitting, he had been standing.

Her grin still in place, she asked, "Would you like to join me?" She didn't expect him to. Doctors had a way of seeming bigger than life, omnipotent in their ability to save human life. She imagined that Dr. Donovan would be meeting someone else to discuss a patient. Or he might need the time alone to regroup. No one could do what an emergency physician did and not require some sort of personal time. Over a cup a coffee. In a secluded spot of the cafeteria.

Nonetheless, she wasn't sorry she asked. Out of politeness alone, she had extended the invitation. For more feminine reasons, she hoped he would accept. Circumstances being what they had been yesterday, she hadn't allowed herself to find him attractive. But today was another day, and circumstances were different.

Tall, with neatly trimmed dark hair and fiercely blue eyes behind round wire-rimmed glasses, Dr. Seth Donovan had about him an unmistakable air of University of Virginia, or perhaps Yale Medical School. Not usually her type, since she preferred a more Bohemian spirit in people, but there was something about him that afforded her an aesthetic pleasure.

His tray joined hers as he slid into the seat across from her. Surprised, she shifted quickly to adjust her legs to accommodate the sudden loss of sub-table space.

"What's the matter?" he asked, that blue, blue gaze penetrating, delving.

"Nothing." The shrug of her brows implied differently. "I didn't expect you'd join me, that's all."

"Why not?" He was almost painfully blunt in his manner. "Didn't you want me to?"

"Yes, of course." A grin completed her expression of pleased amazement. "But I would have thought you'd be busy or distracted, you know, thinking about a patient or something like that."

He sipped the black brew in his cup. "I'm not on duty yet. I don't have any patients."

Over the rim of her own cup, she studied his features just as she studied his puzzling remark. It dawned on her then that she had made several assumptions about him that were incorrect. She had inadvertently lumped him into a generic category of doctor, but he wasn't like other doctors, either in this hospital or out. His time with the sick or the injured was short-lived. Patients were admitted, he did his thing and then processed them on to the next logical course of action. That was the extent of his involvement.

"When do you have to go on duty?" she finally asked.

A flick of a glance to his watch preceded his reply. "In fifteen minutes. Actually, today is my day off. I'm covering for another doctor this morning."

"That's awfully nice of you."

He dismissed the compliment with a shrug. "Comes with the job."

"Maybe." Turning her head, she slanted him a charming glance. "But you gave up a morning to sleep in. That's no small sacrifice."

That earned her a smile, the first he'd given her. She appreciated it with a purely feminine delight. Fit, broad-shouldered, somewhere in the forty-something range, he was a handsome man. The curving of his lips only emphasized that and the fact that she was not immune to all that intelligent, masculine appeal.

"You sound like you haven't slept late in a long time, Miss Chandler."

"If you're going to discuss my sleeping habits, you'd better call me Amy."

"All right, Amy, when was the last time you slept late?"

"I don't remember. Probably on a weekend."

"What about during the week?"

"I nine-to-five it."

"Doing what?"

"Graphic design."

"On a computer?"

"Ninety-five percent of the time."

"And the other five percent?"

"Then I'm on a drawing board."

The speed of the exchange left her mentally breathless. She couldn't remember the last time that had happened. "What about you?" she pressed, unwilling to relinquish this rare heightening of her senses. "When was the last time *you* slept in?"

"Nineteen-ninety."

She laughed, liking the irreverent humor underscoring what she suspected was really a truthful response on his part. She didn't know much about an emergency doctor's schedule, but she imagined it was hectic, stressful. That he could find humor in that pleased her, and she would have said as much if the beeper at his waist hadn't sounded.

He shut it off without giving it a glance, or seemingly even a thought, for that matter. Leaning back in the seat, he narrowed his eyes, tipped his head to one side, and regarded her openly, as if trying to discern something. Amy stared right back, squelching the self-conscious sensation that threatened. Finally, he lifted his chin in a gesture indicative of a man who had come to a decision of some kind.

They exchanged the customary farewell platitudes, topped off with mutual smiles, and then he left without giving her another look. Amy knew that for a fact, for unlike the good doctor, who never once looked back over his shoulder, she swiveled completely around in her seat to watch him walk away.

Seth Donovan looked back over his shoulder as he cleared the doorway. The back of Amy Chandler's head met his gaze. Despite that, he decided that, as views went, this was the best he'd had in a long time. It wasn't often he found anyone who could take him by surprise.

He was a man immune to surprises. Eight years in an emergency room had a way of desensitizing a person to shock and wonder. And yet, Amy Chandler with her wedgewood eyes and effervescent charm made him think of those little blue flowers his grandmother used to grow out behind her house . . . and a transparent silk teddy exposing womanly curves. Contradictory reactions to be sure, and in that came the element of surprise. He liked the sensation.

He carried it with him as he passed through the halls, letting himself savor the pleasure it afforded him. For a short while, before he had to tuck such pleasure away for future enjoyment, he appreciated Amy Chandler's smile and manner.

No shy, retiring woman here. She had a gaze as direct and forthright as a ray of sunlight shining though primordial crystal. And her open nature reeked of self-assurance. Cool and polite, she'd slipped effortlessly into capriciousness, obviously comfortable with both facets of her character.

She was a confident woman. He liked that.

That was the last personal opinion he allowed himself. As he approached the double doors leading into the emergency department, he shut off Seth Donovan the man and regrouped as Seth Donovan, M.D., P.C. He called it his centering mode, the trashing of emotional garbage, the storing away of problems, personal or otherwise. The process was first nature, something he slipped into as naturally as sleep. By the time he reached the nurses' station, he was completely focused.

It was that easy, that intrinsic—most of the time. There were days when there was breakthrough bleeding of the unwanted baggage—days when, like any other human being, he had to struggle with himself for mastery of the mind and emotions. Those days were few, and today was not one of them.

Today, everything was in order, both internally and externally. His mind was set, and the nurses' station had its typical appearance of carefully controlled chaos.

"What's up?" he asked Holly Grant. Irreverent, bottom-line, unflappable Holly Grant. She'd been emergency nursing longer than he'd been a doctor. In practical experience alone, she was rare. For the morale of the ER, she was indispensable.

"What's up?" She gave him one of those big,

buxom smiles that meant he was going to start the shift on the lighter side of medicine. "Take a look at this."

He flipped open the chart, relenting to a smile when he reached the notes on the description of a patient's complaint.

"A tree? The woman says she has a tree growing out of her 'private parts'?"

Holly didn't even try to keep from laughing. "That's what she says."

No, very little surprised him, but in this instance, his curiosity was definitely aroused. A forty-five-year-old woman with normal vital signs thought a tree had taken root inside her vaginal cavity.

"All right, set her up for a pelvic exam."

"Mind if I assist on this one?" The bright light of mischief played all over Holly's face.

He gave her a droll look. "What's the matter, Grant, the morning too slow for you?"

"Nope, but this one's a first for me."

Which said a lot. Between the two of them, they'd witnessed enough human drama played out to make up several lifetimes. "Suit yourself."

"Great." She left with just enough energy to make him laugh. Holly was primed; he could see it in her posture and her step. What she wouldn't accomplish out of professionalism, she'd carry out though interest and curiosity, following his instructions to the letter and then some. By the time he needed to do his thing, she'd have everything perfectly organized.

She didn't disappoint him. When he entered the examining room, she and a second nurse, Bonnie, were standing ready. The patient was lying flat, the requisite white sheet covering her lower torso and legs.

"Good morning; I'm Dr. Donovan."

The woman muttered a subdued greeting, her pale, flabby face flushing in patent embarrassment.

"What seems to be the problem?" He knew what the chart said. He also knew that, for a million different reasons, people regularly lied about their medical problems. What this woman had told the nurse out at the triage desk might or might not be true. He wanted to hear from her exactly what was wrong.

"Well," she began, nervously plucking at the top of the sheet. "I have this . . . this, well, this here tree, I s'pose, comin' right on outa my private parts."

With his face as scrupulously void of expression as he had ever made it, he simply nodded before launching into the standard OB/GYN questions. "When was your last menstrual period?"

She couldn't give him the exact date, but she assured him it was last month.

"Any problems?"

She scrunched her face to one side and then the other. "It hurt more'n normal."

"Any chills, fever, unusual discharge?"

No to all three.

"What about intercourse?"

She blinked her eyes wide. "I ain't been with no man in four years, five months, and a week."

And yet she couldn't remember the date of her last period. "All right. Let's take a look."

Sure enough, she had a vine growing out of, as she liked to put it, her private parts. From where he sat on the low stool between the woman's spread thighs, the little leaves looked absurdly green.

Holly had been right. This was definitely a first. As a race, humans were inordinately preoccupied with every orifice in their bodies. He had believed that there wasn't one item that hadn't been shoved, hidden, or tucked somewhere inside the body that he hadn't, at one time, had to extract. Obviously, he had been wrong.

He absorbed that slap of reality with a certain sense of gratification. As the nurses went about prepping the woman, getting her feet into the stir-rups, he could not shake the sensation that life had tested him and he had passed . . . momentarily. The results of the examination tested him again.

What the woman had called a "tree" was actually a potato. *A potato that had sprouted vines.* He smiled. Just a little smile, just enough to alleviate the balloon of humor that was inflating in his chest by the second. Just enough to keep his fingers steady and gentle and his manner polite and professional.

All in all, the procedure was simple, even if it was unusual. He had to admit that the unusual was what he liked second best about his job. Helping people was number one. It always had been.

He left Ore-Ida to the nurses, reminded of his purpose once again. In all the years, helping people had never lost its appeal or its importance. It was what had gotten him though the crazy years; medical school and residency, the excruciating hours, the stress, a marriage that hadn't been able to survive the strain. That single factor of helping people was what gave his life balance in a world that tilted perilously close to the edge every day. That was why he'd decided to become a doctor.

There were those who scoffingly accused him of being altruistic—people, physicians included, who either couldn't or wouldn't understand that his motives were ridiculously simple. He wasn't an adrenaline junkie, living for the next frenetic high. Nor was he a power monger, wrapped up in a perverted need for hero worship. He did what he did because, as corny as it sounded, helping people was good and it was needed.

If that made him a cartoon character, so be it. There were times when he felt a great affinity for Daffy and Donald. And there were times when Porky Pig's summation of "That's all, folks" said all there was to say about life.

"That's a first for me," Holly joked when she joined him at the nurse's station.

He glanced up from the report he was completing for Ore-Ida's records. "Did she mention *why* she had a potato up there?" Not that it mattered, but he was curious.

"She said it was some old family remedy," she told him over the sudden wailing of a baby in room three.

"For what?"

"Cramps. Trouble is, she forgot she'd inserted the thing."

The baby's wailing turned into a full-blown scream of distress, the perfect accompaniment to the crash of what sounded like a suture tray somewhere down the hall. Phones ringing, monitors blipping, radio calls, moans, and the sound of weeping. He noted them all peripherally, conscious of them in the way one is of one's arm or leg—there, and yet for the most part, taken for granted.

He'd learned a long time ago that the blocking out was a necessary defense if he was to keep his sanity. The same way that protecting his personal self from most of what happened in the department kept his sanity. The same way that locking the "outside" world on the other side of the swinging doors maintained his sanity. For his own sake as well as the patients', he couldn't afford to get caught in the backfire of having the two worlds cross.

With remarkable ease, the memory of Amy Chandler slipped right past his defenses, as if his mind didn't know the meaning of self-control. He wasn't pleased by this. Neither was he completely disappointed. The truth was, Amy Chandler had made a big impression on him, both this morning and yesterday.

Of the three siblings, she was the youngest. It hadn't been difficult to figure that out. Both the brother and the sister looked as if they'd been roughed up by life a bit. If the same held true for Amy, it certainly didn't show. What had been noticeable was her spirit.

The middle sister, Claire O'Riley, was the weepy type, emotionally fragile. The brother, for all of his being steeped in the masculine role, had only been putting up a good front. From Amy he had detected fear, but also a sense of steadfast purpose that bordered on courage, as well as concern and love not only for her mother but for the family as a whole.

The sense of family had been strong in the Chandlers. Like an invisible aura, it had encased them and given them strength. It was a special bond which he envied.

Emotional bleed-through. Son of a bitch, he had it bad today. He wished he could blame Amy Chandler, but it wasn't her fault that he couldn't separate, couldn't regroup and center. For reasons that were beyond him, he was suddenly Seth Donovan at his most human, wishing for the ideals he'd harbored in his youth.

Eons ago, when he'd been raw and too idealistic for his own good, he'd believed that he could have the same kind of life that most men had—the wife-and-kids thing. He'd even tried that route, but with no success. As one of his professors in medical school had offhandedly mentioned, marriage was one of the first casualties in the medical profession. It required spouses to be blessed, or cursed, with extraordinary tolerance and selflessness.

Those spouses existed. So did good, solid, enviable marriages—only that hadn't been the case for him. What he and Gail had had were shared dreams that had soured under the demands of a profession that could absorb a person's very life, and a love that, in retrospect, couldn't have been as consuming and powerful as they had believed. Even sex, as great as it had been, had eventually died for lack of energy.

He blamed himself for the failure of the marriage. He'd had no damned business getting married when he had, but he'd wanted it all. The job, the wife, the family, the house in the suburbs. For a while in those early pressure-cooker years of his career, he had deluded himself into thinking it had been his. He'd given everything he could. Sadly, it hadn't been enough.

So now the house in the suburbs was a condo on the water. His wife was an ex, and he defined family in terms of his parents and his thirteen-year-old daughter.

Melody, thirteen going on twenty-one. She was at that hideous phase girls go through, with hormones flying out of control. Pubescent crazies, he called it, and it was normal. He thanked God for that, even though it was difficult being with her at times. Every other weekend and four weeks a year constituted those times, although that was beginning to change.

Mel had her friends and her interests. Boys, malls, and giggling gossip made up her world. Her father didn't always figure into that equation. Neither did her mother, but Gail was with her most of the time. Gail lived through the daily traumas that were shaping the adult Melody would someday be.

What he experienced was closer to playing catch-up. Two weeks could be forever in the life of a thirteen-year-old. She could change personalities a dozen times in fourteen days. Despite the frequent calls from Gail that kept him informed, he never knew what to expect from his own daughter. He had begun to feel left out.

As never before, he wished for the old ideals he had once harbored of family—the ideals that had been so reminiscent in Amy Chandler.

Blue eyes, short, dark hair that contrasted almost starkly with her fair complexion: Amy Chandler was more than a reminder of an emotional keepsake. She was an interesting, vibrant, unique woman. All combined, that made her appealing as all get-out.

A pair of policemen ushered in a man staggering from God only knew what. Seth instantly shifted mental gears, but not before he let himself think of Amy Chandler one last time.

Chapter Five

The rhythmic squeezing sensations of Peggy's orgasm knocked Mark's senses into another dimension. That was all it took for him to reach his own climax. Arms wrapped tightly about her shoulders, he heaved himself into her, ground his eyes shut, and thrust until he was empty, sated, and more at peace than he had been in a long time.

Sweat dripped along his spine and down his temples. His breathing gradually returned to normal. Against his chest, the twin pillows of Peggy's breasts felt welcomingly soft. On some undefined level, he was aware of his own body, of Peggy's, and of the morning light seeping in around the blinds. Morning . . . after a bitch of a night.

His momentary bliss was replaced by concern for his mother. Concern and a certain sense of guilt over the fact that he had temporarily forgotten his mother and just screwed his wife *and* enjoyed himself as much as was humanly possible. Feeling like a little boy who'd gotten caught with his hand in the cookie jar, he levered himself away to flop onto his back and throw an arm over his eyes.

Peggy's hand followed to lie low against his belly. "What's the matter?" she asked, her voice drugged with the remains of spent passion.

Had Peggy posed the question an hour from now, he might have been able to camouflage what he was really thinking. She'd asked now and she knew him too well. She'd sensed his too-sudden withdrawal both physically and emotionally and, as was her way, delved right to the heart of the matter.

Now her inquiry hung there—now, when he was at his most vulnerable. He always was right after sex. It was as if the price to pay for coming was a temporary destruction of his defenses. As never before, he was grateful for the bond of trust they'd created over the years.

"I feel like shit," he said.

Peggy swiped the strands of blond hair back off her brow as she came to her elbows. "Why?" It was easy to hear in her tone that she was confused and amused.

"Because we just had sex."

"So?"

"So I've been getting my jollies off while my mother is in the hospital."

"There's no reason to feel guilty. Your mom is going to be fine. The doctors said so."

He dropped his arm away to stare her right in the eye. "Yeah, but she's not home yet."

With a roll of her sleepy gray eyes, Peggy squirmed about until she was lying on top of him, her slender curves fitting his as perfectly as they always had. "Mark, don't do this to yourself. After yesterday, you're entitled to want some kind of reaffirmation of life.''

"What?"

Her humor slipped into a long sigh. "You got hit pretty hard with your mother's mortality. It's only natural that you'd want a tangible reminder of life. So you made love." She pressed her lips to his. "To your wife. It's okay; it's allowed. We've got the marriage license to prove it."

For some reason, her analysis didn't sit well with him. It reeked of weakness, of his failing as a man. "We made love because I woke up with a hard-on." A condition that many a man even half his age would envy.

"How romantic," she drawled, giving him a mock glare.

"I didn't hear you complaining."

"I didn't because you've always turned me on. And because I love you. Honestly, I don't care why me made love."

"Jesus, Peggy, you make it sound as if you granted me a mercy fuck."

The sigh she let loose this time was rife with ripening frustration. Rolling to her own side of the bed, she peered up at the swirls of plaster on the ceiling. "I swear, you are ninety-eight percent fragile male ego. It's a good thing I love you. It's a good thing I'm patient."

He eyed her through a haze of annoyance on the brink of erupting. His mood was suddenly that tenuous. "Screw ego." The demon in the back of his head added, *and screw you, too, for probably being right.*

Shame and a discomfort deep in his gut sent him to his feet, but once there, he couldn't figure out where he wanted to go or what he wanted to do.

The condition had been plaguing him too much lately.

Swearing, he sat on the edge of the bed. From behind him, Peggy quietly asked, "Why are you so defensive this morning? Is it because of your mom?"

"I don't know. Most likely." It was as good a lie as any. He knew full well that the nagging uneasiness, the feeling that his life wasn't all he wanted it to be, had never been stronger. For Peggy's sake, he expanded the lie. "I guess yesterday shook me up more than I thought. Sometimes being the head of the family gets to me."

"You don't always have to be the strong one, you know."

"Claire expects it. Mom and Amy, too, I think."

Peggy snorted out her opinion of that. "Claire is a wuss. It would do her good to finally get a backbone."

"Go easy, Peg."

"And you're wrong about Mom and Amy. They're two of the most capable women I know." She scooted over to kneel behind him, thighs spread to encase him. "Almost as capable as me." Her arms circled him as she pressed against his back. "So don't mess with me, mister." One of her hands lowered with lovingly indecent intent. "I've been known to bring men to their knees."

He could hear the humor in her voice, could picture that sassy smile of hers, the one that challenged him and lured him at the same time. She'd been wearing that smile the first time he'd seen her nearly twenty years ago.

In a single second, he was a college senior again, cocksure of himself, restless with academics, ready to take on corporate America. With graduation a few short months off, he'd lined up three job offers, two within his area of concentration and one in general office management. Only half a semester and exams had stood between him and the real world.

Enter Peggy Fitzgerald. Freshman to his senior. Blonde to his brunette, lofty philosophy major to his more hard-edged advertising. They were exact opposites, and perfect complements to each other. He'd known that the minute she'd looked at him over the shelves in the college bookstore, lifted one delicate eyebrow, and given him that sassy "you don't know what you're in for" smile.

Her hand found its targeted mark and he sucked in a breath. Blood began to surge.

"See," she teased, "there's no need to stress. Your body knows it even if your head doesn't."

It was difficult for his head to work at all with her hand doing what it was doing. It certainly was too much of an effort to dwell on discontentment or being strong for his sisters. "Don't you have to get the kids ready for school?" The clock showed eight-fifteen.

"They've got the day off," she breathed in his ear. "Teacher work day."

He didn't need any further encouragement. In a swift move, he dragged her into his arms. Not once in the ensuing half hour did he even think of pity or mercy, doctors or work, or dissatisfaction with what he'd made of his life.

With the morning newspaper tucked under one arm, Peggy snagged the carton of orange juice out of the refrigerator, danced around the dog underfoot, and still managed to pick up the phone on the third ring.

"Hello." Setting the orange juice on the counter, she cradled the cordless phone between her jaw and her shoulder while scooping dog food into Furry Dude's bowl. Five-year-old Julia waddled in, still scrubbing sleep from her eyes. Peggy blew her youngest a kiss, set water on to boil for the oatmeal Julia was sure to want, and through it all kept track of the conversation she was having with the president of one of the local women's civic groups.

Five minutes later, latest club disaster averted, she went about the business of getting breakfast for the kids. They hurried in from various parts of the sprawling house, drawn by the scents of French toast and bacon. Once seated, Peggy indulged in one of her favorite pastimes: simply sitting and eyeing each of her offspring with motherly pride.

Her gaze rested on Sarah, the eldest of the three. At nine, she was prim and proper, bright, and absurdly concerned about life's little details. Even in the third grade, she was determined to be a lawyer. Over her coffee cup, Peggy smiled and thought how much like Mark Sarah was, not only in temperament but in looks as well.

Tyler, too, had inherited Mark's good looks, but that was where the similarities ended between father and son. The seven-year-old was as laid-back as his father was driven. At times the differences grated on Mark's nerves.

And then there was Julia. Peggy admitted that little Jules was the best and worst of both herself and Mark. That five-year-old temper was matched by the unrelenting drive to keep up with her siblings. Yet on a moment's notice, Julia was the most loving and giving child Peggy had ever encountered.

Almost ten years' worth of children, Peggy reflected, encompassing the three in her gaze. Ten years of careful tending, of molding characters, of trying to instill moral fiber and responsibility. With all her heart, she hoped she and Mark had succeeded.

Over the din of her children's table talk, she considered her husband. She was worried about him; she had been for some time. She couldn't put her finger on what was eating away at him, but something was. If she didn't know better, she would think he was having an affair.

She shoved away from the unthinkable, coming to her feet so quickly, she nearly turned her chair over.

"Jeez, Mom," Tyler said. "Are you in hyperdrive or something?"

"Sorry," she returned with a slightly forced smile. Immediately she busied herself by loading the dishwasher. "Guess I had too many Wheaties."

"You didn't eat Wheaties," Sarah observed, her eyes wide and far too discerning for someone her age.

"She knows that," Julia shot back to her older sister. "Mom knows everything."

"She does not," Sarah countered.

"How do you know?" Tyler asked.

Sarah gave her brother a condescending glare, as if to say *you poor stupid male*. "Shut up, Tyler."

"He doesn't have to," Julia asserted around a mouthful of oatmeal.

"Yeah, I don't have to do what you tell me. Just because you're the oldest, you think you're so great."

Sarah smiled angelically. "I am."

Julia obviously thought she had evidence to the contrary. "You pooped in your pants last week."

Sarah screamed in outrage. Tyler exploded in taunting laughter while Julia, having scored heavily in the ongoing sibling rivalry, dissolved into delighted giggles. Over the clamor of Furry Dude barking, she exchanged a low five with her brother.

To Peggy, Sarah wailed, "Mom! It was an accident. You know it was an accident."

"Enough, all of you," Peggy informed them, and that included the dog.

Sarah hung in there. "But Mom."

"But nothing." Her gray eyes rife with a commanding grit that would have done an army general proud, Peggy issued her orders. "Jules, finish your breakfast. Tyler, leave your sisters alone. And Sarah, lighten up. Not another word, goofy-eyed glance, or 'accidental' touch until breakfast is over."

The three knew better than to cross over the line Peggy had set. On that score, she congratulated herself. If she had taught her children nothing else, she had taught them common sense. They knew she could and would pull rank in a heartbeat. On this rare day off from school, with toys and friends waiting, it was just plain foolish to rile a mother who never, *never* issued false threats of "go to your room."

Breakfast was finished in relative silence, and in short order. A little ruefully, Peggy noted that she may have tempered all the energy of her children, but she certainly hadn't contained it. There was no containing youth. In minutes the kids were out the back door.

The sound of their muted laughter drifted into

the kitchen, bringing Peggy contentment and a happiness that ran to the very heart of her. By comparison, the still hush of the house was saturated with far less. Helplessly, her mind drifted to her fears. For a few minutes, the kids had distracted her, kept her from probing too closely into the whys of Mark's recent moods. But there were no distractions now—nothing except cowardice or obstinate folly to keep her from examining the issue.

Was he having an affair? Her stomach twisted in on itself at the possibility. She shut her eyes, her bottom lip trembling despite her efforts to keep it steady, despite the voice in her head that told her she was crazy for doubting Mark.

He loved her. In a hundred different ways, he told her so every day. Then why the strange moods? Every time she'd asked, he'd had an excuse. This morning it was his mother. Last week it had been annoyance over a business account. Three weeks before that, he'd explained his distraction away by saying he was tired.

And so the reasons went. But for six months? Something other than life's daily challenges was behind the subtle changes she'd witnessed in him.

According to his latest physical, he was in perfect health, so she was sure he wasn't keeping a medical problem from her. And Lord knew, any man who could make love the way Mark did wasn't lacking for stamina.

The family finances were sound. The mortgage on the house was steep, and the balance on their MasterCard was outrageous, but they owned outright both cars and the sit-down mower. Three more payments to the orthodontist, and Sarah's braces would be paid for.

Chandler Graphics had never been in better shape. A slew of accountants and attorneys confirmed that quarterly. And even if they didn't, Peggy knew that Mark was too savvy a businessman ever to fail at any venture.

So the question remained: what was wrong with Mark that he could drift off the way he so often did? Her answer: nothing was wrong with Mark. He had everything a man could want. Health, family, money, and the satisfaction of being successful.

The truth in that sent her down an avenue of thought that drained the joy from her day and slumped her shoulders as she continued to sit. Whether she wanted to or not, she had to ask herself if she was the cause for Mark's dissatisfaction.

Did he find her lacking? Their bout of lovemaking this morning would indicate otherwise. Nonetheless, a very basic human insecurity impelled her to question her own worth.

She was a thirty-eight-year-old woman who had a worthless degree in philosophy. In the early years of their marriage, she'd played at being an aide at the local library until the babies had come along. After that, she'd stayed home to do what she loved best: raise her family and care for her home.

Such domesticity didn't come without a price. Her reading list included Dr. Seuss instead of John Grisham, and she sat on the Board of the Williamsburg PTA instead of that of a mega-corporation. She had no interest in nor time for politics, but she'd be the first to criticize the nearest grocery for selling imported products over American.

Thanks to three pregnancies, her breasts no longer held the perky muscle tone they once had. A few stray white hairs had begun to thread through the blond. And even though she was still a size nine and her face held fewer lines than those of her friends, Mother Nature had definitely been having her way.

Regardless of all of that, she was happy with herself, with taking care of the kids; she loved them and Mark. But was that enough to keep his interest? Was being supportive, caring, loving, and as intellectually stimulating as she could manage enough for him? From the way he looked right through her at times, she didn't think so.

"Kids outside already?" he asked, entering the kitchen with his jacket slung over his shoulder.

She thrust her anxiety into the nether regions of consciousness and then damned herself for doing so. She'd been avoiding the issue far too often of late, and it wasn't a habit she wished to promote.

"Yeah," she answered, stacking dishes because it was far easier than pushing for the truth. In her heart, she wasn't certain she was ready to hear it. "The swing set beckons. What about you? Are you going to the hospital?"

"For a while. I want to see how Mom is doing."

At the sink, she didn't let herself look at him, didn't let herself dwell on how great he looked in his dress slacks and white shirt and tie.

"I thought I'd drive out later myself. Sharon next door will take care of the kids. She owes me ten times over for sitting with her bunch."

"Sounds good to me, and Mom would like that. You okay?"

"Sure." She answered automatically, turning then to face him squarely. That slight display of interest on his part was all that was needed to assuage some of her hurt.

"You don't sound like yourself."

In a credible imitation of the Peggy he was seeking, she flashed her grin and quipped, "All that early-morning sex must be affecting your ears."

"It affected something, **all right**, but further south. My ears are fine."

"So's the rest of you," she drawled, his lazy smile warming her insides.

"You should talk."

"I'm glad you realize that," she teased with outward flippancy. Inside, she needed to be reminded that he was as attracted to her now as he'd been when she had been eighteen or twenty-five or even thirty-six.

"How could I ever forget it? What you do to my libido should be outlawed."

Sweet words, yet they weren't the ones she wanted most. She wanted, needed, to hear him say that he loved her, that he couldn't live without her, that the reason he had seemed distant all those times was because he had been reflecting on how lucky he was to have her as his wife.

What she got instead was the ringing of the phone, and Mark reaching for his jacket. What she got as she ignored the ringing was Mark planting a kiss on her forehead instead of her lips, and a gentle pat on her shoulder rather than a lustful grope of her ass.

The disappointment weighed her down and made her feel, to use Mark's earlier words, like shit. Silently she raged at him for making her feel that way, and at herself for allowing it. In the end, she was left with her anger, her confusion, and the horrible, unshakeable suspicion that her marriage was slipping out of her grasp.

Chapter Six

"I'll be glad to take Mom home," Claire insisted for the third time. For the third time, Amy caught the note of desperation in her sister's tone.

"I don't know, Claire," Mark deliberated, taking it upon himself to decide what he thought would be best in this situation.

Irked by his characteristic condescension, Amy countered with, "If Claire wants to take Mom home, it's fine with me."

He continued to look doubtful. "Are you sure?" he asked of Claire.

"Of course I'm sure," Claire maintained. "I can handle this. Besides, John told me I don't have to go in today, whereas the two of you should have been at work an hour ago." From her seat in the only chair in the hospital room, she turned to her mother. "What do you think?"

"Leave me out of this," Ellen protested on a laugh.

"Claire's right," Amy told her brother. "I'm on a deadline with that Sanderson account and I'm sure there's some owner-of-the-company thing you've got to do."

Mark relented with a laugh of his own. "Don't let anyone ever tell you that you have a way with words, Amy. Stick to drawing."

"Then it's settled?" Claire prodded.

Mark shrugged, but Amy was more definite. "Yes. You take Mom home." It was obviously important to Claire.

"Good." Claire looked to the empty doorway. "Now, if we can only get Dr. Jamal to sign Mom out."

Ever the one to take charge, Mark made for the door. "I'll speed things up."

In typical Mark fashion, he worked his magic. It never failed to amaze Amy that he could make the world dance to his tune. By the time their mother was in the adjoining bathroom changing into her street clothes, Mark had returned with a satisfied smile and had taken up a post at the foot of the bed.

"I'm sure this makes sense to someone," he commented, checking over their mother's chart.

Amy reached for the records, her curious expression suddenly turning pained. "Someone's made a mistake."

"With what?" Mark asked.

"Mom's blood type."

He craned his head forward to look over her shoulder.

"Right here," she pointed out. "They've got her typed as O negative."

Claire wondered aloud, "So?"

"So," Amy clarified, "she can't be O negative. Dad was O negative."

"Well, so am I," came Claire's comment.

Mark agreed. "Me, too."

Amy gave them both a distorted smile. "Well, I'm not. I'm A positive."

"I don't follow what you're saying," Claire said.

Amy could not contain her disbelief. "Think back to high school biology, folks. There's no way that two O negative parents can have A positive children."

"Are you sure?" Mark questioned.

"Of course I'm sure. Mrs. Freeman drummed that stuff into my head. Children of two O negative parents are *always* O negative." She lifted the chart. "Which makes this impossible. Mom has to be A positive."

"Maybe Dad wasn't O negative," Claire suggested. "Maybe he was A positive."

Mark shook his head. "No, he was O negative, all right. When he had his gall bladder removed, I donated blood for the operation."

"Well, then, someone has screwed up," Claire averred, glaring at the chart.

"No kidding," Amy echoed. "Thank God Mom didn't need a transfusion."

"What's going on?" their mother queried from behind them.

As one, they turned, Amy with an irate lifting of her brows. "The hospital has messed up."

"Oh?" Ellen laid her hospital gown over the foot of the bed. "With what?"

"Your blood type," Mark said. "They've got you down here as being O negative instead of A positive."

Claire fumed. "You'd think that with all the money this place makes between patients and insurance companies, they'd be able to get something as simple as blood type right. I have half a mind to sue someone."

"For once, I'm inclined to agree with you," Mark told her.

"Really?"

"Almost, but it's probably a simple mistake. Most likely they have the correct information in another set of records."

Amy wasn't so sure. "Nothing is simple about medicine. This could have been real trouble for Mom." She shook her head, sending her gaze about the room to let it finally rest on Ellen. "Mom? Are you all right?" Their mother's face contained no more color than the sheets. She grabbed hold of Ellen's hand. "Mom?" For one horrid moment, Amy was sure her mother was having another stroke.

Ellen came to life in a flurry, patting her hair, smiling hugely, looking like her old self, as if she could not wait to leave. "I'm fine, never better."

"You sure?"

"Of course I'm sure. I'm not daft. I know when I'm fine."

Amy exchanged a bemused look with Claire, who shrugged with her face as well as her shoulders and prompted, "Let's get out of here. We've all had enough of this place."

Claire was so glad to be away from the hospital, she didn't pay any attention to her mother's silence in the car. Nothing was going to ruin her day, nothing, although Mark had come pretty close earlier at the hospital.

His reluctance to trust her to see Mom home safely had made her feel subhuman, like an incom-

petent fool who didn't know up from down. He
had a way of doing that to her, only this time she
hadn't allowed it. It was important that she be the
one to care for their mother without help from
either her brother or sister, so she had dug in her
heels on the matter.

Mark had been graceful about it, although she
sensed he had not been pleased. She'd bet anything that he would call and check up on her within
minutes of getting Mom into her house. She could
picture him in his office, timing her drive on his
watch, counting out the minutes down to the last
stop sign. She should let the phone ring, just to
let him stew in his own self-righteousness, and to
remind him that she wasn't a little kid any longer.

He saw her that way; she knew he did—the little
sister needing the support of an older brother. To
some extent she did. He was great with her kids
and sympathetic with her, but she wished for once
that he would let her choose when she needed
help and on what issues and in what capacity.

If she hadn't been aware that Amy shared, to a
small degree, the same sentiments, Claire would
have been troubled by her selfish and unkind feelings. Thankfully, Amy fell under the same big-
brother umbrella of mentality. She commiserated
with Claire and even once or twice had put Mark
in his place for assuming attitudes and airs that
weren't his to assume.

Feeling aggravation erode her good mood, she
refused to think of Mark and focused her attention
back on her mother.

"Are you sure you're feeling okay?"

Ellen dragged her gaze in from her window. "I'm
sure."

Claire would have liked to have been better convinced. Her mother sounded normal and looked only slightly pale, and yet she wasn't quite herself. "I think you need to rest as soon as you get home."

"I've got things to do."

"I'll do them for you." Claire flicked her a smiling sideways glance as she pulled into the driveway. Proud that she was dealing with the situation so competently, she said, "That's why I'm here, remember? Don't be stubborn about this, please. You know what the doctor said."

"To take it easy for the next week," Ellen groused.

Claire had to laugh at her mother's standard balking at medical advice. "Everyone wants to help out, even your sisters. Aunt Dot and Aunt Betty are bringing you dinner tonight. Come on, Mom, it won't be that bad."

"Yes, it will." For the first time since they'd left the hospital, Ellen seemed to come fully to life, spurred, Claire was sure, by a perceived challenge in the doctor's orders.

Swiveling about as much as the seat belt would allow, Ellen stared indignantly at her daughter. "I'm not used to sitting around the house, you know. I have friends and hobbies. I have clubs and responsibilities, you know. I have a life of my own, you know."

Claire turned off the ignition before answering. Her mother was entitled to be out of sorts, but her rare defensiveness hurt nonetheless. "I didn't say you didn't have a life. All I said was that you have to rest for a while." And as quickly as that, all the positive, confident things she had been feeling were dashed into a forlorn heap of good intentions gone bad.

Staring out the windshield at nothing in particular, Claire lamented her inability to make things work out as she wanted. Today she had wanted to be the responsible one. All she'd done was annoy her mother into an unusual snit. She could well imagine what Mark would have to say about that. The criticism wouldn't be blatant, but it would be there in his casual suggestions or in his body language that once again, poor little old Claire had· messed up.

"Come on," she muttered. "Let's get inside." Screw the fact that her dejection was hanging out there for her mother to see. A lifetime of the same had taught her that there was no hiding this kind of emotion. There was no use in trying.

It took Ellen sitting in her favorite living-room chair for Claire to regain some of her optimism. Being able to fix lunch and call the pharmacy for her mother's prescriptions further boosted her spirits. And the fact that Mark did not call was encouraging. By the time *Guiding Light* was on TV, Claire had recovered completely. Gently but implacably, she delivered a no-nonsense command to her mother to stay put, even sleep if she could.

"What are you going to do?" Ellen asked, giving no outward signs of her earlier annoyance.

"I thought I'd run some errands for you, pick up your prescriptions, stop by the grocery store." On an afterthought, she added, "And I want to check with Mark or Amy and see if either of them has called the hospital about the mix-up with your blood type."

Just thinking about what might have happened sent a shaft of pure fury through Claire. Old age alone was precarious enough on one's health. It was unconscionable, criminal in regard to her mother, that a hospital could add to life's uncertainty.

"I wish you wouldn't make a fuss over that," Ellen said.

"I'm not making a fuss."

"I'm sure it was just an innocent mistake. Like Mark said, someone probably copied the wrong information down; that's all."

"Probably," Claire agreed, bending to kiss Ellen's cheek. "But I don't want there to be any mix-up where you're concerned."

"You've got more than enough to do without worrying over that."

"If I don't worry over it, I can guarantee you that Amy or Mark will."

Ellen released a breath that in no way resembled a sigh. The exhalation bordered on pent-up energy escaping a tightly sealed vacuum. To Claire, the sound was peculiar enough to make her ask again, "Are you feeling all right?"

The instantaneous reassurance, whether a lie or not, was not forthcoming. Her mother continued to sit as though in indecision, worrying the knuckles of one hand against the other.

"What is it, Mom?"

Lined lips parted as if to speak before rolling in on themselves. Finally, in a slow cadence, Ellen admitted, "I suppose I'm tired, is all. The last two days have finally caught up with me."

There was so much resignation in the beloved voice, Claire felt a stab of sorrow. Errands were dismissed as she pulled the hassock near and sat at Ellen's knees, feeling very much like a mother to her mother. "It'll be all right," she soothed. "Really it will. Dr. Jamal said you might feel depressed about the stroke." She tenderly gathered one of the arthritic hands in her own. "It's only natural. The best thing you can do is think positively, think happy thoughts: your grandchildren, your flower garden."

Ellen's expression remained unchanged. Claire persisted. "Well, then, think about all those times Dad made you laugh."

At the mention of Sam, a light that Claire could only describe as mellow suffused her mother's eyes. "He was the finest man I've ever known," she whispered.

"He loved you with all his heart."

"And you children, too." Her fingers gripped Claire's. "I'm glad he wasn't here for this."

"Why?" Claire was genuinely surprised. "Dad wouldn't have been anywhere other than right at your side."

"I know. I wouldn't have wanted him to go through that."

"Mom, you were there for him. You can't expect him to have done any differently. That's what your marriage was all about. You can't have regrets about that."

Ellen shut her eyes, holding on to the memories or blocking them out; Claire couldn't tell.

"I miss him."

"We all do, Mom."

With quiet, sure emphasis, Ellen shook her head. "Not like I do. He was my best friend, you know."

"I know."

"We went through some very rough times together. That can be hard on a marriage."

"Whatever the two of you did obviously worked."

"Thirty-six years. If your dad were alive today, it would have been forty-four, you know."

"It's tough losing your spouse."

Ellen offered up a wistful smile before stroking her fingers down Claire's cheek. "You should know." Motherly pride rose up to replace the melancholy turn of lip. "I'm so proud of you for carrying on with your life the way you have."

The vote of confidence was a panacea to Claire's ofttimes fragile sense of self. That did not necessarily mean that she believed her mother entirely. The day-to-day struggle of coping wouldn't allow Claire to mindlessly accept the compliment. "Oh, I don't know, Mom," she said with a chuckle. "I screw up more times than not."

"We all do, but you've done well for yourself and the kids."

"I try. I don't always succeed."

"No one does."

"You did."

"I was older than you when my husband died. My children were grown, not babies like yours. It makes a difference."

Claire let herself accept that. Feeling buoyed for that acceptance, she teased, "You always know what to say and what to do."

"Not always. I'm not perfect."

"Pretty close," she maintained in loving loyalty.

"I've made mistakes, Claire, but I've always loved you children. Always. There isn't anything I wouldn't do for any of you."

"I know. We all do.

"Remember that, always."

Chapter Seven

Amy's internal palette had been hovering near fuchsia for days. Ever since her mother had been released, fully recovered, from the hospital, the red of elation and the purple of gratitude had tinged most of Amy's waking hours. One look at Seth Donovan standing in her office doorway, however, and life took on a startling golden glow.

"Dr. Donovan." He was the last person she ever expected to see in her office. "This is a surprise." More so for his being out of context. Until now, she had not envisioned him anywhere other than in the hospital.

"Is this a bad time?" He glanced to her computer monitor.

In those three seconds, she had completely forgotten the layout in which she'd been so engrossed. Almost flustered, she saved her screen, all the while explaining, "No, not at all. Please, come in; sit down." She didn't even try to keep the curiosity or the smile from her expression as she swiveled her chair around to face him. "What brings you here?"

Sitting, he thrust one leg out before him, his pose that of a man completely at ease in his surroundings. "I came to see if your breakfasts had improved lately."

She had been anticipating some comment or inquiry about her mother; it was what she would have expected. Surprised again, she realized with a start of pleasure that this was not a professional visit. She reached behind her for her cup of tea. "I'm afraid this is it this morning."

"It's almost eleven. That's all you've had?"

"This and two others just like it."

Linking his fingers over his stomach, he chided with a smile, "That's not very nutritious."

She couldn't come up with a suitable defense, so she went on the offense. "What about you? What did you have for breakfast?"

"Nothing. Which is why I'm here."

"Toast and juice?"

"Lunch. I thought you might like to join me."

The man certainly knew how to get to the heart of a matter. Reticence didn't seem to be his style, nor subtlety either. For all he knew, she could be involved with someone, yet there he sat looking like anything but a doctor in his well-worn jeans and white oxford-cloth shirt, unfazed by the fact that they barely knew each other, point-blank inviting her to have lunch with him.

"Is this something you have to think about?" he asked. Behind his glasses, a hint of tension flickered in the blue gaze.

"No. It's just that you've taken me by surprise."

"Don't you like surprises?"

"Some more than others." This one more than

most. "I'd love to have lunch. Can you give me five minutes?"

It was closer to ten, but she noticed he didn't seem to mind. He wandered about her office, studying displays in the same intense way she had seen him study her mother's medical chart.

"Did you do all of these?" he asked.

"Yes."

He shook his head in blatant admiration. "I'm impressed."

"Don't be."

"Why not?"

"There's nothing here to be impressed with."

"That's a matter of opinion." He looked at her for a moment too long before nodding to the artwork advertising the opening of the symphony season. "I don't know much about graphics and advertising, but I know what I like, what strikes a chord."

Amy, too, knew what she liked. She also knew that any work she considered truly worthy of merit was at home: her drawings and paintings, the pieces she did for herself and for the sheer joy of creativity. "So what exactly strikes a chord with you?"

His reply was instantaneous. "Honesty. Directness." Turning fully to face her, he gave her one of his lazy, one-sided grins, which was totally incongruous with the challenge in his eyes. "Modest graphic artists."

Warp speed, shields up, fazers on stun—it was all Amy could think. For years she had condemned herself for speeding through life and then having to pay the consequences, but she had nothing on Seth Donovan. He had her feeling mentally breathless, which was not altogether unpleasant. The sensation ignited feminine nerve endings lethargic from disuse.

The feeling was tenacious and more long-lived than she would have thought possible. By the time they were seated in a cozy Japanese restaurant, her internal palette had forsaken its customary order for something more closely resembling a Jackson Pollock kaleidoscope of colors.

"How's your mom?" He posed the query as a friend might, rather than as the physician he was.

"Good. Better than any of us would have expected."

"I'm glad. She's a nice lady, very determined. She knows her own mind. I like that."

"You're being kind," she vowed with a gentle scoff. "She'd be the first to tell you that she's as opinionated as they come and as stubborn as the proverbial mule."

"There's nothing wrong with that."

"That's because you've never had to convince her to do something she's dead set against."

"Such as getting a physical every now and then?"

"That and a hundred other things." Despite her mother's ofttimes annoying stubbornness, Amy could not deny the love she felt for Ellen. The insecurity of days past threatened. "Thank you for helping her the way you did."

"I don't want your gratitude."

"Why not?"

"It isn't warranted. I did what I've been trained to do."

"Which was to care for my mother. I don't know how you expect me to overlook that."

Seth leaned back in his chair, head tilted to one side, his left hand resting lightly on the table. Amy would have sensed his displeasure even if he hadn't so obviously withdrawn from her. A silent tautness suddenly seemed to saturate the space between them.

"Is that why you agreed to have lunch with me? To thank me?"

"No. Of course not."

"Are you sure? What about subconsciously? Maybe there's a tiny grain of gratitude still floating around in your psyche that needs to be expressed."

He had slipped from affable to defensive because, Amy realized, he thought she might be with him out of some misplaced sense of appreciation. Clicking her back teeth, she considered how best to handle this. She could lie to him, disavow her gratitude in order to spare the male pride he so patently thought was in jeopardy. Or she could reply with simple honesty, the same honesty he had claimed struck a chord within him. The former would be easier for them both, but not in the long run.

The implications underlying her thoughts were not lost on her. She was just getting to know this man, and she was already thinking in terms of future time for them.

Her usual caution with men was nowhere to be found, so she actually went mentally searching for all the warnings her head ordinarily sent up in situations like this. What she got for her mental safari was a sense of intrigue. Seth Donovan had accomplished a rare feat in record time: he stoked her imagination. For that reason alone, she would be nothing less than honest with him. It was up to him to deal with those truths.

Squelching the beginnings of a betraying vulnerability, she said, "Of course I'm grateful to you. I'm not going to deny it. You helped my mother when she was most in need." She tipped her head to an angle to match his, raised her brows encouragingly, and smiled. "I find the compassion inherent in that extremely appealing. That's why I'm having lunch with you. I can't help it if I'm attracted to your sensitive streak." She let her smile broaden with irreverent rebuke. "All this testosterone nonsense of resenting a perceived pity, however, is pretty lame."

Chin tucked, he regarded her steadily. "Lame, huh?"

"Extremely. But I'll forgive you because you're so good-looking."

He scoured the inside of his cheek with his tongue before relenting to rueful laughter. "Your mother isn't the only one who knows her own mind."

Liking his humor, she teased, "Don't ever forget it."

"Somehow I don't think you'll let me."

"Then we're bound to get along."

And they did. Amy could not remember when she had ever enjoyed a man's company more. The energy level between them reminded her of atoms imploding in a constant discharge, one right after another. Laughter came easily, as did the subtle, new-relationship digging for all the vital stats.

"Do you see your daughter often?" she asked on the ride back to her office. She had not been surprised to learn that he had been married once. Attentive, compassionate, he struck her as the husband type.

"Often enough." Despite his keen attention to traffic, a gentleness crept into his voice. "She's a great kid."

Amy liked his assessment and the fact that it had

come so effortlessly. She had listened to too many parents who never had anything good to say about their children. "I get the impression that she comes by it naturally."

"Yeah, Gail's done a great job with her."

"I'm sure she has, but I was talking about you."

He gave her a sidelong glance underscored with skepticism.

"You doubt me?"

"Let's just say," he mused aloud, "that my influence has been minimal."

"Oh, I don't know," she disagreed without a second thought. "Somehow I don't see you as the sit-back-and-do-nothing type. You're far too intent and determined for that."

He had pulled into a parking space in front of Chandler Graphics. Killing the engine, he shifted sideways to face her, stretching his right arm across the back of her seat. "Think you've got it all figured out, don't you?"

"Perhaps." A tilting of her head from side to side emphasized her opinion that, when it came to him, the jury was still out. She had learned that beneath his secure exterior he was multilayered, multifaceted, possessing more than his share of normal strengths with a few weaknesses thrown in for balance—qualities that kept him from being a cartoon character. What she hadn't had time to discover was the extent and nature of all those qualities. She'd like to, though. With an eargerness she hadn't felt in years, she admitted she wanted very much to discover everything there was to discover about Seth Donovan.

That was why, when he hooked his hand behind her head and drew her near for a kiss, she didn't hesitate. She accepted it with a sense of satisfaction and joy, as if her body and mind had been waiting years to feel this particular man's warmth and intensity. Neither disappointed. In fact, they lured her to return the kiss, unmindful of time or place.

In broad daylight, where anyone could be—and most likely more than a few from inside actually were—watching them, Amy disregarded all sense of privacy. In that, she was well met. The kiss deepened, tongues and straining breaths mingling in earnest repertoire.

"Jesus," Seth muttered, the first to break away, although not entirely. His hands lingered, one at her neck, the other resting on her ribs just below her right breast.

"Is He home?" she whispered, shaken. The kiss had been that profound. "I'm in need of some divine intervention myself."

"I want to see you again."

The idea of refusing never occured to her. "Me too."

"I'm on tonight. Tomorrow? Have dinner with me?"

Taking a breath to stave off one last latent twinge of wariness, she nodded, knowing full well what she was getting herself into. Seth Donovan was no naive boy to be content with a few tongue-ola kisses followed by a quickie grope in the dark. Everything she had learned about him proclaimed him to be a man in the fullest sense of the word. Sooner or later—her brain declared the former—he was going to want to make love to her, and not because he was hard-up or horny. Seth Donovan was after more in life.

"I get off at five," she told him.

"How about if I pick you up at seven?" He couldn't seem to keep his hands still. Unlike his eyes, which remained laser-beam fixed, his fingers at her nape massaged in small circles while his hand at her ribs flexed rythmically.

"Fine." She was in imminent danger of melting right on the spot. To her great relief, he released her with a final whispering kiss and the promise to call her tomorrow.

"How was lunch?" Cicily drawled the minute Amy walked in the front door.

"Good. We had Japanese."

"Looked French to me." Cicily clucked her tongue and shook her head in what Amy thought was a pretty bad show of innocence. "I must have been looking at dessert."

Amy ignored the comment and the following laughter as she headed for her office. As she flipped on her computer, she decided she had to have been out of her mind to have abandoned her normal sense of reserve. It was, of course, Seth's fault. He had her so overwhelmed, she had forgotten to ask him to check on her mother's blood tests.

To her surprise, she had the chance to do so later that afternoon. He called her just as she was shutting down for the night.

"Are you at the hospital?" she asked. Adrenaline made a heady rush through her veins. Her end-of-the-workday weariness was instantly abolished.

"Yeah. I've got the graveyard shift tonight."

"I'm sorry." It sounded awful to her.

"It's not that bad. Actually, I enjoy it for the few times a week that I'm scheduled. You see different problems at two in the morning than you might usually see at noon."

"I bet, but aren't you tired? You've been up since before we had lunch."

"I slept for a few hours this afternoon."

The mental image of Seth Donovan stretched out naked beneath the covers of a king-sized bed formed in her head. She thrust it aside for Seth's sake. For her own, she would have gladly lingered in the reverie.

"Well, I'm glad you got some rest. I'd hate to think of you falling asleep while literally in the middle of some poor patient."

"Never happens."

"You mean you never make mistakes?"

"I do my damnedest not to."

"That reminds me." She shifted in her chair, reaching out to toy with her mouse on its blue pad. "Who should I speak to if I think a mistake was made with Mom's blood tests."

"What?"

She heard the faint trace of caution enter his voice and proceeded carefully. "Mom's chart indicated that her blood type is O negative, and that can't be. I was wondering what we should do to correct the error, or who we should talk to about having new tests done so that her records are accurate."

"You can bring her in and have her retested, but are you sure about this? The lab doesn't screw up very often."

Amy's innate reply was, *well, they sure screwed up this time.* But she didn't voice that opinion. She knew it was a knee-jerk reaction, born of love and protectiveness for her mother. She tempered her response. "I'll talk to my brother about bringing Mom in again."

"If you like, I can check through the paperwork at this end."

"I don't want you going to any bother."

"It won't be."

"Are you sure?"

"I wouldn't have offered if I didn't want to help."

Once again she was struck by his generosity of spirit. She was deeply touched, and more attracted to the man than she had been minutes ago. "Thanks, Seth," she said, fully aware that her voice had softened with her feelings.

Seth had to have heard it, too. When he spoke, his voice was a mellow purr. "No problem. I'll take care of things at this end. You take care of yourself."

"I will. You, too."

"I'll talk to you tomorrow."

With the exception of lunch with Seth, "tomorrow" turned out to be very much like yesterday. Work came complete with the pressure of deadlines, an irate client or two, and the inevitable foibles that glitched every layout. Amy sailed through them all, though, anticipation adding a layer to her already thick skin. She went home that evening feeling as if she hadn't done anything more taxing than puff on the feathery seeds of a dandelion.

Home was a two-bedroom cottage she rented on Lyons Creek in Poquoson. On clear days, she could see all the way to the Poquoson River, which fed into the Chesapeake Bay. On stormy days, the sky and water churned into a pewter backdrop that had served as inspiration for more than one of her paintings.

Select canvases were hung randomly throughout the house. Most were stored in the second bedoom, her studio. Seth was quick to make comment when he arrived to pick her up.

"These are wonderful," he said. Bent low, he

slowly flipped through the canvases stacked neatly against the wall. "Oils, right?"

"Yes."

"Do you sell any of them?"

"No."

"You mean you just keep them stored in here like this?"

"At times. Mostly I use them to decorate my walls. I change wall displays the way most people change socks."

Over his shoulder he smiled her way. "Fickle or temperamental?"

"Neither. It's more a case of crazed creative energy needing an outlet." She needed as much variety within her private domain as she required outside it. She had figured out a long time ago that it was easier, not to mention more economical, to change paintings than it was to give into the recurring whim to buy new furniture.

"So if I come back next week, your living room is going to look different?"

"Probably."

He turned to face her. "What about three days from now?"

"It might."

"And tomorrow?"

She supected that he wasn't referring so much to her decor any longer as he was to his welcome in her home. In her life. "You have no respect for time," she breathed softly, sensing again his rush toward something that was as yet undefined.

"No," he shook his head. "Just the opposite. I know how fleeting time can be. I don't want to waste any of it. Does that bother you?"

Rolling her eyes from side to side, she explained, "I'm not used to your hyperwarp style."

"It's an occupational hazard, I suppose. The pace in the ER doesn't lend itself to plodding through life."

"I don't think you can blame this entirely on work. Obviously, something in your personality lends itself to the frantic pace of your job." Without realizing it, she crossed her arms over her chest. An instant too late she realized how telling her body language was.

"Don't go all defensive on me," he cajoled.

"I don't mean to. The truth is, I'm feeling out of my league with you."

"There's no need for that. I'm a man like any other."

He was as unlike any other man as one could get, and the indelicate scoff she gave said as much. From the very start, she had responded to him in ways that were wholly out of character for her. The kiss in his car was proof positive of that. Her susceptibiltiy to that kiss was simply the icing on the cake.

"Do you think we could take things slow?" she asked.

"What would be the purpose?"

"To give my brain and my body a chance to get in sync."

"Are they out of sync now?"

"Very much so. My body wants to ignore the messages my brain is sending."

"Sex is a good thing." His bluntness cut right to the heart of the matter. "It's normal and healthy."

"So is sleep. That doesn't mean I give in to the urge every time I feel like it."

"Maybe you should."

"Do you?"

"No."

"Then why aren't you following your own advice?"

"I don't know." His brows knit over the rims of his glasses. "With you, I can't seem to slow down. More to the point, I don't want to." His expression said it all. He was perplexed by his lack of restraint. And he didn't like it one damned bit that he was a victim to himself. Raising his hands in a gesture of surrender, he said, "I'll try, Amy."

As concessions went, Amy thought Seth's was just about the most meaningful she had ever been given. He was so obviously at odds with himself, and he so blatantly wanted her, that she couldn't help but feel a warmth infuse her. "That's all we can ask of each other, that we try."

"I'm not promising to keep my hands off you, though." He sounded as if the thought would be impossible even for a saint.

"I'm not asking you to." She couldn't contain her grin.

He jutted his chin to the left. "As long as you understand."

Oh, she understood all right. Dr. Seth Donovan had set his laser-beam blue eyes on her, and her life was never going to be the same.

Chapter Eight

"I had a great time last night," Seth said. His early-morning voice sounded like gravel over the phone.

"Me, too." Propping herself up against her pillows, Amy snagged the phone between her ear and her shoulder. "I had a wonderful time." The meal had been delicious, the conversation engaging. Better than both had been the long, wet kisses on her living-room sofa that had followed. "Are you at work?" She could detect hospital noises in the background of Seth's voice.

"Yeah."

"What time did your shift start?"

"Seven."

The clock on her nightstand read ten of eight. "You couldn't have gotten very much sleep." He hadn't left her house until after one that morning.

"Enough."

She wondered if that was his way of telling her that sleep had been as long a time in coming for him as it had been for her. Even now, she was feeling the effects of sexual frustration. She knew for a fact that he had driven home with a raging case of thwarted lust.

"Well, if it makes you feel any better, I'm just about to get ready for work myself."

"Are you still in bed?"

"Mmm."

He was silent for a moment before he muttered, "Damn."

"What?"

"You couldn't have lied?"

"Why?" she asked with a curious laugh. He was sounding miserable.

"Because after last night, I'm not having any difficulty picturing you at the moment."

His confession pleased her. There was something infinitely enticing about knowing she could disrupt the thoughts of such a dynamic, intelligent, handsome man. "Don't picture too hard. I'm not my best at this hour."

"I intend to be the judge of that very soon."

Again she was pulled up short by his blatant determination to get into her bed. There had been other men who had wanted the same, but none had been so barefaced in their intentions. And once denied, they usually stopped calling her, period. "Seth," she breathed, drawing his name out.

"I know I promised not to push, but give me a break. You're hell on my libido."

If she had not heard the smile in his voice, she could have been annoyed with his persistence. "I'm learning that patience is not your strong suit."

"I like to think of myself as tenacious."

She would have called him dogged. She had come to realize that he could be intensely single-minded about certain aspects of life: specifically his daughter, his job, and his ethics. The man was grounded in honesty, hence his habit of getting right to the heart of things. That, too, reflected his impatience. The combination had Amy feeling slightly unraveled. It wasn't something she could remember feeling about any man in her past—certainly not Greg, and she had been engaged to him. Considering she had known Seth only a few short days, she knew she was in deep.

"Amy, you still there?"

"I'm sorry. I checked out for a second."

"I hope it was one of those creative interludes and not a response to me."

"You know what my response is to you," she replied. If he could be brutally blunt, so could she.

Again he fell silent. Again he broke that silence with a muttered "damn."

"Problem, doctor?"

In choked laughter, he accused, "You're a real wiseass, aren't you?"

"Who, me?" she protested in outrageously feigned innocence, enjoying herself more than she would have thought possible.

"If I were there, you wouldn't be so smug."

"If you were here, I get the feeling we wouldn't be talking at all." They'd be all over each other for a good-morning bout of steamy lovemaking.

The image sprang up like a slap in the face, stunning her with the ease with which her subconscious had apparently been tantalized by Seth's seduction.

"Oh, we'd be talking, all right," he informed her in an intimate tone. "But the FCC has rules against saying those things over the phone."

What started out as gentle teasing had escalated

to foreplay with stunning speed. Unfortunately, Amy didn't realize until too late that she had talked herself into a very tight corner. There were comebacks by the dozens that she could give him, responses that would take the verbal gambit to another level. True intimacy lay there, and she knew she wasn't ready for that.

"Amy?"

Against her pillows, she drew her legs up to her chest and her elbows close to her knees. "Um, I'm here."

"Damn, I'm sorry." It was as if he could see her mental and physical retreat from miles away.

"Don't apologize. It's just that I keep forgetting you're different from other men."

"That's good, I hope."

Tipping her head from side to side, she confessed, "Yes and no. I like you; I'm attracted to you. I don't want to play games with you, but—"

"But I'm moving too fast for you."

"Yes."

"And you'd like me to slow down."

"A bit." She shook her head at that. Perpetual-motion Amy Chandler asking someone else to slow down.

She could picture him nodding at his end of the line, adjusting his glasses for good measure. "I can live with that."

"You can?"

"It won't be easy. I'm not going to lie about wanting you, Amy, but I'll wait. Just don't get impatient with my impatience."

He may want sex—he was a normal man—but the fact that he was willing to bide his time for her sake spoke to a vulnerable spot within her. "I won't."

Muted voices from Seth's end intruded. She could hear him respond before saying to her, "I've got to go soon. EMS is bringing in a car wreck."

"Oh, God, please go."

"I've got a minute or two yet, but I wanted to tell you about your mom's blood tests. I'm looking at the lab work right now, and there's no doubt your mother's blood type is O negative."

"What?" She stilled, not even blinking. "Are you sure?"

"Positive. Two tests were done and they're both O negative." The intrusive voices came again. "I've got to go, Amy. I'll call you later."

She sat unmoving long after Seth had hung up, long after the phone clutched in her hand had begun to beep raucously. Only then did she move, her limbs working without their usual grace, her brain too bombarded with implications and questions for it to innately and easily carry out normal functions.

Denial clashed with fact. Repeatedly, she wanted to dispute what she knew about blood typing, but she could not. She had carried that seemingly extraneous info with her for years; had even joked about needing a brain flush to rid her of all those little ABO, positive, negative combinations. She knew fact for what it was, and it was fact that two O-negative parents always, *always* had O-negative children.

Claire and Mark were O negative. Dad had been, too. And so was Mom. The whole damn family had the same blood type—except for her.

Half an hour later, she was knocking at her mother's door, a shower forsaken to haste, jeans and a sweatshirt substituting for the outfit she had planned to wear to work. *Work.* She couldn't even think about her job. She felt as if she had left part of herself back in her bedroom, as if only the shell of her person watched as her mother opened the door.

"Hello, sweetheart. What are you doing here?"

For the very life of her, Amy wasn't sure. She wanted reassurance and guidance. She wanted her mother to explain away the incomprehensible, to grab hold of her daughter's world, suddenly on the verge of spiraling out of control, and anchor it with love and reason.

The urge to blurt out the confusion and dread made Amy nauseated. She could not think of a way to begin. Laying a hand over her stomach, she stalled. "I needed to see you. I . . . had—I wanted to—" She gave up as she headed for the kitchen, the heart of the home in which she had grown up.

She stared about her, seeing all the familiar nooks and crannies. Memory served up a dose of bittersweet tenderness in the form of remembered images: the family gathered about the table for dinner, Mom at one end, Dad at the other. Desperate, she yanked away from the sight, turning to find her mother standing in the archway leading into the hall.

"Amy, what is it, dear? You're as white as a ghost."

Amy did indeed feel haunted, caged in, shaken to the core of her. The basis for her entire life had been ripped apart. Her identity, her personal history, lay in question, and before her stood the only person who could restore order and peace.

"I was on the phone this morning with Dr. Donovan." Placidly spoken words, uttered on automatic pilot while the rest of her prayed and begged and demanded that her mother say there had to be a mistake.

"What did he want?"

"I had asked him to check into your blood type." Body tensed, breathing shallow, she stared wide-eyed.

Ellen paled visibly. As if she were about to speak, her lips parted ever so slightly, but she remained silent, her lips clamping shut to still their quivering. Like a wilting flower, she sagged into herself, her face seeming to age by decades, the ever-present light of spirit dimming in her eyes.

In the hideous silence, Amy felt her sense of self shift off-kilter. "Tell me," she croaked. "Tell me that the hospital really did make a mistake, that you're A positive and not O negative. Tell me, Mom."

Ellen's eyes filled with tears before they slowly shut.

"Mom?" It was the plea of a child. "Please."

The whispered entreaty was met with the hushed sounds of Ellen shifting away from the doorway. Arms hanging limply at her sides, she sank onto one of the chairs at the table, her gaze fixed on her lap.

"Mom?" A demand for understanding saturated the single word.

Ellen held up a shaking hand. "Please." Her voice sounded as dusty and cracked as centuries-old parchment.

"Please what? Please don't ask why my blood type is different from everyone else's?"

Ellen's tears slipped over sunken cheeks. "Oh, God."

"Prayer won't help." Feeling betrayed beyond

all sense of decency, she lashed out, "Tell me the truth."

The truth burst forth in wrenching sobs that shook Ellen's body and filled Amy with the kind of anger she had never before experienced. They had lied to her. For her entire life, her mother had lied to her about her very identity. She didn't know who she was.

"I'm so sorry," Ellen whispered. "I never meant to hurt you."

"Well, you have!" As if her body needed an additional outlet, she paced to the far counter only to spin and rush back. "How could you have done this? Why didn't you ever tell me?"

"Please, don't yell." Remorse and shame permeated the plca, so pitifully apparent that Amy's anger was tempered just enough to stem the full tide of her outburst. Holding on to a thread of self-control, she took the seat beside Ellen, facing her squarely.

"I never thought this day would come," Ellen whispered.

"Tell me." Numbness was beginning to set in, desensitizing coherent thought into dulled, fragmented particles.

Ellen shook her head, nodded, and shrugged. "It's been my secret for so long. I never meant for you to find out." She shook her head again. "Never, never."

"Dad. What about Dad?" His voice came back to her: *my little peanut*.

For the first time, her mom lifted her head and attempted to look straight at her daughter. "He knew he wasn't your biological father."

The breath left Amy so suddenly, she had to grip the table to steady her reeling balance. He had known he wasn't her father; he had known all along, even when he had called her his peanut.

"Who?" It was all she could think to say, and then she added, "Why?"

"Amy, please."

"I have a right to know."

"It's personal."

"Fuck *personal*." Ignoring her mother's cringe, she pressed a hand to her chest. The numbness was suddenly gone. In its place were resentment and dread zinging crazily back and forth. "This is my life we're talking about, not a made-for-TV movie. You've just told me that Sam Chandler isn't my father and you expect me to simply walk away as if you'd said 'looks like rain today'?"

Ellen retained her silence for so long that Amy doubted she was going to say anything more. She finally relented, as Amy knew she would have to. Now that the secret was out, there didn't seem to be any reason to maintain the why and how of it.

Still, Ellen's words emerged slowly, reluctantly, her gaze withdrawn, her shoulders slumped. "Your father and I were going through a bad time in our marriage."

"So you decided to have an affair?" Amy accused.

"Don't condemn me," Ellen flung back, her own temper always susceptible to the same. "You don't know what was going on between your father and me. You don't know what we shared or didn't. You don't know what it's like to . . . to stand by and . . ." Tears choked her voice. "To stand by and . . . and watch your husband's attention drift away, year after year. I loved him with all my heart and it wasn't enough."

No, Amy had never seen any of that. All she knew of her father, of Sam Chandler, was a strong-willed man devoted to his wife and children. "Dad loved you."

"Yes, he did, but for a while he wasn't content with his life. I don't know; some people call it a mid-life crisis." She scrubbed a weary hand up and down her arm. "I suppose it doesn't make any difference what you call it."

"Did he have an affair?"

"No." Her answer came easily, as if she had had years to be comfortable with her certainty. "Or if he did, he never admitted it. I believed him, I still do. He got too wrapped up with his job to have any time for another woman. That's all he ever thought about, you know, scrambling to keep up with the younger men coming into the company, proving to himself and everyone else that he was as sharp as they came. Even thirty years ago, the insurance companies were competitive. Sam scrambled with the best of them and, in the process, forgot that I even existed. He was good about Mark and Claire, setting time aside for them, but I might as well have been dead. That hurt."

"Is that why you . . ." Amy could not complete the question.

"No. I wasn't after revenge, even though I was angry enough when I met Alex."

The name ricocheted through Amy's head. "Is that my . . . my father?"

Ellen leaned forward, looking very much like her old, stalwart self. "Alex was the man who sired you, but Sam was your father."

"Alex who?"

"Does it matter?"

"Yes."

Again, the lapse in Ellen's response. She looked askance, scrubbing one hand against the other.

"Bouchet. I met him at the grocery store, in the frozen-food aisle. Our carts bumped and his peas ended up in my basket."

Amy crudely thought that far more than bumping had resulted, with peas being the least of what had been exchanged. "What happened?"

Shrugging with her brows, Ellen said, "Nothing, everything. We laughed, talked for a few seconds. That was all. I checked out and loaded the bags into my car. Alex surprised me by helping. We talked some more, laughed some more. I enjoyed myself, really enjoyed myself."

The tears that had dried up returned. "I hadn't realized until then how needy I'd become, how desperately I wanted your father's attention and love. And here was this handsome man I didn't even know, looking at me like I was the most beautiful and interesting woman he'd ever met. For the first time in over a year, I felt good about myself. I felt like a woman again, pretty to a man."

All Amy could think was, how did one go from the grocery store to making love with a stranger? For some reason the logistics seemed important. "How . . . what did you do then? I mean, did he ask you out?"

"Not right away. I didn't see him for a while, maybe a month or so. And then one day we met again in the grocery store. I remembered him." She paused, drew in a shaky breath. "I was glad to see him. He'd been on my mind all that time. Whether that was wrong or not, I don't know, but nothing was going right with Sam. We argued a lot. Alex made me smile and laugh and feel good even for those few short minutes we had together. I can't tell you how happy that made me. I liked it. I liked him, so when he asked me to have a cup of coffee, I did.''

Ellen's voice took on a far-away note, as if she were reliving those private moments from thirty years ago. "It was the most difficult decision I'd ever made. I had always taken my marriage seriously. I'd honored my vows to Sam, and for the first time, I knowingly turned my back on both.

"I felt guilty, you know, but I also felt as if I owed myself something, if that makes any sense. I couldn't think of anything I'd done to deserve the way Sam had been treating me. So I let myself enjoy Alex's company for a cup of coffee. That was all I wanted; it was safe and harmless. I never thought it would be more than that.''

"But it was?''

Nodding, Ellen wrapped her arms about her waist and stared out through the kitchen windows. "We met a few more times for coffee. Every time, I told myself I had nothing to be ashamed of. I was just having coffee. And Alex, oh, he was so kind and thoughtful. His wife had been dead for five years and he was as lonely as I was. Funny, you know? I had a husband and two children, friends and relatives, and I was lonely.

"I didn't feel that way with Alex. And I made him feel better, too. He admitted that after we met that first day, he had been going into the grocery store every day hoping to see me again. He'd buy one or two items at a time just to give himself the excuse and opportunity to see me. I was so flattered and touched. . . .'' Her words trailed into silence.

Amy didn't need to hear any more. She could well imagine what had happened next.

The numbness was back, obliterating all and any sensation, even the anger and the resentment. For years she had assumed she knew her mother, knew everything there was to know about her. All these years, she had been wrong.

Consumed by something that felt like a hollow sadness—for her mother, for her father, for Alex— she asked, "Where is he now?"

"Passed away. He died in a car accident before I found out I was pregnant with you."

"So he never knew about me?"

"No."

"Did he have any children?" Like a shot out of the dark, it dawned on Amy that she could have half-siblings somewhere.

"No, no children. His wife hadn't been able to conceive."

"And . . . and extended family?" Her head was suddenly reeling with this new possibility.

"None that he ever mentioned. I honestly don't know if he had any sisters or brothers."

Who would be aunts or uncles to Amy. She gripped her head for no other reason than that she felt she had to get a grip on her brain. One second, she couldn't think straight, and the next, questions tumbled one right on top of another. And underscoring the mélange was the pendulum swing of emotions.

"How did Dad take it?"

"About me being pregnant?"

Amy nodded.

Ellen's reply was a long time in coming. "He knew the baby couldn't have been his. We hadn't— you know—for some time."

"Was he angry?"

"Oh, you can't imagine. Angry, hurt, dazed. He asked me if I wanted a divorce."

"You didn't?"

"All I ever wanted was for him to love me the way I loved him."

"Did he blame you? Did he understand why you did what you did?"

A thin smile crept along Ellen's lips. "Do you?"

Startled to have the query turned back on her, Amy exhaled, incapable of answering. She could not divorce herself from the situation, could not be unbiased. She had been lied to all her life by the two people she trusted above all others. She could not set aside the anger and sense of betrayal and come to terms with that in a matter of seconds.

And yet, neither could she imagine the wretched hurt her mother had felt. She couldn't imagine how it felt to be ignored by the very person you love best in life.

"I'm angry; I'm hurt. I'm . . . I don't know what I'm feeling."

"It was the same with your father, but once he was over the shock and we had finished yelling at each other, he finally realized that he had pushed me away. He was more sorry than you could imagine. From that point on, he was a changed man, the man I fell in love with and married." Reaching out, Ellen grasped Amy's hand. "And he loved you, Amy. You know he did."

Of that, Amy had no doubt. In the midst of her reeling world, she could honestly admit that Sam Chandler had been all and everything a loving father could be. "I know."

"I don't want you doubting him. If you lose faith in anyone, it should be me, but I tell you this. I wouldn't go back and change a single thing, not one single thing." She squeezed Amy's fingers. "If I did, I would have never had you."

The tears came then. "Why didn't you ever tell me, Mom?"

"It's not something you tell a child. You would have only been hurt and confused. Your father and I thought it was best that we keep it private, between him and me. We were only thinking of you."

From the entryway came the toxic sound of Mark's voice, slicing through the quiet hush with devastating virulence. "What about me and Claire, Mom? Did you ever once think about us?"

Chapter Nine

From way down deep inside, Mark felt a surge of anger begin to seethe. It boiled up in ever-expanding increments, rising slowly past his stomach, lungs, and finally into his neck until his field of vision glazed over with a film that pulsed and quivered.

Riding the anger was the need for denial. He didn't want to believe what he had overheard; it reeked of a betrayal that savaged the essence of his carefully constructed world. At the core of that world was his parents' influence: their beliefs and ethics, their moralities and convictions. Those intangibles were the truths in his life, and he believed in them, just as he had always believed and trusted in his parents. It was past all bearing to discover that, in part, the truth had been a sham all along.

"Mark."

It was Amy who spoke. Her voice dragged him back to reality, making him realize that he had blocked out everything around him: the room; his mother before him, Claire standing just behind his left shoulder, her utter stillness woven right into the charged atmosphere in the kitchen. Distantly he remembered that he had been giving Claire a ride to work that morning when they had decided to check on Ellen first. Surprise of all surprises had been waiting for them when they had walked into the house and overheard their mother's confession to Amy.

"Mark," Amy said again, then fell silent, as if she did not know what to say next.

He had no such trouble. "How could you have betrayed Dad?" The question, like his gaze, was directed solely at his mother. "He loved you."

Ellen's mouth pulled into a thin, quavering line. "It was between me and your father."

"The hell it was," he shouted. "This affects us all."

"Don't yell at her," Amy ordered.

Claire added, "Calm down, Mark."

He ignored them both. "All these years you were preaching to us about right and wrong, and love and devotion, and it turns out to be nothing but sanctimonious bullshit. While you were talking out one side of your mouth, you were off screwing another man."

"Stop it!" Amy yelled.

"Don't tell me you can defend her?"

"I don't know what I'm feeling, but you have no right to talk to her that way."

"She slept with another man. You of all people should be furious."

"I . . . it's not that simple."

"Jesus H. Christ! A baby could figure it out."

Her voice uncertain, Claire spoke up. "From what Mom said, she had her reasons."

He swung on her. "No reason is good enough."

"Please, stop yelling," Amy said. "It's only making matters worse."

"Things can't get much worse." Everything was changed. The family would never be the same again. He stared at Amy, seeing her as his *half-sister*. Jesus Christ, she had a different father. It was a struggle to assimilate the fact.

"Mom's right," Claire insisted. "Whatever happened was between her and Dad, a long time ago."

"This isn't something we can bury in the past. We're feeling the consequences now. How can the two of you ignore that?"

"We're not ignoring it," Amy reasoned.

"What do you want me to do?" He flung a hand in his mother's direction. "Pat her on the head and say all's forgiven?"

His sneering tone ignited Amy's temper with visible results. "You're way out of line."

"Mom was out of line, not me."

"You don't have any right to pass judgement," Claire maintained.

"You think she's blameless? You think she's a saint?"

"At least I'm not behaving as if I'm holier than thou," Claire sneered back. "At least I'm trying to be understanding, which is more than you're doing." She planted herself halfway between him and Ellen. "This is so like you, Mark. You've got this attitude that you're so perfect, like the rest of us are ignorant and helpless, like we don't have a single brain cell. Well, I've got a news flash for you, big brother. You aren't perfect and you don't know everything. So I wish you'd stop trying to bully us into feeling the same way you do."

He could not believe what he'd just heard.

Incredulous, he exhaled as he asked, "You're siding with her?"

"No one is choosing up sides."

"It sounds that way to me."

"That's because you're upset and not listening," Amy contended.

"Damn right, I'm upset. I'm fuckin' pissed."

"Not in front of Mom," Claire scolded.

"Grow up, Claire."

Amy lifted her hands in much the same way a referee might. "All right, stop it, both of you. We all need to calm down before we say anything more."

"Just because you say so?" Mark sneered.

"No," she snapped back, "because it's the right thing to do. We're all upset and shocked. We need to stop and let things sink in before we discuss this further."

"What more is there to discuss?" As far as Mark was concerned, the deed was done. His father had been betrayed. His mother was guilty of adultery. He could not understand how his sisters could view the matter any differently. They were down the middle of the road, leaning heavily toward forgiveness if their attitudes and expressions were to be believed. Shaking his head in complete confusion, he asked Amy, "How you can stand there and forgive her?"

"I . . . I don't . . . I can hardly think straight."

"She lied to you for twenty-nine years. You're just going to ignore that?"

"I told you, I don't know what I'm feeling, and that's the point, Mark. If anyone is entitled to *feel* anything, to feel angry, it's me, not you. For God's sake, give us all some time to come to grips with this."

Slowly, thinking Amy to be out of her mind, he

nodded and, just as slowly, shifted his gaze to Claire. "I suppose you agree with her."

Claire's brows arched and fell before wavering into place. "I need time." She looked to Ellen. "I'd like to talk to Mom."

He had come up against a stone wall. Worse, there was no going around, over, through, or under this one. There was simply no way he could make his sisters see reason. Feeling as if he wanted to put his fist through the wall, he pivoted and stormed out of the house.

Half a mile down the road, hands clenched about the steering wheel, he realized he didn't know where to go. The office was out. He would bust a gut if he had to carry on with business as if nothing had happened. Just as intolerable was the thought of going home. Peggy would want to know what was wrong, and he wasn't sure he could tell her yet. And if he did, she would hover and worry. He couldn't stomach that right now.

Striving to stave off the frustration and anger slicing him into bits, he ended up driving around aimlessly. When he finally did stop, he found himself two blocks from Buckroe Beach. Without conscious thought, he headed that way and parked.

He had never had an affinity for the water, so he thought it odd that he should be there. Then again, he reasoned that as volatile as he felt, the deserted expanse of sand and water was probably the best locale for him at the moment.

Ordinary, mundane thoughts raced through his mind as he sat behind the wheel: he should call the office and let them know where he was; a bottle of bourbon sounded tempting; the interior of the car was warming up quickly. But he neither reached for the cellular phone nor started the car to drive to the nearest liquor store. As for the sweat beginning to dot his upper lip, he rolled down the window. Other than that, he sat and stared. And silently railed.

There was no stopping the tsunami of emotions that crashed in on him. The resentment, anger, and utter sense of loss, all temporarily contained while he had been driving, saturated him without mercy. In silent self-defense, he scrubbed his hands over his face and tried to understand.

He had heard every word his mother had said—the explanations, the reasons, the arguments—but he couldn't get past them. He wasn't able to comprehend the how of it, not from his mother. Other wives might have cheated on their husbands, but not Ellen Chandler.

In that moment, he didn't know who she was, but rather, who she wasn't. She wasn't the truthful, constant, devoted woman he had always believed her to be. She wasn't the strong mother. She had carried a lie with her for almost thirty years. That had to say something about her lack of character. Some might argue that strength had been needed to maintain the falsehood for so long, but he couldn't see it that way. Weakness had prompted her actions in the first place, and fear of discovery had kept her silent. That was cowardice, not strength. And Claire and Amy had fallen for it.

In a renewed spat of anger, he recalled Claire's outburst. Where in the hell did she get off saying he thought of himself as perfect? If anyone was guilty of delusional thinking, it was her. She always had been flighty and temperamental. Given that, he shouldn't have been surprised by her reactions, but Amy? Jesus Christ, Amy was so grounded.

He turned his thoughts to her only to find that

his brain reached another wall. Obstructed by that insurmountable blockade, reality suddenly took on a very unreal quality. Amy was the same little sister, but not; the same person he had always known her to be, but not. Mentally he scrutinized each feature, searching for the subtle nuances that proclaimed the difference in parentage. The exercise was a waste of time. She was a carbon copy of Ellen.

Jesus, God, his mother. He couldn't find it within him to comprehend what she had done, let alone forgive her. For him it was a black-and-white issue; a trust had been shattered and there was no going back. How his father had come to terms with it, he would never know.

Into his consciousness snaked an inescapable accusation; his mother hadn't been the only one to perpetuate the lie. His father had known the truth, too, and had never said a word.

Futile, hated tears clogged the back of Mark's throat. There was no stopping them from filling his eyes as a hideous sinking sensation dragged at his stomach. The combination left him disoriented, with too many questions and not a single answer that made sense.

For the first time in his life, he felt lost and impotent. To a man accustomed to shaping the world to suit himself, the feeling ate at him like acid on tender flesh.

Chapter Ten

The downstairs toilet was clogged; the cat had chewed through the hem of her best pair of woolen slacks; Bethany was running around in a tizzy, complaining at the top of her lungs that she couldn't find the yellow scrunchie to go with her outfit, and Michael had the TV blaring. It was all Claire could do to keep her sanity.

"Bethy, stop whining. Michael, shut that damn thing off and get your book bag."

Bethany shouted down the stairs, "But Mom, I can't go to school looking like this."

Over Ren and Stimpy's early-morning frolics, Claire shouted back, "I don't want to hear it, Beth. Not this morning." She grabbed the remote control and blanked the TV screen. "Michael, I'm not telling you again. Get your book bag."

"Ah, Mom, I was just getting to the good part."

"If you miss the bus, I'm not taking you to school."

Bethany wailed, "Mom!"

"Get down here now, Bethany."

Michael made a flying lunge from the sofa to tackle the cat. He landed inches from cracking his head on the coffee table just as Bethany stomped into the den, pouting as only a prepubescent girl of ten possibly could.

"Mom, I have to have my yellow scrunchie. I can't go to school looking like this."

"You look fine," Claire assured her.

Michael laughed, "You look like puke."

"Shut up," Bethany snapped.

Sitting on the floor with the cat in his arms, Michael taunted, "Make me, puke face." Obviously believing himself the funniest person on earth, he dissolved into great gusts of laughter. Bethany screeched out her indignation, picked up the nearest throw pillow from the sofa and sent it at her brother's head.

Claire saw the results even before they happened, called out a warning and an exclamation of dismay, but there was no stopping the inevitable. The pillow hit Michael's glass of grape juice on the coffee table and splashed purple in every direction.

"That is enough!"

Even the cat stilled. Michael sat motionless, his eyes rounded. Bethany stood unmoving, both hands pressed to her lips. In the silence, Claire was certain she could hear her blood pressure jump another ten points.

"I'm sorry, Mom," Bethany whispered.

"Me, too, Mom," came Michael's mournful apology.

Claire gripped her forehead as if she might physically contain the anger. Thankfully, she knew when to remove herself, both literally and figuratively, from a potential disaster.

Gritting each word out, she ordered, "The two

of you get your things, get out to the bus stop, and I don't want to hear another word." With that, she headed for the kitchen. Every step of the way, her patience unraveled until all that remained was a single tenuous thread. It snapped as soon as she returned to the den and realized that the can of spray carpet cleaner was empty.

On her knees, the scent of grape thick enough to choke on, dishrags spread all around her, she scrubbed at the ruined carpet as if her life depended on eradicating the stain. No matter how she mopped and scoured, though, she could not inflict her will on the forces of nature. Patches of purple remained. She wasn't going to get the carpet clean. She was completely and totally helpless.

She doubled over and pounded the floor, feeling utterly alone. In her heart she blamed Dan, blamed him for leaving her to fend for herself, for leaving her lonely, for not being there to support her and hold her when she needed him most.

"I hate you," she screamed, slamming her fists into the floor. "Do you hear me? I hate you! You weren't supposed to leave me. It wasn't supposed to be this way." Struggling to make it through her days while he rested in bliss. Her life was falling apart and her husband wasn't there to help her.

Head bent to her knees, her hands limp before her, she let the tears come, not caring that she was ruining her makeup and fixing it would make her late for work. She just didn't care. Yesterday had finally come crashing in on her and she did not have the energy to cope.

She had had that talk with her mother. She had taken it all in, kept her composure, borrowed some of Amy's mind-set and refused to make any judgements. She had even managed to get through work and a restless night, but she was paying the price now—in spades. She felt stripped down to nothing, used up, tired.

It was a while before the tears stopped. She didn't sit up, though. She couldn't summon the energy, wasn't even certain if she had it within her. For the moment, it was all she could do to hunch into herself and let the quiet bathe her senses and spirit.

With the dregs of her emotions spent, she was feeling empty, purged of the extremes, wide open, and helpless to whatever might claim her. Oddly enough, it was serenity, of all things—the kind she hadn't experienced in a long, long time. Where the sense of calm came from, she didn't know, but it was as though she had climbed a previously insurmountable mountain and reached the other side.

Swiping at the streaks of mascara ringing her eyes, she finally sat back, still feeling that strange hollowness where confusion and anger had been. But as the seconds passed, a timid realization toyed with her mind, flicked about her awareness, and finally took root in her heart.

She could not blame her mother for having gone to another man.

Almost afraid to admit she had thought such a thing, she stared unseeing about the room, stunned to find herself so easily accepting her mother's infidelity, *and* casting blame on her father for treating his wife the way he had. His behavior had amounted to desertion—not in the physical sense, but surely in the emotional.

She understood the feeling. Hadn't Dan deserted her, too? Perhaps not intentionally, but he was gone. All too well, she understood the feelings associated with being abandoned, the hurt and resentment. And the fear, too. There was always the dread and dismay of failing as a woman somehow. In all of this, she could sympathize and commiserate with her mother.

As bonds went, this one was peculiar. For the life of her, though, she felt closer to her mother than ever before, linked in ways that were unique and unlike anything that was ever likely to exist between Mom and Amy. And certainly between Mom and Mark.

The jackass. His asinine behavior had been unfair and uncalled for. It was, however, typical Mark, all high-handed and self-righteous. She was glad she had told him off, although at the time she had been too upset to think clearly, too stunned to tell him even a small part of what she really thought. If she had him here now, she would be tempted to get in his face and let it fly.

The satisfaction she derived from the idea made her smile. She came to her feet on a surge of energy that only moments ago had been depleted. She felt nothing so much as she felt she was starting over—fifteen minutes late, true, but by the time she walked into the bank, she had on her best professional smile, and her makeup would have done Max Factor proud. As she made her explanations to John, she definitely had her act together.

"I'm sorry," she told him. "We're still having some fallout from Mom's stroke."

From behind his desk, John looked worried. "Is everything all right?" His sandy brows pulled together over sincere gray eyes. "Do you need to be with your mother today?"

"No, it's nothing like that." She waved his offer away. "We're all trying to muck our way through. You know how families can be in a crisis."

"Don't remind me. I have a sister and two brothers."

"Well, then, you know how screwed up things can become."

"Screwed up? That's an understatement."

She appreciated his understanding just as she appreciated his crooked grin.

"How's your mom feeling?" he asked.

"Better. She's taking her medication."

"Good, but let me know if the situation changes or if you need extra time off."

Even more than his grin, she appreciated his compassion. It boosted her spirits for the better part of the morning and gave her an added touch of strength when she got on the phone to Amy.

"Hi. Are you busy?"

"Not any more so than usual," Amy said.

"How are you?"

"I don't know."

"I didn't expect you to be at work. I tried your house first and got your machine."

From her end of the line, Amy exhaled slowly. "If I had stayed at home, I would have brooded. At least here I can keep my mind busy until I can sort things out in my head. Besides, I'm on deadline with two accounts. With the mood Mark's in, I don't think he would have appreciated me calling in sick."

"What do you mean?" she asked.

As if she were pausing to look around, Amy whispered, "It's bad, Claire. I've never seen him like this, not even after Dad died. I tried to talk to him this morning, but he walked away. He won't discuss it."

"Oh, that's real mature."

"He's having real problems with this."

"If anyone should be having problems, it's you. Do you know if he's talked to Mom?"

"No, but I doubt it."

"Have you spoken to her?"

"This morning. I stopped by to see her on my way to work."

"How is she?"

"Sad because she's upset everyone."

"I'll call her." Better yet, she'd pack up the kids after school and drive over to see her. More than anything, she wanted to give her mother a hug that spoke of love and forgiveness and understanding.

"I think she needs to hear from you, Claire. She's blaming herself, and I'm afraid of what the strain might do to her."

"Oh, God, not another stroke. Mark better shape up. I don't want him upsetting her."

"Right now I don't think he can think past his own reaction."

"That pisses me off. Who does he think he is? You know—"

"Please don't, Claire. I can't handle it right now."

Hearing the pain in Amy's voice, Claire was instantly contrite. "I'm sorry. You're right." She lowered her voice. "I'm worried about you, Amy."

"You and Barbara Chan. She's been hounding me all morning. She knows something's wrong, but I can't bring myself to confide in her yet."

"How are you, really truly?"

Her sister's reply was not immediate. When Amy did speak, her voice was halting and laden with tears. "Confused."

"Are you mad at Mom?"

"I don't . . . No—yes. I really can't say. Part of me feels numb. It's like waking up one morning and not knowing who you are. I'm still me, but everything has changed."

"No, it hasn't. You're still my sister. I still love you." Her response was innate. She hadn't even taken the time to consider what her own feelings about Amy might be, but it seemed no time was needed. Nothing had changed except that she felt closer to Amy than ever before. "Mom still loves you."

"I know, but in some ways I feel disconnected."

"That will pass with time, don't you think?"

Amy said nothing. Claire didn't know if her sister had shrugged her answer or had dissolved into silent tears. "Amy?"

"I've got a lot of thinking to do," she said at length.

"Do you want me to let you go?"

"Yeah, probably."

"Do you want me to come over when the bank closes?" She checked her watch. "It's going on one now."

"Don't bother. I'll be all right."

"Are you sure?"

"No, but I can't afford to fall apart."

"Okay, but call if you need me."

"I will. And thanks, Claire."

"For what?"

Through choking tears, Amy murmured, "For not deserting me."

Claire's own eyes filled with tears. "What are big sisters for?"

At least ten times in the ensuing hour, Claire answered her own query. Big sisters were for support, friendship, and love. They were for caring and nurturing, giving and sharing. She had offered all that to Amy today and she could not remember having done that before. Neither could she remember feeling better about herself.

"Something funny?" John asked.

Claire was packing up for the day, filing loan applications into neat piles that would be waiting for her tomorrow. At John's query, she looked up to find him standing on the other side of her desk.

"No, why?"

He scanned her face. "I don't know. You look as if you were telling yourself a joke."

"Oh." She grinned again, more to herself than to him. "No, no joke. I was just running some things through my head."

"Must be good things. You look great."

His compliment hit her broadside. She played it cool, though, stifling the urge to whip her head up and gawk at him in pleased wonder. She tossed off another smile as she stacked up the folders. "What would the feminist leaders have to say to such a sexist remark?" she teased. And then, just to make sure he didn't realize how potent his compliment was, she carried the files into the vault, gently badgering back over her shoulder, "I don't think it's politically correct to say those kinds of things anymore."

"There was nothing sexist about it. I made a simple comment about how you look." Swinging open the interior vault door, John contended, "If we follow your line of logic, I'd be sexist if I said you look like hell."

She laughed, giving him a shaming glance. "Okay, you've made your point."

"You don't, by the way—look like hell, that is."

"Thank you." She shut the file drawer and faced him with a flirting grin. "I'm so relieved. I was beginning to lose sleep."

"So, are you going to tell me?"

"What?"

He leaned a shoulder against the door jamb to ask, "What you've been thinking that's got you looking and feeling so great."

"Nope."

"Why not?"

Because, she mentally replied, if she did, the discussion would turn serious, and she didn't want to relinquish the lighthearted élan that had sprung up between them. She was enjoying herself too much. And too, she had never confided her personal thoughts to John. If she did now, they would surely cross some invisible line. Their relationship would never be the same. That could be good or bad; she didn't know which, but keeping it the same was safe.

The end of her rationalization made her blink, then frown, then silently fume. Good old insecure, emotionally dependent, vulnerable Claire, always striving for status quo because it was safe.

"Claire?"

Seeing John stand straight, Claire realized her shift in mood was obvious. "I'm sorry, I just realized something."

"What?"

"I'm a wimp." For her children's sake she maintained and even managed, but on a personal level, as a woman and a person, she relied on others to get her through. First it had been her parents, then Dan. After his death, she had reverted back to her mother and, to some extent, Mark and Amy.

Here at the bank, she was good at what she did because she did what she was told—extremely well, but she followed John's direction. She was not innovative; she was not gutsy. To put herself on the line was unthinkable, and that attitude was repeated time and again in her private life. The reason? She was afraid. She was, in a word, a wimp.

John cocked his head to one side, as if he hadn't heard correctly. "A wimp?"

"That's right, and I'm sick of it." Sick enough that she suddenly wanted to throw off the caution that had ruled her life for so long, and to thumb her nose at the Fates.

"You're not a wimp. You're one of the most put-together people I know."

That was because she had made sure to project that very image, but John didn't really know her. He didn't see her day-to-day struggle to keep the insecurities at bay. Looking at him now, she was tired of the pretense. She wanted to be as "put-together" as he assumed she was.

In a straightforward, even tone she answered his original question. "I was smiling because, for the first time that made any difference, I helped my sister. I've never been very good at that." In all honesty, she had been piss poor at it, but she wasn't ready to confess that much. Baring her soul was taking its toll. In her attempt to be "put-together," her insides had begun to quake. "I guess I was smiling because it felt good to know I was being helpful."

"It's a good feeling."

In her own mind, she was guilty of so much that she half-expected him to criticize her. Instead, he was nonjudgmental and accepting. For that alone, she was prepared to like him. Before she could think better, she said, "You're a nice man, John."

The instant the words were out, she felt her insides shrivel up into something she was sure would have resembled a year-old raisin. Her newfound courage flew right out the window, taking her sense of purpose with it. "I'm sorry; I suppose I shouldn't have said that."

"Why not?"

She wasn't exactly sure, except that she had indeed stepped out of the workday role and trespassed into a more personal realm. A bit lamely, she explained, "It wasn't a very professional thing to say."

Shoving his hands into the pockets of his slacks, he shrugged. "There's room for being friendly here, Claire."

"I know, but you're my boss."

"Does that mean you have to be hostile to me?"

"No, but I don't want you to think . . ." She finished by waving her hands.

"I'm not thinking anything, Claire." Smiling his off-center smile, he peered into her eyes. "Don't worry about it. You think I'm a nice man. I happen to think you're a nice woman."

Like a little girl, she was tempted to blurt out, "You do?" Her mind repeated a variation on the theme. *He thinks I'm nice; he thinks I'm nice.*

Striving again for "put-together," she quipped, "Thanks." And was so proud of herself for surviving the moment, she could have cried. Laughter came to her rescue. John joined in and mere survival escalated into true enjoyment.

"I guess I better be going," she said at last. "Mike and Bethy will be home soon." But she didn't move. As if her body wasn't ready to relinquish its share of pleasure, it ignored her brain's messages to move her legs.

"Do they have a key to get in?" John asked. "Just in case you're late or caught in traffic?"

"They both do, but I don't like them walking

into an empty house. They're still a little young for that. Some people think I'm overprotective, but . . ." Again, she finished with a wave of her hands.

"I think you're smart."

Her tolerance for flattery was about to go into overload. In the space of a few minutes, he had told her she was put-together, nice, and now smart. *Smart.* This last bit of praise meant more to her than the other two combined. It meant more to her than all the compliments in the world rolled into one, and because of that, she could not summon up an offhanded witticism. She couldn't shrug off the impact it made on her senses.

Helplessly, dead certain her feelings were written all over her face for John to see, she stared at him in silence. All kinds of frantic warnings were going off in her head. She knew she should say something, but there she stood, in the middle of the vault with her boss, and she could not make a single sound, let alone turn those sounds into an intelligent statement.

And she knew why. In the blink of an eye, every one of her feminine instincts had been ignited. This had happened before between them—her awareness of him on a basic man-woman level—but not to this degree. Suddenly, she was thinking in terms of John closing the three feet between them and kissing her.

"I have to go," she blurted out. This time she did move, straight for the vault doors. Thankfully, John stepped aside. Thankfully, the bank lobby was empty. They were the only two there.

"Claire?"

"I'll finish up with those loan applications first thing tomorrow morning." To hell with courage.

She was scared silly. She had not felt what she was feeling now for any man except Dan.

"Claire, what just happened here?" He was right behind her, crowding her.

"I don't know."

"Yes, you do."

She reached into her bottom drawer for her purse. "I'm ... I'm—no—I ... nothing happened."

"Something did," he insisted. With surprising gentleness, his hand settled on her arm to turn her to face him. She knew before their eyes met that she was lost.

She stared up at him like the vulnerable little girl she had been most of her life, waiting for him to take charge. It was, after all, what she did best in stressful times. But no direction was forthcoming. He dropped his hand and stared back, obviously waiting for her to do something, anything: yell, laugh, throw her arms around his shoulders and kiss him hard.

"Damn," he muttered after what felt like eons of time.

"What?"

Clearly stunned, he whispered, "You know damn well what."

She did, of course, and was about to apologize, because that, too, was habitual in times of stress. If she had to stand there too much longer, he was going to be treated to bitchiness and the inevitable crying.

The first sting of tears threatened. "Damn."

He cast an assessing glance about the entire room. "We need to talk."

She nodded, shook her head, nodded again.

"Is that a yes or a no?"

"Both. I don't know."

"Come on, Claire, tell me what you want here. If I've made a monumental mistake—"

"You haven't. I mean, we both felt . . . I mean, you were right in that something happened."

The sigh he heaved was laden with relief. The expression in his gray eyes was saturated with wonder. "All right."

It came to her with an insight that amazed her that John didn't know what to do next any more than she did. Such confusion was endearing enough to give her the needed strength to square her shoulders and leave.

Chapter Eleven

Amy rarely worked in clay. However, on this Saturday morning she slammed ten pounds of stoneware onto her work table with all the force she could muster. The act of wedging, of pounding the clay, was intended for removing air pockets. Amy's intentions had nothing to do with air bubbles and everything to do with venting.

For three days, she had been existing in an emotional vacuum, unwilling to attack the issue of her true parentage. Raising the clay to shoulder height again, she knew her time of waiting was over. Willing or not, she could not put off the inevitable any longer.

The clay hit the wood with a satisfying sound that echoed around her studio. Not so satisfying was her state of mind. No matter how many times she replayed the conversation she had had with her mother, she was left feeling adrift. She was angry and accepting, understanding and resentful. For every emotion raking her insides, she also felt its opposite. The disparities were what had finally pushed her to slamming clay in pure frustration.

Of one thing she was absolutely certain, though. She loved her mother. That didn't mean she could fully accept what Ellen had done. For as long as Amy could remember, she had wanted a marriage equal to that of her parents. It was demoralizing to realize that the very ideal she held most dear had been, for a while, so horribly flawed.

She slammed the clay with a vengeance, offended with her own naïveté. She had trusted; she had believed.

From the kitchen came the sound of the phone. She ignored it, knowing her answering machine would pick up. The caller would be either her mother or Claire, Barbara, or Seth.

Her arms stilled. In the past days, she had placated Barbara with miserable excuses for her inert behavior and had said everything she was capable of saying to Mom and her sister. Not so to Seth. He had left a combined four messages at work and on her machine, but she hadn't been able to return his calls. Something inside her instinctively shied away from talking to him. It was as if in him she felt her betrayal more keenly. She had known him for a short time, but he had made her think of marriage and the kind of trust and commitment she had associated with her parents.

"Parents." She scoffed the word right out loud, unable to contain the mockery underscoring her amazement. She was suddenly possessed of an extra parent, although she still thought of Sam Chandler as her father. She didn't know what to think of Alex Bouchet. Some would say he amounted to nothing more than a sperm donor. She could not be so cavalier. His "donation" had resulted in her life. So what did that make him?

A knocking at the front door prevented her from pursuing the answer. It lay a long way off, buried, she was sure, in hours of soul-searching. So perhaps it was best that she let herself be distracted. She did not have the energy to traipse down that particular lane of personal discovery. Far easier was answering the door.

The minute she did, she wished she had paused to look out the window. She would have been forewarned that it was Seth who waited for her. She could have used a few seconds to prepare herself mentally. Seeing him again was indeed difficult, and the look on his face was not encouraging. He was obviously not pleased that she had been avoiding him, and his expression hovered somewhere between irritation and concern.

"Hi," she began, not knowing what else to say. Standing in the open doorway, she kept a firm grip on the doorknob.

He scanned her face before dragging his scrutinizing gaze down the length of her. Only when he had obviously seen his fill did he say, "I thought you might be sick or hurt."

It was a logical explanation as to why he was there, or why she had not returned his calls. He had been worried and, as a doctor, had come to see for himself if he could help. Feeling lower than pond scum for worrying him, she started to tell him that she was fine, but the words got caught. She wasn't fine. If she were, she would not have avoided him and he would not have been disturbed into coming to see her.

"Come in." To leave him on the porch was unthinkable. Her fledgling feelings for him wouldn't allow that, and out of basic human decency alone she felt she owed him an explanation. What that might be, precisely, she didn't know. They were more than acquaintances, almost friends, not quite lovers, and she was still scrambling around for a firm foothold on life. How much could she or should she tell him?

Hands still tinted gray with a fine layer of dried clay, she scrubbed both palms down her jeans, stepping aside as he entered. "I got your messages." There was no use in denying the truth. "I'm sorry I didn't call back."

"Are you?" Regarding her intently, he adjusted the set of his glasses on the bridge of his nose.

Amy doubted she was strong enough right then to deal with his directness. "Am I sorry? Yes." Seeing the confused irritation in his eyes, she said, "Things have gotten messed up."

"With us?"

How simply and easily he stated that. "In a way."

"What way?" When she closed her eyes and shook her head ever so slightly, he asked, "Have I screwed up?"

"It's not you."

"What's going on, Amy?"

She opened her eyes to see a vulnerability in his gaze that she would never have imagined in such a strong man. She had come to realize that at the core of the forcefulness of his nature lay a vein of sensitivity, but she had not known to what depths that sensitivity ran or how fragile it truly was. It was there for her to see now, and against her will, she was touched when she least wanted to be. Her palette was full, the facets of her life swirled into a muddy mélange that precluded her coping with any more difficulties. And yet, Seth's distress was real. She could not ignore the hurt she had caused him.

Heaving a sigh that spoke of her internal upheaval, she started to thread her fingers through her hair when she remembered the clay on her hands. "Give me a minute to clean up."

His expression was a dead giveaway that he did not want her to leave, even if it was into the next room. He nodded instead, and thankfully let her retreat to the kitchen while he remained in the living room. She used the time to try and gather her thoughts. To that very moment, she did not know what she was supposed to be feeling. Unlike Mark, who was furious, and Claire, who was forgiving, her own sentiments lay in the nebulous somewhere-in-between.

She supposed her quandary was painted all over her face when she returned to the living room. It explained why Seth gave her another of his penetrating, searching looks.

"Why don't you sit down?" she suggested. She curled up in the corner of the sofa, wrapping her arms about her drawn-up knees. An apropos position to begin with, made even more so by Seth's pose. Seated on the edge of the stuffed chair facing her, his forearms braced on his widespread knees, he leaned toward her in an assertive, determined posture. "I really am sorry, Seth."

"Why don't you explain what's going on?"

"It isn't easy."

"What can I do to make it easier?"

Exhaling sharply, she shot the ceiling a punishing look. "Nothing."

"How about talking to me, telling me what happened to freeze you up? You've already told me that I'm not to blame."

"You're not," she assured him.

"Then something else has to have happened. Have you changed your mind? Is there another man?"

"No."

"Is this your way of telling me that you'd rather not see me?"

"No. It's not that, Seth. There is no one else, and I like you. A lot." The line of his shoulders lost its hammered cast, and she smiled ever so slightly. "Probably more right now than ever, but seeing you is tough. I know that doesn't make sense, but something . . . there's a problem with my mother—"

"Medically?" he cut in.

"No, she's as fine as can be expected."

"So what's the problem?"

Helpless to keep the hurt from infusing her voice, she whispered, "I'm not sure I can tell you. I'm . . . not ready. There's a lot I have to work out yet."

"Let me help."

She had been right to doubt her ability to deal with his directness. It cut right to the heart of her. Shrugging as she shook her head, she said, "I know it's instinctive for you to want to cure the problem, but you can't fix this one, Doctor."

He bristled visibly. "This has nothing to do with my being a doctor. This is personal, man to woman. We had the start of something great going on and I want it back." Straightening, he challenged, "Don't you?"

"Yes."

"Well?"

"Well," she snapped, feeling pressured, "I have to come to terms with a few things and I can't do that with you around.'' She came off the sofa in a rush that took her to the windows. There she planted a fist against the sash and bowed her head, striving for control of emotions on the verge of crumbling.

''Amy.''

She started at the feel of his hands on her shoulders. Without a word, he kneaded the tense muscles with a surgeon's sure touch, skillfully, generously. In self-denial, she wanted to step out of reach, but the physical contact was an unexpected blessing that she was too needy to relinquish. It eased her strain with devastating thoroughness and finally, in the end, broke the delicate hold she had on her composure.

The tears came, silent shudders she couldn't contain. Seth turned her and gathered her close, surrounding her with a strength and warmth she eagerly absorbed. It may not have been the wisest thing for her to do, but she hugged him fiercely, needing to feel strong and warm again, needing a sense of being whole. Seth was all of that and more.

So she stole some of his well-being; there would be no giving it back, and let him feed her soul and her senses. In the aftermath of the last dismal days, to feel so replenished was more satisfying than anything she could have imagined, until she felt his lips travel from her cheek to her lips. And then satisfaction was redefined by the pressure of his mouth on hers.

If kissing him was ill-timed or foolish, she didn't stop to consider it. The taste and feel of him added to her sense of well-being, of wholeness and strength. Her mind rejoiced in that. Her body followed suit. Seth's was a heartbeat behind.

Reason and caution were instantly annihilated.

Seth's passion had been harnessed from the very start of their relationship. At her answering response, she knew the reign was slipped. He yanked off his glasses, and then with hands and mouth created a breathtaking heat between them that had her forgetting blood types and long-kept secrets.

She half-expected him to set a mad-dash pace. What she knew of his nature lent itself to haste. However, she realized very quickly that she didn't know as much about the good doctor as she thought.

Seth Donovan might hustle his way through most of life, but there on the sofa in her living room, he was painstakingly unhurried, stretching each pleasurable minute into prolonged moments of sensual delight. He knew the human body as only a physician would, but played on that knowledge as only a caring man could. From removing her shirt and bra to ranging kisses down the flat of her belly, his every touch was designed for her enjoyment.

And she did enjoy, not only the receiving but the giving as well. To feel Seth come alive under her hands, to hear his muttered groans, to see his blue, blue eyes narrow and his jaw tighten was gratifying to her on a purely feminine, and up until then undiscovered, level.

Cupping his face between her palms, she regarded him intently, and wondered who this man was that he could affect her so completely. He kissed her again, and her question wavered and dimmed until it was just a ghost of a thought to be fully obliterated by the force of his body entering hers.

Their joining was sublime, the quintessence,

Amy felt, of sharing. He thrust, she received, she gave, he took; a never-ending circle that spiraled, intensified, and all too quickly culminated in a climax that arched her body tight. Seth joined her before she could begin the inevitable downward float toward reality.

Limbs entwined, the bright morning sun blazing through the windows to superheat bodies already warmed from within, Seth was the first to stir. He levered himself to his hands to peer down at Amy. Once again, she saw an incongruous flash of uncertainty in his eyes.

"Amy? Are you all right?"

"I don't know." Reaction was just setting in. Swallowing against the effects of reason, she glanced away and would have scooted out from under him, but his weight held her in place.

"I didn't realize," he whispered.

"What?"

"That it's been such a long time for you."

Knowing how he could tell, and still feeling him very much embedded within that telling flesh, she exhaled, "Please don't be a doctor right now." Her defenses were down; she was woman at her most vulnerable. She needed the caring man he had been while making love. "I don't usually do this." And with good reason. "Oh, God." Every headline she had ever seen on AIDS, every statistic she had ever read on pregnancy, curdled the remains of her serenity. "Let me up," she muttered and, this time, shoved to extricate herself from their embrace.

"Take it easy, Amy."

Shifting about to gather her clothes, she asserted, "I don't believe I did this." She found her shirt tangled up with his pants. "What was I thinking?"

"This was going to happen sooner or later."

Over her shoulder, she shot him an indicting glance. "Yes, but not the way it happened today."

"So we slipped up. We'll handle it, but I sure as hell don't regret it." He was talking to the back of her head while she sat working the buttons on her shirt. "And I sure as hell don't have any sexually transmitted diseases, AIDS included. So that leaves only the matter of pregnancy."

"Only?" Still sitting, she spun to face him. "*Only?* Spoken like a true man, or is that 'Doctor Seth' getting in the way again? Being pregnant may be an *only* to you, but it would be everything to me."

"I'm not belittling the possibility of you being pregnant, but it would be something we faced together." His touch gentle, he curved his fingers around to the nape of her neck. "All I'm trying to say is that I would never abandon you. I'm as responsible for this situation as you."

She wasn't inclined to being reasonable, but there was reassurance in his caress, and conviction enough in his words to allay some of her worries. Freed from the panic that had seized her brain, she mentally checked her calender. The timing could have been a whole lot worse. Unfortunately, she placed absolutely no faith in the rhythm method of birth control.

"Better?" he asked, dipping his head in order to look into her lowered eyes.

Instinct took over. "I need a few minutes to myself." Not waiting for his reaction, she headed straight for the bathroom and the much-craved privacy of a hot shower. She had always done her best thinking in the shower, the resulting white noise filtering out extraneous thoughts and leaving her mind wide open to true creativity. It was from that aesthetic right side of her brain that she hoped to find deliverance from her fears and problems.

The hot water worked wonders on her muscles and even eased her tension over the scene on the sofa. She was not going to go borrowing trouble. And too, Seth had made his promises, for all they were worth. A week ago, she would probably have believed him wholeheartedly. Thanks to her parents' deceptions, such trust was slow in coming now. Whether Seth held true to his word remained to be seen.

That he hadn't left while she showered and changed clothes was encouraging. He found her in her studio, the one room in the house where some of her identity was intact. Leaning against the door frame, barefoot, his shirttails hanging loose over his jeans, glasses back in place, he stared at her as if trying to read her mind. She didn't think she made interesting reading, but apparently she looked as awkward as she felt, because he crossed the room to draw her into his arms.

In its own way, his offer of comfort was as tempting as making love had been, the underlying compassion a thousand times more beguiling. And she was powerless to her own susceptibility. Leaning her head onto his chest, she shut her eyes. In that position, it would have been easy to pretend that all was perfect in her world.

"What was that for?" he asked on the tail end of her heaving sigh.

"It's been a rough week, and this feels good."

His fingers flexed along the small of her spine. "Can you tell me what's happened?"

She lingered over her response, not because she debated whether or not to confide in him, but because she was stunned to realize that she suddenly wanted very much to do so. In becoming lovers, they had become friends, and friends shared their problems with each other.

"You know Mom's blood tests I had you check into?"

"Yeah."

"They were right all along. She is O negative. So was Dad." Her voice cracked. "The problem is, I'm not. I'm A positive." She knew she had made her point. The muscles in his chest contracted, then gradually eased. "Dad wasn't my biological father."

The flexing of his fingers on her spine ripened into a soothing caress. "Adoption?"

She shook her head. "It seems my mother had a brief affair thirty years ago. I was the result."

"I take it you never knew until this week."

"That's right."

"Damn, Amy, no wonder you've been upset." He tightened his arms. "What a kick in the ass."

All she could do was scoff at his understatement.

"Can I help?"

"I don't see how. I don't know what to do or what I'm feeling."

"I imagine confused."

"It's as though I've been living a lie for twenty-nine years. My parents aren't the people I've always believed them to be. The basis for my identity has been axed. I don't know who I am any more."

"It'll take time."

"I'll slowly go out of my mind."

"Take it day by day. The worst thing you can do is anticipate next week or six months from now."

Her future, like her past, had been wiped away by a lie. Without warning, all her childhood memories, all those cherished heirlooms she had held

dear, were tainted, flawed by a deception that forever altered the meaning of family. In its altering,
came a change of Amy herself, for at the core of
her lay the essence of her family. Or what it had
once been.

The unit had been ripped apart. Mark had withdrawn, as had Mom. Claire alone seemed to have
withstood the upheaval—insecure, vulnerable Claire.
The irony was nearly humorous enough to make
Amy laugh. Anger played closer to the surface,
however. Anger and resentment for being forced
to redefine who she was.

Chapter Twelve

They had not made love in more than a week. In all that time, he hadn't even hugged her. He had been tense and distant with her and short-tempered with the kids. At night, he tossed over his half of the bed and onto hers. Whenever she asked what was wrong, his response was "nothing," or a variation on that theme: "I'm tired."

Peggy admitted that Mark had had his moody moments over the years, most noticeably in the past few months, but nothing, *nothing* to equal this latest bout of depression—if that was the right word for it. She sensed in her husband anger as well as sadness, disgust as well as discontent. Each could and had flashed simultaneously and independently, confusing her as much as hurting her.

Carefully shutting her car door in front of Chandler Graphics, she tossed back her blond hair and decided that she had been hurt enough by Mark's moods, his silences, and his excuses.

"Hi, Cicely." She offered the office manager her

most pleasant smile. If it was strained, so what. She felt strained to her absolute limit. "Is he in?"

Cicely nodded. "As ever, and you've caught him at a good time. No meetings, no conferences."

"Great." She headed down the hall to the impressive office at the end. On the way, she paused at Amy's door only to find her sister-in-law wasn't at her desk. Not that Peggy had considered asking Amy for some insight into her brother, but she would have appreciated Amy's effervescent smile. Sunny or otherwise, one was unlikely to be forthcoming from Mark.

Her prediction was right. At her entrance, he looked up from the papers in front of him, surprise in evidence where she would have preferred to see pleasure.

"Peg, what are you doing here?"

"I came to see you," she replied, imbuing her voice with lightness. Only she knew that it was forced. She doubted Mark was observing anything past himself these days.

Leaning back in his chair, he quirked his brows upward. "Are you out shopping or something?"

"No." As calmly and deliberately as she had shut her car door, she closed the office door. "I came here specifically to talk to you."

As if he knew where she was headed, he closed up, his face taking on the brittle cast Peggy had seen too often lately. "I'm working, Peg."

"Then you'll just have to stop." Their eyes met, his wary, hers hopefully reflecting every ounce of determination she felt. It was difficult to tell. They desperately needed to talk, but she feared what she would hear. "I'm serious, Mark. You've put me off for days, making excuses and pretending that nothing's wrong." When he started to speak, she interrupted, "Don't tell me everything's all right, because I know it isn't. Something is bothering you, and I want to know what it is."

He threw the door a pained glance. "Can't this wait until we're home?"

"No. I've waited for over a week." And the fact that he would attempt to evade the issue once again further fueled her resolve. Issuing orders was not normal byplay for them, but she commanded now. "Tell me what's wrong."

He swore under his breath as he shoved to his feet, sending his chair backward to bump against the wall. Wholly unimpressed, Peggy took up a stance on the other side of his desk, folded her arms beneath her breasts, and waited. If it took a certain amount of stewing for him to reach a comfort zone, so be it. She would be damned if she'd let him off easily, especially after the week he had put her through.

His behavior had undermined her usual self-confidence. Unable to believe his assertions, she had looked inward for answers, searching herself as if she were the cause of her husband's dissatisfaction. She wasn't; she had told herself so dozens of times a day. Now she needed proof of that from Mark, along with affirmation that he still loved her.

The possibility that he didn't was what she feared the most. It was what had her swallowing Tums as if they were candy and waiting by the front windows for him to come home every night. Even knowing she had become a cliché of a desperate middle-aged housewife hadn't been any solace to her. A long time ago, she had chosen to make her husband and family her life. It was too late now to lament in bitter hindsight the choices she had made.

Staring at his back, she rolled her lips in over her teeth to prevent herself from asking, "Are you having an affair?" It wouldn't be the best way to proceed, for either of them. Instead, she simply prompted by saying, "Mark, please. Is it me? Have I done something to make you this angry?"

His muttered curses were discouraging, but when he turned to face her, she could see the utter depth of his sadness. In all the years she had known him, she had never seen him look as he did then. Instinct, old and automatic, urged her to take him in her arms and comfort him. A newer, protective reflex, erected at the hands of her husband's insensitivity, kept her knees locked.

"I'm sorry, Peg. I've been a regular bastard."

"I agree. Now, are you going to tell me why?"

Startlingly, he seemed to edge closer to tears. "It's all fucked up, Peg." He lifted one hand in an impotent gesture that could have implied anything. "Mom has fucked up my whole life."

"Your mother?" Peggy was stunned. "What does she have to do with this?"

A grating scoff came as his reply.

"Is her condition worse than we've been told?"

"It isn't that. This goes back a long way."

"You're scaring me," she told him, not following him at all. Hope hung precariously, teasing her with the kind of relief that would assuage the torment in her soul, baiting her with the knowledge that his love for her was still solid. She was afraid to yield to those hopes.

Unexpectedly, out of her wishful thinking came a truth and she saw it for what it was. She had been as good a wife and person as she had always been. Her fears had been for nothing.

She was so giddy her legs began to tremble. The

temptation to collapse into the nearest chair and suck in huge, bracing gulps of air was overpowering. Unable to hide her reaction, she blurted out, "Is this why you've been so upset all week? Because of something your mother's done?" At his nod, she demanded, "Why didn't you tell me?"

"I can't, couldn't."

She crossed the room as she had wanted to moments earlier and slipped her arms about him. "Tell me, Mark. You can't go on like this. I won't let you. You're hurting yourself, and me and the kids."

"I didn't mean to."

"Tell me."

His words came in halting phrases, a disjointed narration underscored by vehemence, shame, and bewilderment. Naively, Peggy had thought herself prepared for anything as long as it wasn't Mark telling her he didn't love her, but she had been wrong.

"She had an affair?" It would have been impossible to keep the amazement from her words. "And your dad wasn't Amy's father?"

"How's that for a kick in the ass?"

"This is unbelievable."

"A real pisser, huh?"

"No wonder you've been off the edge. My God, how's Amy handling this?"

"I don't know." He stepped back to knead at the nape of his neck.

"How can you not know? Haven't you talked to her?" No sooner did she ask than she had her answer. Mark's withdrawal had been complete. He had no more talked to his sister than he had to his wife. "She's got to be hurting, Mark."

He spun on her. *"I'm* hurting."

"I don't doubt it, but it can't be the same."

"Damn right, it isn't. My mother betrayed my father. She betrayed all of us."

"She deceived your father, but apparently they made their peace."

"Yeah, well I haven't."

Beyond the obvious outrage, she could not define the extent of his mood. "What exactly are you angry about?"

"Isn't it obvious? My mother lied to us all these years. She slept with another man, for Christ's sake."

"That doesn't mean she loved you any less, honey. Is that what you're thinking? That carrying her secret prevented her from loving you?"

"I don't know what the hell she thought. No, I take that back. She was thinking about herself. She sure as hell wasn't thinking about my father."

"You don't know that."

"The hell I don't."

"That's not fair, Mark."

He jabbed an irate finger her way. "You're beginning to sound like Amy and Claire, defending Mom."

"I'm not defending your mother; I'm not forgiving her. It isn't my place to do either. Nor is it yours."

"I'm involved. I'm her son."

"True."

"That gives me every right to be angry."

"Angry, yes; you're also being judgmental."

"I'm reacting the only way I can, and you of all people should see my side of this."

"Because I'm your wife?" she scoffed. "This isn't about sides; you against your mother, your mother against your father."

"You got that right. She acted against Dad."

Peggy threw her hands up in disgust. He was still very much in pain and, in the way of all wounded animals, could not reach beyond himself. It explained why he couldn't try to understand his mother's circumstances, and why he hadn't thought of the upheaval in Amy's life. His tunnel vision on the issue was frustrating to the point that she knew discussing it further would be a waste of time. Until he came to terms with his own reactions, there would be little reasoning with him.

Deciding to abandon the matter, she focused on the more immediate. She laid her hand on his arm, tipping her head to one side in a gesture as sympathetic as the sound of her voice. "I can't begin to imagine what you're going through, so I won't insult you by saying I understand. I don't. Your relationship with your parents is unique, the personalities and emotions complex. Now you've been hurt, and everything has gotten even more complex."

"It's gone to hell."

"You feel that way now, hon, but it won't do any good to carry this rage around with you."

He jerked away from her touch. "What am I supposed to do—pretend that I'm okay with this?"

"No, but anger never solves anything."

Rolling his eyes, he jeered, "Jesus, Peg, spare me."

"I wish I could." Ignoring his disdain, she stepped close yet again, breaching the defensive barrier he kept erecting. "I'm not the enemy in this war you've declared with yourself. I love you, and I want to help."

He visibly withstood the effects of her hug, his posture unbending. She ignored it though, and in the end, after long, tense moments when she felt Mark's erratic breathing against her chest, her persistence paid off. His arms slowly circled her before contracting in a crushing embrace.

"I'm sorry, Peg," he breathed into her neck. "I'm so goddamned sorry."

As she would comfort one of her children, she soothed this man who had come to be her life. "You better be," she breathed back, her normal sassiness present for the first time in days. But just as quickly as her impudence arose, it died, dragged under by the tow of regret and grief for all the hurt they each had suffered. "Things will work out, Mark; I know they will."

"God, I hope so. These last days have been so bad."

"I know." Leaning back ever so slightly, she peered up at him. "Can you get away from here? Can you take a break?"

"I wish."

"You're the boss. You can do whatever you want."

Before he even spoke, she felt his refusal in the way his chest expanded with a weighty sigh. "Maybe another day."

She had no choice but to let it go at that, and she was disappointed. As a couple, they needed to cement their bond with time together. Holding hands would suffice; lunch would be better; but a room at the Holiday Inn down the street was what she truly wanted—and needed. He had yet to tell her that he loved her, which was little wonder given his frame of mind. That did not preclude her needs, however, so if he couldn't think to say the words, she would settle for a physical expression. Knowing it wasn't forthcoming, she eyed his desk, imagining a tumultuous quickie. It had happened once before, in the heat of passion, after hours. She had felt wild and wicked and, with her panty hose torn, her blouse and bra unbuttoned, completely loved. By contrast, standing in her husband's arms now, she felt empty and discontented, the more so because she knew she could prompt the response she wanted. A simple *I love you* would do it, but pacification wasn't what she was after.

She wanted Mark's unrestrained, heartfelt love, bestowed freely and spontaneously. Sadly, he was incapable of such giving, and most likely would be until he could accept his mother once again.

Chapter Thirteen

Seth eyed his daughter over the rim of his Styrofoam coffee cup and wondered if she was wearing a little too much makeup. Lipstick, blush, eye shadow, and mascara: he had seen her wearing various combinations but never the entire works— and certainly not for breakfast at McDonald's on a Saturday morning. He would bet anything she wasn't normally allowed in public that way.

"When did you start putting on an entire face?" He regarded the effects of her heightened cheek color against the tangle of brunette curls waving down to her shoulders. The added color accentuated the delicate bone structure she had inherited from Gail, and made her look closer to seventeen than thirteen.

Melody toyed with her plastic fork, nudging pieces of pancakes into puddles of syrup. "What?"

He gestured with his chin. "The makeup. Does your mother let you out of the house like that?"

She gave him her best thirteen-year-old sniff of disdain. "Mom doesn't always tell me what to do."

He could see the sneer coming, the parents-are-so-stupid look meant to pulverize him. He fought to contain his grin. "Think twice before you roll your eyes at me, Mel. I'm not your mother."

The warning was an old one, issued to remind Melody that Gail might tolerate disrespect, but he would not. And Melody knew it.

"She's so dumb, Dad; she still thinks I'm a kid."

"Mel." Another warning. He and Gail might not be a viable couple any longer, and she might not be the strong disciplinarian that he was, but that did not mean he would tolerate hearing criticism about her, especially from their daughter. Nor did it mean that he would allow that daughter to pit parent against parent.

Frowning, Melody glanced away before squinting back at him. "I'm grown up, Dad."

"Almost. Where are your glasses?"

"I left them at home. They make my nose look huge."

He ignored her pout. "Since you have my nose, I'll try not to be insulted."

"I didn't mean it like that. You're a man; your nose looks good on you."

"I know what you meant." He knew better than to enter a debate on her looks. That was a minefield in waiting. She was in that awkward stage: not quite the young woman she believed herself to be, not precisely the child she could no longer abide. She was insecure with her appearance, nose and all, and there would be no convincing her that she was beautiful—at least not from him. She wanted affirmation from some guy she considered a stud, not her father. Nodding to her breakfast, he prodded, "Finish your pancakes."

"I'm not hungry."

"Sure you are. You're just worried you'll eat off your lipstick." Seeing the shock of discovery in her eyes, he attended to his own meal and with exaggerated nonchalance added, "You can always put more on, although I like you better without it." He didn't say he thought she was too young to be plastering her face. In this case, the direct approach would be a major mistake.

Not for the first time since he had picked Mel up last night, he had to temper his natural, blunt inclinations. As volatile as she was these days, the combination of temperamental teenager and bottom-line father would make for a disaster he wanted to avoid. He truly liked his time with her and didn't want it ruined. So he bent enough to keep the peace without compromising his principles.

"Any new boyfriends these days?" The question was two-pronged in that it kept him abreast of the latest in her life and also distracted her from her myriad discontents. Unfortunately, he had forgotten to be less direct. He mentally held his breath, waiting for her to break into a wail of mortification. It was possible with a thirteen-year-old.

Thankfully, she tilted her head into a one-shouldered shrug, a whimsical smile tugging at lips now sans lipstick. "Well," she drawled around a mouthful of pancakes, lowering her eyes to her plate, "there's this guy in my third-period math class that is so cool."

"Oh, yeah?" He was surprised and pleased she had chosen to confide in him. They were close, but not necessarily confidants on every matter. "What's his name?"

"David."

"What makes him cool?"

Her eyes lit up as she leaned forward in her seat, no longer the moody teen but the eager child of years ago. "He has long hair that he like, you know, ties back, and he wears one earring, just one, in his left ear."

Seth had visions of some skinny, pimple-faced throwback to the sixties with a mop of grungy hair and bell-bottom jeans. "An earring, huh?"

"He's totally cool and he's really smart: knows every answer in Miss Bennett's algebra class—I mean every single answer, Dad. He's on the honor roll every quarter."

That was encouraging, although not enough to prevent Seth from constructing the proverbial chastity belt for his little girl. Mathematical whiz or not, David was no doubt in possession of the standard dose of hormones. At the thought, Seth locked the belt and threw away the key. "So, are you two a thing?"

The wail he had anticipated earlier came forth, but its effects were sweetened by a laugh. "Dad, you're such a father."

He smiled in return. "It's in my job description. You're my daughter. I love you; I'm concerned."

"You don't have to worry. We're not like dating or anything."

It was the *anything* he had indeed been worried over. He had lost count of the number of pregnant girls Mel's age he had seen in the ER.

"We're just friends," she went on, her tone of voice saying she wished it were different. "His parents think he's too young to date."

Smart parents. "What does David have to say about that?"

Again, she shrugged. "I guess he's okay with it. Besides, he's pretty busy with soccer. He wants to go to college on a soccer scholarship so he can become a computer designer. His parents aren't wealthy or anything, so it'll be hard for them to come up with all the money."

In Seth's book, David's stock just increased tenfold. "He sounds like a great guy."

"Really?" Those blue eyes so like his own rounded in obvious pleasure. "You think so?"

"I wouldn't have said so otherwise. I'd like to meet him some time."

Without missing a beat, she came back with, "He's got a game this afternoon. We're playing Norfolk."

With expectancy tingeing her every word, the hint was far from subtle, the underlying hope impossible for him to overlook. "Sure."

"Really? We can go to the game?"

"Why not?" He didn't have anything special planned for the afternoon other than grocery shopping and grilling steaks for dinner. And possibly stopping by to see Amy.

He hadn't seen her all week, partly out of necessity and partly out of design. His schedule had been a real bitch, but even if it hadn't been, Amy had made it clear she needed her space. As frustrating as that had been, he had backed off, settling for the sound of her voice over the phone every day instead of the feel of her in his arms.

It took no effort for him to recall every nuance of their lovemaking. The memories had gilded his waking hours, but after an entire week, memories weren't enough. He needed to be with her, and not necessarily to make love, although that would be great. When it came to sex, she was two-hundred-proof lust, and he would be lying if he said he didn't find that extremely appealing.

However, that was not what prompted him to want to see her. The simple fact was, he missed her, missed seeing her smile, missed the faint scent of her perfume, her insights and opinions, the warmth of her hand in his.

He checked his watch. "What time does the game start?"

"Two."

It was going on ten. Amy would be up, possibly working in her studio. Adjusting the set of his glasses, he leaned back in his chair and carefully considered his daughter. Even more carefully he asked, "What would you say if I asked a friend to come along?"

"What friend?"

"A woman I know. Would you mind?"

Melody's elation went straight to unholy glee, bypassing suspicions and teasing irreverence altogether. "A girlfriend? You've got a girlfriend?" She gripped the table with both hands. "Dad, this is so cool."

Jealousy might have been expected. Resentment wouldn't have been beyond the realm either. In fact it could have been a real possibility. This was the first time a woman other than Gail had entered into the father-daughter relationship. Looking at Melody's smiling face, he released a small sigh of relief, glad that she was prepared to like Amy. That, more than anything, made him realize just how important Amy had become in his life. And it reminded him what a great kid he had in Melody.

"Who is she, Dad?"

"Her name is Amy Chandler. She's a graphic artist." He sketched through the details on how they'd met, and reduced the full extent of their relationship down to "we've been seeing each other. I'd like you to meet her."

"So I can check her out?" she teased back.

"She's a nice person. I think you'll like her."

"Cool. Does she like soccer?"

He didn't know, but he intended to find out. A call on his cell phone later, he asked Amy, "Do you like soccer?"

"I suppose."

"How about soccer played by a bunch of middle school kids?"

"I really don't know. I've never thought about it."

Mel silently mouthed that she was headed for the ladies' room. "Well, think about it. Mel and I are going to watch her school team play this afternoon, and we'd like you to come with us."

"You *and* Mel? Melody doesn't even know me."

"I've told her about you. As she puts it, she's cool with the whole thing."

A low groan prefaced Amy's reply. "I don't know, Seth. I don't think I'd make very good company."

"Bad week, huh?"

"You don't know the half of it. Mark is making life hell for everyone. The way he's been treating me, you'd think I carried the plague."

Mentally he skewered her brother. "All the more reason for you to get out. Don't let him ruin your life."

Again she hesitated. "I've got a zillion things to do."

"Anything life-threatening?"

"No."

"Then they'll wait." Before she could put him off again, he urged, "Come on, Amy, I miss you. I haven't seen you all week. As much as I like the sound of your voice, it's no substitute for the real you."

"I've missed you, too."

Her whispered words went straight to the heart of him. "You have?"

"Yes, and I'm sorry about hibernating."

"Don't apologize. As you said, you've had a rough week." Which was one of the reasons he was pressing so hard. She needed to get her life back on an even keel. He wanted to help in any way he could. "Look, you don't have to make up your mind right now. Mel and I are at McDonald's. We'll stop by in a half hour. That will give you two a chance to meet." And it would give him the chance to gently bully her into joining them. Actually, he had no intention of taking no for an answer. "I think you two are going to get along great."

They did. Melody was completely impressed by Amy's art work, throwing "cool" around as if it were the only adjective she knew. And Amy was as pleased as she was charmed by Melody's enthusiasm.

"My art teacher is such a dweeb," Mel exclaimed as she circled Amy's studio for the third time. "He never lets us do anything interesting like, you know, paint with oil paints or chisel stone."

"I don't think it's anything personal against you or the other students," Amy suggested.

"No?" Melody blinked her blue eyes wide.

Shaking her head, Amy explained, "The supplies and tools needed for oil painting and stone sculpture are pretty expensive. Public schools tend to save costly supplies for the advanced groups in high school who plan to make art a career."

"I never thought of it that way. I just thought Mr. Blevins was being a nerd."

"Oh, he probably is," Amy laughed.

Seth felt as if he had found the cure for cancer. For days, Amy's genuine laughter had been buried under an avalanche of emotional stress. It pleased him to know that her natural élan hadn't been destroyed, merely contained.

With help from Melody, that spirit and humor flourished through an afternoon of middle school soccer, in which David, who was neither pimple-faced nor grungy, scored two goals, and into the early evening as Seth put three steaks on the grill.

"I don't know how you talked me into this," Amy said. She was perched on the rail of his deck, looking very relaxed. Seth liked the color in her cheeks, put there by the sun. "But I did enjoy myself." She glanced out to the dock, where Melody sat throwing bread crumbs to the ducks. "She's terrific, Seth."

"I think so."

"And beautiful. Lord, what I wouldn't give to have her legs."

He scanned the length of her trim jeans. "I like your legs just the way they are." After a suggestive pause, he added, "And the rest of you, too." Unable to resist, he stepped near and skimmed her lips with his.

"Hey, you two," Melody called out in laughing tones.

Seth lifted his head the fraction of an inch needed to peer at his daughter. To Amy he said, "She's got a warped sense of humor." Ruefully, he returned to the grill to ponder how his daughter had become his chaperon.

Over dinner, she took devilish delight in taking the role to its limits. "I hope you two are practicing safe sex," Melody blandly advised.

Seth all but choked on his salad before he managed to swallow and find his voice. "That, young lady, is none of your business."

"Sure it is, Dad. You can't be too careful these days." Quickly, she turned Amy's way. "No offense, Amy."

"None taken," Amy assured her, but Seth noticed her cheeks were pink.

"I'm just watching out for your best interests, Dad."

Recognizing the very same speech he had give her dozens of times, he told her, "You're trying to reverse roles, and it isn't going to work."

"Why not?" Her expression might have been innocence incarnate, but there was no disguising the ill-concealed laughter she struggled to suppress.

"Because I'm an adult, I'm your father, and you're embarrassing Amy."

"No, I'm not. Am I embarrassing you, Amy?"

Amy's own smile was close to the surface. "No."

"See, Dad, Amy's cool. She's a twenty-first-century kind of woman. She's open-minded, she's informed, she's in charge of, like, you know, her own destiny. A woman's got to be these days."

"I expect you to remember that the next time David asks you to dance." He punctuated the command with a searing look that effectively restored the natural order of authority. Melody retreated to safer topics of conversation, engaging Amy in nonstop questions about computer design.

For the most part, Seth listened, peripherally aware of a rich inner pleasure derived from the rapport being established between Amy and Melody. On a more cognizant level, his brain toyed with the likelihood of Amy being pregnant. It was a real possibility he had not forgotten for a moment all week. Mel's teasing comment on safe sex only served to magnify the issue in the forefront of his awareness.

The emergency doctor was nowhere to be found as he dissected the matter; his emotions were fully engaged. Hope warred with joy for supremacy, the responses surprising him into reaching for his glass of water. It dawned on him suddenly that, deep down inside, he wanted Amy to be pregnant; he wanted them to have created a life together. Given that he had always assumed that future babies would come when and if he ever remarried, he was coldcocked by his realization.

Unable to help himself, he stared at her. He had been drawn to her right from the start. Physically, emotionally, and intellectually, they were perfect complements to each other, balancing each other's strengths and weaknesses, temperaments and personalities with flawless ease. He hadn't let himself think so far as marriage, but he couldn't stop himself now. With the three of them—maybe even a fourth—sitting as they were, he envisioned the family he had longed for in his younger days.

"What do you think, Dad?"

To cover his lapse of manners—he was still staring—he adjusted his glasses on the bridge of his nose and produced a convincing smile for Mel. It wasn't that difficult. He was inundated with the sensation of having found his way home.

"I'm sorry, I was thinking of something else."

From Melody's lopsided frown, he gathered she thought he ranked at the very top of the strange-animal list. "I asked if it would be okay for Amy to show me how to oil paint. She's cool with it."

He turned his questioning gaze Amy's way.

"I'm cool with it," she verified, then leaned in to taunt, "That's why I made the offer."

He absorbed the jab with good grace. "Then far be it from me to stand in the way."

Melody gripped the air with both hands. "Yes. I can't wait to tell David. He's going to be totally jazzed when he hears. Can I call him now, Dad? Can I be excused?"

What the hell. Dinner was over, and he hadn't seen his daughter this excited about anything in a long time. "Go on, but I want you off the phone in thirty minutes." She was out of the room instantly. "NASA needs to harness that kind of energy," he said before returning his gaze to Amy.

Contentment flowed through him, and he was momentarily at a loss. A dozen different comments boomeranged in his head. What finally emerged was a simple "Thanks."

"For what?"

Offering to teach her how to paint was the least of it. "I suppose for liking her."

"You don't have to thank me for that. She's a delight."

"Most of the time. I'm sorry she embarrassed you."

Her smile was cracked about the edges. "She didn't—not too terribly, anyway." She paused to look toward the hall, nibbling on the inside corner of her lip. "Do you think she knows that we did it, or was she simply guessing, trying to pull your chain?"

Her hesitancy bothered him, especially since it was his daughter who was responsible. "A little of both." He tossed his napkin onto the table. "I'm sorry, Amy."

"No, no, don't be."

He left his chair anyway and came to squat down beside hers. "She had no right."

"She had every right, at least to wonder." Laying her hand along his cheek, she smiled. "You're her father. She loves you very much."

"That doesn't excuse rudeness."

"She was just testing her limits. We all go through it. And besides," she added, dropping her hand to his neck where his pulse beat. "I'd rather have her honest audacity than bitter resentment. She could have hated me; in fact, I'm surprised she's accepted me as well as she has." Her fingers curled to grip the front placket of his shirt and give it a teasing tug. "So count your lucky stars, Dr. Donovan. It's better this way."

He couldn't resist. With her touch warming a spot in his heart and her eyes filled with tender emotions, the temptation was too great. He kissed her, having to content himself with the brief, fierce contact. "Come on, why don't I take you home."

She was as quiet as he for the drive back, which suited him. He didn't like useless chatter, and he was pleased that Amy seemed perfectly comfortable with their silence; but then, she was a woman comfortable with herself, or she had been when he had first met her. The news of her father had derailed her, but he had no doubt that she'd right herself soon enough. He admired that kind of strength of character.

"I'd come in," he told her as he parked the car in front of her house, "but I'm afraid that if I get you alone, we'll end up in bed, and Mel's waiting."

"It's a moot point anyway." The lights from the dash played off her features. "I got my period this afternoon."

He absorbed the news in much the same way he

would a jab to the stomach, and had to call on his years of emergency doctoring to suppress the full extent of his disappointment. It was there, though, a not-so-gentle wounding he tried to philosophically shrug off.

He told himself it was for the best and, in a mere flash of a second, recounted every sensible reason there was that Amy was not going to have his baby. Sensible or not, though, he was still saddened.

"I'm sure you're relieved," he assumed in a carefully neutral voice.

"Yes." She eyed him curiously. "Aren't you?"

"Honestly?"

"Honestly."

He took a deep, slow sigh. "No. I was kind of hoping."

The breath she expelled was as harsh and quick as his hadn't been. "How can you say that? We're not ready to have a baby. We've hardly begun seeing each other."

"I didn't say my reaction was logical, Amy. You asked me how I felt and I told you. I wouldn't have minded if you were going to have my baby."

"Oh, Seth," came her muted wail.

"Don't sweat it. You're not pregnant."

"That's not the point. You're thinking way too fast here."

"It can't be helped. I've never made a secret of how I feel about you."

Her expression incredulous, she returned, "You've never made any secret of the fact that you want me sexually, but we haven't discussed feelings— yours or mine."

"I didn't think I could have been any more clear in how I felt. Why do you think I've been in such a rush with you?"

"It's part of your nature."

"A part I can control if I want. With you I don't want to slow down. I don't see the need because my feelings have been engaged from the start." He stared her dead in the eye. "I love you, Amy."

"Oh, my God. Seth, we only met a little over two weeks ago."

"Time doesn't have anything to do with it." He shifted to cup her face in his palms. "I love you. It's that simple."

Her fingers clamped about his wrists, her eyes drifted shut. "Don't do this to me."

"Why not? You feel something for me, you can't deny it."

"I'm not trying to, but my life is such a mess right now. I can't begin to think about love."

"It isn't something you think about. You either feel it or you don't." His fingers tensed. "So which is it, Amy?"

Her eyes opened as slowly as they had shut. In the troubled gaze, he saw her answer before she gave it voice. "Yes, I do feel it. I have right from the start, but I'm not sure I can handle it right now."

"What's there to handle? I would think it would be a simple matter."

"It would be except that you're already thinking about babies." She turned her head away, dislodging his hands. "Does that mean you're thinking of marriage, too?"

"That's where I'm headed."

"Well, I'm not," she clarified, her head spinning back. "Damn it, Seth, I don't even know who I am any longer. How can you expect me to think about marriage?"

"It doesn't have to be right away. I know that, but you have to admit—"

"I don't have to admit to anything, least of all about marriage." She scrubbed a hand through the short strands of her hair, her voice becoming increasingly acidic. "Excuse me if my faith in that particular institution has been shattered." Exhaling again, she muttered, "I used to believe in marriage so trustingly, just like a naive kid."

"You weren't naive," he told her, reaching out to slip his hand over her shoulder.

"That's exactly what I was. I believed what I saw between my parents. What a joke—I didn't know it was a lie."

"Not all of it was a lie. They had a few rough years. No marriage is without its troubles, but what they had, had to have been built on a solid base in order for them to have remained together. If they hadn't loved each other, if they hadn't cared, they could have gotten a divorce."

"All that says is they were strong people, willing to work out their problems. It doesn't say anything about fidelity or commitment or the kind of love that's supposed to last forever." Tears rose up, clogging her voice. "I thought that's what my parents shared."

He was helpless against her misery. Seeing it tore at his insides. Gathering her close, he whispered against her temple, "They did love each other, Amy. That's why they dug in their heels and refused to give up. Maybe that's what the last-forever kind of love is all about: doing everything you have to do to keep the passion and commitment alive."

"It's so hard for me to believe that any more."

He absorbed her inner trembling with his body.

"You will again in time. Until then, have faith in yourself, and in me."

"I have more faith in you."

"Then for now, that'll be good enough."

Chapter Fourteen

"Here's the proof of the flyer you wanted to see." Keeping her voice and her expression professionally cool, Amy handed her brother the work she had just printed out, half expecting him to crumble the sheet into a wad and toss it into his trash basket. It wouldn't have surprised her. His reactions had not been the norm for weeks.

"It's fine," was all he said after a quick but thorough scan. He handed the sheet back, his gaze lifting unsteadily to hers.

She stared right back, having the advantage of height to literally peer down her nose at him. He might be the boss, seated behind his considerable desk while she stood there waiting for his approval of her work, but that didn't make him any less of a jerk. His manner had thawed enough so that they spoke to each other, but not so much that he displayed any real affection. They had work in common, and that was as far as their relationship went these days.

She buried the hurt, rode the resentment. "I'll

finalize this, then,'' she told him, turning for the door. She refused to beg him for scraps of brotherly affection. And she'd be damned if she would try again to reason with him.

"Amy."

His voice stopped her on the threshold. The quirked brow she aimed his way asked "what?"

In an awkward move, he came to his feet and shoved his hands into his pockets. "The flyer is very good."

"Thank you." Silently she sneered, asking herself if that was supposed to appease her, to make up for all the senseless hurt he had caused not only her, but their mother as well. Her brow still arched, she waited.

"How's work going?" came his next question.

It was all she could do not to laugh in his face. "Good." For weeks he had been treating her— them all—as if they were a scourge on the earth, and now he wanted to know about her work? The side of her brain that cautioned reason argued that he was making an attempt, trying to bridge the gap he had created. The other side of her brain, the emotional side, told reason to stuff it.

Again she turned for the hall. Again hc stopped her.

"Amy."

This time, she could not keep the sneer from showing. It was there in the exaggerated tilt of her head and the fist she planted on her hip. "What, Mark?" That her eyes narrowed was in keeping with her emotions. They were a blazing scarlet.

"Don't get all hot under the collar on me."

"Why not? I'm entitled."

"I don't want to get into an argument."

"Frankly, I don't care what you want." She straightened. "I've got work to do."

"Let it wait."

Again the sensible side of her head pleaded with her to resist her temper, to consider the fact that he was making an obvious stab at reconciliation. It took some doing, but after long seconds she relented, not so much as to retrace her steps, but she didn't walk away, either.

"All right," she conceded. "I'll let it wait. What's on your mind?" She couldn't resist thinking that what he had for a mind could easily pass for a pea.

Scrubbing at the back of his neck, he dredged up an uneasy laugh. "I see you're going to put the ball in my court."

The typical business bullshit kind of remark was the last thing she wanted to hear. "You're the one who wants to play games, Mark. Not me. Now, if you're done scrambling about for something to say, I've got a life to put back together."

"How is your life?"

That was what she had been after, the personal injury of brother to sister. It rankled, nonetheless—a case of too little too late. "What do you care?"

"I care."

"Oh, please." Discretion was being flayed alive, losing inches by the second. "You haven't cared about anyone but yourself for weeks."

"It's been a tough time."

"For all of us, Mark."

"I know."

"No, you don't. You've acted as though you were the only one affected, like you were personally sinned against. And you've made the rest of us pay the price. Especially Mom."

His expression chilled. "I don't want to talk about Mom."

Temper threatened to explode. "How convenient."

"It isn't," he snapped. "It's a bitch. This entire mess is nothing but a bitch and I'm trying to cope the best way I know how."

"Cope? You haven't coped, you've condemned. If that's your best, it's pitiful."

His own temper tinged his words. "Excuse me if I'm not as strong as you'd like me to be."

"The only thing I expected from you was support and understanding, the kind we've always shared. We could have helped each other through this, but you've made that impossible, turning on Mom, ignoring Claire, pretending I don't exist."

"I never—"

"The hell you didn't." That he could, for one instant, think he hadn't cut them all out of his life tore the last of her restraint to shreds. "You sanctimonious ass. You act the caring, benevolent big brother as long as everything in your perfect little world is exactly the way you want, but the minute life hands you a problem, you desert us."

"Christ, Amy, keep your voice down."

"Why the hell should I? You think everyone around here doesn't know something is wrong? They have eyes. And feelings. You've treated the staff like dirt, and they haven't done anything to deserve it. None of us has."

"Mom—"

"What Mom did was between her and Dad," she yelled. "It doesn't involve you. At the very most, it involves me." She pressed her hand to her chest. "Me, Mark. I'm the one wondering if I should go looking for sisters and brothers and a spare grandparent or two. I'm the one whose definition of father will never be the same. I'm the one who's lost her identity.''

Sauntering forward, she jeered, ''Your history is still intact. You still know who your father was, so where do you get off wallowing in all this anger?''

''Mom lied to all of us.''

''So did Dad. He never said a single word either. Why aren't you angry with him?''

''Because he was the victim in all of this.''

''That's a matter of opinion.''

''How the hell can you say that?''

She planted her hands flat on this desk and leaned forward. ''Because I wasn't there. And neither were you. We can't possibly know what went on, what they were feeling.''

''The hell I can't.''

His unreasonable stubbornness had her rearing back, exhaling in stunned amazement, and at last, understanding. All of Mark's actions suddenly made sense, and she mentally kicked herself for not seeing the truth sooner.

''You know, ever since Dad died you've assumed the role of head of the family. I guess it was only natural; you being the senior ranking male Chandler. But somewhere along the way I think you crossed over some lines. Somewhere along the way, you began to think you were Dad.''

''For Christ's sake, that's not true.''

''I think it is,'' she challenged, growing more certain by the moment. ''I think in trying to take up the slack for Dad's absence, you went a little further. You've tried to assume his place in our lives.''

''That's bullshit.''

''No, it isn't. It explains why you're so bitter about

what Mom did. You're reacting as if you were Dad, casting blame and feeling betrayed. Those are all things that Dad could have, and may well have, done. And he'd have been justified, but you aren't." She leaned forward again to enunciate each word in separate syllables. "Because you aren't Dad."

She could see she had well and truly impaled him on that one. The fact that he had no comeback was evidence. His spinning around to slam his palm against the window jamb was confirmation.

Anger aside, she didn't know what he was thinking. It went without saying that he certainly was not having an epiphany. Mark didn't like being told what to do, let alone what to think. And his excess of male pride prevented him being proved wrong, especially by his youngest sister, half or otherwise.

Well, too bad. She refused to take back a single word. To the marrow of her bones she knew she was right. It was up to him to deal with it—if he could. As was his way, he would stew about this for a while before he reached any conclusions, but she knew him well enough to know that in that conclusion he could very well tell her to go to hell. She prayed it wouldn't come to that.

Knowing there was nothing left to be said, she turned away, entered the hall, and came to an instant stop. People lingered in various doorways looking her way, obviously having heard, if not the content of the argument, then the angry tones. From the looks in their eyes, she had their sympathy. She didn't want it.

In her office, she shut her door, slumped into her chair and closed her eyes. It didn't surprise her in the least when the door opened and Barbara rushed in.

"Are you all right?"

Feeling as if she had been wrung out, she managed a weak smile. "I'm not sure."

"We all heard the arguing."

"How much did you hear?"

"Just the loud parts. Not enough to know what's going on."

"Thank God for little favors."

"I'm sorry, Amy."

"Why? You didn't do anything."

"Yeah, but you two might have wanted your privacy."

She shook her head in disgust and toyed with a pencil, only to toss it back to her desk. "Mark should have thought about that before he decided to open his mouth."

Barbara leaned a hip against the desk, laying a hand on Amy's shoulder. "I knew something was bothering you. You haven't been yourselves."

"I know, but I couldn't tell you."

"Do you want to now? It might help to talk about it."

"You sound like Seth."

Barbara grinned. "Dr. Yummy? I knew he was more than a great set of buns and killer eyes."

"You've only seen him once, and that was when he showed up here to take me to lunch."

"Yeah, but what a sight it was. I tried to think of a hundred ways to send myself to the emergency room, but I don't like the sight of blood—mine in particular."

Barbara's irreverence never failed to cheer her up. Now was no exception. Despite her battered nerves, she had to smile a little. "You're cracked."

"I know, and don't you just love it?"

No, what Amy loved best about Barbara was her generosity. "Thanks, Barb."

"Hey, what's the saying about friends?" Without waiting for Amy to answer, she said, "Let me get us both a cup of tea and then you can talk my ear off." At the door she warned, "And I want all the details, not the CliffsNotes version."

Amy watched her friend exit, feeling better already for Barbara's unwavering friendship. Nothing between them had changed. At a time when so much had, she appreciated the steadfast loyalty more than ever. It went far in helping to reestablish a portion of her sense of self.

Oddly enough, the argument with Mark had done much the same. The release of anger had been cathartic, and made her feel somewhat like the Amy Chandler of old. Not completely. She doubted she would ever be that person again.

It was all Mark could do not to put his hand through the window. His anger was that volatile, that close to the edge. He had been in this precarious place only twice before in his life, and he knew it was a dangerous place for him to be. One tiny little shove and he would cross over.

Only once before had he actually lost it. It had taken three men to physically control him. For that reason alone, it was a good thing Amy had left when she had. Another two seconds of listening to her bullshit and he would have erupted.

Her accusations slipped into his consciousness, and he instantly regretted his weakness in not keeping them locked out. Her charges were so ludicrous, so insulting, so demeaning that his vision actually blurred.

By conscious effort, he fought for control, talked himself away from the rage, reminding himself again and again of the time and place. He was surrounded by the trappings of his career, his livelihood. Common sense, caution, and civility weren't merely needed; they were fundamental.

He spent an agonizing ten minutes sitting on the sofa with his office door locked, concentrating on breathing normally. Then and only then, after his temper had drained sufficiently, did he lean back, confident that the anger was contained—not eradicated, but under control. That was when he got up and poured himself two shots of Jack Daniel's. The first scratched downward like a sheet of sandpaper. The second was smooth enough to make him pour himself a third. This one he took back to the sofa, where he silently, vehemently denied every accusation Amy had made.

If he had taken up the slack when his father had passed away, it was because it was a man's place to care for his family. And his mother and sisters had needed his grounding influence. They had made it apparent in a hundred different ways, relying on his help and advice. How the hell could Amy misconstrue that to mean he had tried to usurp his father's place?

Sam Chandler was and always had been irreplaceable, his life the impetus of the family. Amy should be grateful that she had a brother who had stepped in and done his damnedest to keep the family intact. He wasn't egotistical enough to think that the family wouldn't have survived without him, but it sure as hell wouldn't have been the same.

Thanks to his mother, the matter was rather

meaningless now. She had shattered the familial bond as surely as she had committed adultery.

He polished off the remains of his drink and thought about going for another when the intercom buzzed. Without thinking, he picked up the phone only to hear from Cicily that Rene Bellieux was waiting to see him.

"Give me five minutes before you send her back," he grated out. In all the commotion with Amy, he had forgotten his appointment with Rene. That he could so easily have forgotten seventy-five thousand dollars had him cursing again as he stepped into his private bathroom.

Exactly four minutes later, the taste and odor of whiskey obliterated by several serious doses of mouthwash, he gladly shoved Amy and his family problems from his mind. As goddamned tired as he was of being stuck in that mental muck, he couldn't extricate himself soon enough. The sight of Rene Bellieux increased the feeling a hundred times over.

He had always found her attractive. She was more so now for the very lack of emotionalism she represented: straightforward business mentality with mile-long legs and seductive brown eyes thrown in for good measure. He greeted her with a burst of enthusiasm the likes of which he hadn't felt in . . . he couldn't remember the last time he had felt so good. His familial problems went the way of trash.

"Rene, how are you?"

"Hanging in there, and you?"

"Fine." He was tempted to say better than fine now that she was there, but knew better. "Have a seat. Can I get you something to drink?"

She waved his offer away with one of her breezy

smiles. "No, thanks any way. I just came from lunch." Her smile turned a touch sour.

"You look like you could use some Tums instead," he joked, settling back against the front of his desk.

Openly disgusted, she lifted both hands to scratch at the air. "Attorneys, the bane of my life," she joked back, crossing one of those forever legs over the other. "There should be a law that makes it a crime to be in their presence for more than ten minutes at a time. And being forced to have a meal with them should be punishable by death."

"I've made it a policy to have as little to do with the breed as possible."

Rene made a swipe at her bangs and laughed, "You dog, you. I'm jealous."

"Don't be. I make up for it by having to contend with professional artists everyday."

"Somehow I don't see you being bested by temperamental personalities." The look she raked down the length of him turned patently assessing. "In fact, I can't imagine you being bested by anything."

The compliment nourished him on several levels, levels he hadn't realized were so starving. Normally he didn't think of himself as emotionally impoverished. Hearing Rene's unqualified endorsement of him as a man pointed out just how far his self-esteem had slipped. That the endorsement had come from a woman as appealing and clever as Rene boosted that sagging self-esteem into the stratosphere.

There was no helping his response. Its impact caught him with enough force to make a liar out of Rene. He was, for a moment, bested by a purely visceral sensation of omnipotence.

Energy flowed, bringing with it the arrogant self-confidence that had made him such a business success. As he hadn't in months, he felt a sense of purpose reminiscent of his younger days. The feeling was intoxicating, empowering, and stimulating, both mentally and, amazingly enough, physically.

Startled, he retreated to sit behind his desk before his body's reaction embarrassed them both. Not that there was anything wrong with having a hard-on; it was simply ill timed. And certainly misplaced. Rene was there on business. While he knew that corporate games could be seductive, he had always associated that seductiveness with the power involved, and not with a woman.

But damn, Rene made him feel good. There had not been anything sexual about the look she had given him. However, there was no separating the sensual, attractive woman from the keen businessperson. The two were meshed into a whole that affected him profoundly.

Admiration, respect, and lust: the mélange was as unsettling as it was exhilarating. And that in itself was stimulating.

"I like to think of myself as in control," he replied. As responses went, it was right down the middle, modest and yet layered with confidence. Little did she know that, right then, he wasn't as in control as he sounded. His body had conspired with pride, and both had attacked his libido.

"Oh, you're that, all right," Rene assured him. "That's what I like about you, Mark, your sense of control. Not many men are so sure of themselves." She flicked her dark brows upward. "That's why I decided to bring Bell Electronic Systems's money to you. The entire three hundred, twenty-five thousand."

The figure stopped him for a fraction of a second, but no longer. The amount was more than they had originally discussed. Much more. As cool as could be, he said, "You've upped the original budget." But inside he was exultant, his satisfaction so sweet there was no containing it. The bulge in his pants increased.

"It only makes sense. Since Father is behaving himself by staying out of it, I made certain decisions as to what I think is best for the company."

He completed the statement in his own mind. Chandler Graphics was best for her company.

Just as there was no separating Rene the woman from the company vice president, Mark could not sever himself from Chandler Graphics. He was the company. He was the heart and soul of it. What Rene had just told him was that he was, quite simply, the best.

In all his life, he had never heard sweeter words. Nor any that were as prized.

Chapter Fifteen

"Are you sure you're up to this?" Claire asked her mother for the fourth time.

For the fourth time, Ellen said, "Yes, Claire. I'm fine." She lifted her hands to indicate her kitchen, her house. "It's not like you haven't left the kids with me a hundred times before."

"I know, but I worry that it might be too much for you."

Ellen gave one of her hefty sighs. "I'm not an invalid, you know. Dr. Jamal says I'm fully recovered."

"Physically, yes, but I don't want you overdoing it."

"The kids are no problem. They never have been."

Under normal circumstances. Life for the Chandlers had been anything but normal. "A lot has been going on." There was sadness in her mother's eyes and lines of depression bracketing her mouth. Neither were there because of the stroke. "Mom, you know how I feel about all of this."

Shrugging first with her brows and then her shoulders, Ellen whispered in deference to Bethany and Mike in the next room. "I never wanted this to happen."

"I know."

"Mark won't talk to me, and Amy is upset, I know she is even if she says she isn't."

"Mark is an ass."

"Claire."

"And Amy will recover."

"I feel like I've ruined everything."

"You haven't, Mom."

"Your brother thinks so, but what am I supposed to do? I can't go back and change the past."

In her mind, Claire resolved to have a long chat with her brother. "They just need time, Mom, but it'll all work out." Seeing her mother's entire body sag in on itself, she added, "I promise." But she could tell that her mother wasn't convinced, and nothing she said was likely to change that.

It had always been that way: her family not taking her seriously, as if her opinions were invalid. But God, how she wanted to be able to reassure her mother; how she wanted to be the one who made a difference.

Disappointed despite the fact that she should have known what to expect, she gave up. Glancing away, she pushed a strand of hair behind her ear and quietly asked, "Will Amy will be by later on?"

"In about an hour. She's staying for dinner, too. Are you sure you don't want me to fix you something?"

"Positive." Purse over her shoulder, she made her way from the kitchen into the living room.

"You don't take care of yourself."

"Mom."

Clearly glad to be able to turn her mind to the mundane, Ellen stepped over Claire's objections. "I'll fix up a plate just in case and keep in it the microwave for you. You can take it home with you if you want and heat it up later."

Claire gave in as she always did, in this instance because her mother needed to nurture. Claire wouldn't take that from her even if it did come at the sacrifice of her own will. "Whatever you like, but I won't be very long."

"Take as long as you want. I'm okay; the kids are okay." Turning to Bethany and Mike, planted in front of their grandmother's television, Ellen prompted, "Right?"

Bethany smiled over her shoulder. Mike grunted out something that sounded like, "Don't sweat it, Mom."

Claire took heart from that and from her own fledgling sense of purpose. "Well, all right, but if you need me I'll be at work. You have my number?"

Ellen patted her daughter's cheek. "Go. Do whatever it is you have to do and don't worry about me." When Claire would have spoken again, she said, "Good-bye," and ushered her daughter to the front door.

Finding herself on the front steps, Claire stared at the door, feeling the pressure of all that had yet to be resolved. Given that, she considered the wisdom of what she was going to do. She should; she shouldn't; she was crazy; she was sane; she had no business; she was long overdue.

The private debate carried her to her car, although in all honestly, the issue itself had been settled in her mind days ago. Her hesitancy came in her reluctance to hurt anyone, specifically her kids and her mother. And Dan's memory.

Habit alone had her feeling guilty, and she was sick of that—disgusted with the kind of mentality that had her questioning her actions and second-guessing her own decisions. She had had a lifetime of that, and she was determined to put forth a new and improved Claire O'Riley.

Before she could rethink, she was on her way back to the bank for the sole purpose of seeing John. She was returning on the pretext of working overtime; that was the reason she had given her mom. And by a stretch, it wasn't a lie. She always had something that needed to be done, but not necessarily tonight, after hours, when the bank was empty and she knew John would be working late.

Go do what you have to do, her mother had said. She intended to. She wasn't certain what that entailed, not entirely. Oh, she intended to see John, but other than that, nothing was clear. All she did know was that she couldn't go on as she had for the past week, being with John every day at work, seeing the questions and expectancy in his eyes, feeling awkward and edgy. The situation had become unbearable.

He was where she expected him to be, behind his desk, engrossed in paperwork, his shirtsleeves rolled up. In its own way, the familiar sight was comforting. At the slight sound she made from the doorway, he looked up.

"Claire. What are you doing back here?"

There was no doubt that he had gotten right to the heart of the matter. If only she could be as straightforward. With difficulty, not sure how best to proceed, she said, "I thought it was time we talked." She exhaled slowly, wondering instantly if she shouldn't have made up some excuse about needing to catch up on work. Then they might have been able to ease into the matter.

He came to his feet in a gradual unfolding of limbs. "We have been tiptoeing around each other."

She cleared her throat, shifted her weight from one foot to the other. "I know."

His expression remained inscrutable. "You made it pretty obvious that you wanted to back off."

"I'm sorry. I needed time." She fiddled with her purse strap. "I didn't know what I was feeling, or how I should handle things."

He accepted her explanation with a nod of his head. "It's understandable. We've both been caught by surprise. I'm glad you decided to talk it out."

Was that what she was doing? As big a step as this was for her, it felt as if something far more momentous than talking was going on. She cleared her throat again. "Can I sit down?"

As if he suddenly remembered his manners, he extended his hand to one of the chairs opposite his desk, then just as suddenly curled his fingers into his palm and nodded to the couch on the side wall. She followed his unspoken suggestion, sinking into the cushions with visible relief.

"Are you all right?" he asked, sitting in a chair that put his knees at right angles to hers, nearly touching.

"I don't know. This is so hard for me. I'm not even sure what I'm doing."

"Don't you?"

He looked so dubious, she wanted to laugh. What emerged was a stifled smile. "It would help if I knew what you were thinking."

"I'm thinking that there's no reason for you to be nervous."

"But I am."

"Why? Because we're attracted to each other?"

Just hearing him put it into words was enough to make her stomach twist. Forgetting every promise she had made not to give in to guilt, she apologized. "I didn't mean for this to happen."

"Neither did I, but there it is." He smiled broadly enough to highlight the crinkle lines about his eyes. "And unlike you, I'm not going to apologize for it." Leaning forward, he slipped a hand over hers where it rested on her lap. "I've been attracted to you for a long time, Claire."

Her mind literally stopped, all conscious thought processes brought to a screeching halt by the touch of his hand. She stared at his fingers and felt whole layers of herself shed away, leaving her as naked and vulnerable as any snake that had shed its skin. To some extent, she felt lower than a snake, betraying her husband with feelings that she had reserved for him alone. For so, so long.

She finally breathed, exhaling on an agitated laugh. "Oh, God."

"No, just me," he said, dipping his head to catch her eye.

"I haven't done this before. I mean, not since, I mean, only with Dan." Helplessly she sought his gaze, hoping to see absolution there and confirmation that she was entitled. "I mean, I never expected to feel this way about another man."

He tightened his fingers about hers. "Then I'm glad it's me." And to prove his point, he edged that much closer and kissed her.

It was a simple kiss, lips slightly opened, more seeking than demanding. But if she lived forever, she knew she would never be fully able to express everything she felt at the first touch of his mouth. The sense of time was overwhelming.

How long had it been since a man had kissed her? Seven years? In all that time, the basic woman at the heart of her had been shunted away, buried beneath mountains of grief, slaughtered by insecurities and the pressures of responsibilities. Too often she'd felt like an asexual nonentity, going through the motions of living without ever having lived at all.

She had forgotten how it felt to be woman, what it felt like to have a man find you attractive. She had forgotten the raspy feel of a man's five-o'clock shadow against her skin, the dizzying flow of anticipation, the unbelievable awareness of every square inch of her body as it came alive. She'd forgotten it all in those seven years, and it came back now in a staggering rush.

"Why are you crying?" John skimmed his thumb over her cheek.

Taking hold of his wrist, she shook her head, unable to tell him. Could he possibly understand what was happening to her? Could she even put what she was feeling into words?

She answered by raising her lips to his again, and found welcome, and joy and arousal. Arousal, when there had been times when she had been sure her body had atrophied from lack of use. She couldn't contain her laughter.

"First tears, now this," John said. "I didn't think I was that bad at kissing."

Scrubbing at her cheeks, she choked out, "You're wonderful. I love the way you kiss."

"I'm glad you approve." His humor drained away, serious intent filling his gray eyes. "Because

I want to do more than kiss you, Claire. You know that, don't you?"

"I know."

"How do you feel about that?"

"Nervous, but okay." To hide some of that nervousness, she laid her hand along his jaw.

"Then we have ourselves a small problem." To soften his words, he clasped both her hands in his. "You know bank policy as well as I."

She did, but she hadn't given a thought to the regulation of no fraternization between employees. They could both lose their jobs. "What are we going to do?"

Her distraught tone brought a one-sided smile to his face. "Take it easy, Claire," he soothed. "This happens all the time."

"Not to me."

"Or me, but trust me, it happens a lot."

"Really?"

"Mmm," he answered. "You'd be surprised who's sleeping with whom. We just have to be careful."

She didn't like the idea of sneaking around, but what choice did they have? Neither one of them could afford to give up their jobs, especially in light of how nebulous their personal situation was. Neither was speaking in terms of love and happily-ever-after. Attraction and sex were as far as they'd gone, and then only theoretically. Still, John was willing to put his job on the line for the chance to be with her. She couldn't help but be flattered.

"What now?" she asked. Having an affair wasn't something to which she had ever given any thought. She honestly didn't know what to do next.

"Now I'd say you need to take your nails out of my wrist."

"Oh, God," she whispered, mortified. "I'm sorry."

"Claire, it's all right." As if to prove it, he kissed her again, the tender exchange quickly escalating into something more heated. When he lifted his head, he coaxed, "Why don't we get out of here?"

The old Claire Chandler O'Riley balked. That wimpy wuss wanted to shake her head and delay the inevitable with stuttering excuses, a few tears, and possibly a loss of temper. The new Claire, the one who had brought her to this very moment, screwed her courage to the wall, swallowed, took a deep breath that was supposed to relax her, and finally nodded.

They ended up in his bedroom in his townhouse, although Claire didn't actually remember agreeing that his place would be best. By the time she could think about it, she was half-dressed, sitting self-consciously on the edge of John's bed, hoping with all her heart that he wouldn't be disappointed with her body. The concave belly she had had at eighteen was gone. And even though she was slender, there was no getting around the fact that she was a thirty-six-year-old mother of two on whom gravity had begun to take a hold.

Not for the first time, she frantically wondered what on earth she was doing. Then John kissed the slope of her breast and made her forget her questions and worries. Not then, nor at any time in the following hour did she fret about work, or her kids or the problems within the family. She did rouse herself enough to panic over birth control, but John was one step ahead of her, calming the last of her fears, so much so that what she experienced in his arms was the most satisfying sex she'd ever had.

And that made her cry. With her head on his shoulder, passions spent and breathing labored, she let the tears come. There was no stopping them. Something inside her suddenly needed to be purged, and tears were her body's solution.

John was instantly alarmed. He rolled over so that he could study her face. "What's wrong?"

"I'm sorry."

"For what? Claire? What is it?"

Opening her eyes, she explained, "I feel as if I've finally put the past to rest. I feel like I have a whole new life to live, like everything is possible."

"Wow." He laughed, clearly relieved. "All that, huh?" One hand settled on her waist; the other one toyed with her hair. "I knew I was good," he teased, "but not that good."

Her laughter burst out past her tears as she hugged him fiercely. "Don't go conceited on me."

"Hey, you're the one who's crying."

"Only because I'm happy." She refused to acknowledge the guilt. She had loved Dan with all her heart, but she wasn't going to blame herself for enjoying making love with John. She tightened her arms around his shoulders, feeling better than she had in a very long time.

Years, she decided on the way back to her mother's. She hadn't felt so good in years. Mentally and physically, she was at peace, although she wasn't so foolish as to think that the feeling was permanent. Reality had a way of reducing contentment to frustrations. On the other hand, she knew that what she was feeling was more than a lingering case of post-sex euphoria. Something had happened tonight, other than the obvious. Something inside her was forever changed. Exactly what, she couldn't pinpoint.

If she was distracted when she picked up the kids, she reasoned it was perfectly understandable. Luckily, she presented a fairly good replica of her old self, good enough that no one gave her a second look. She expected them to; as altered as she was feeling, there should have been some outward sign.

Halfway home, she realized she was behaving like a virgin all over again, and she laughed. After that very first time with Dan, she had done what women have done for centuries; she'd studied her reflection in a mirror to check for any indications that she had lost her virginity. It was an elementally female reaction to one of the most significant rites of passage women experience.

She was reacting no differently now, and it didn't make the slightest difference to know she was being silly. Having made love to John was not going to be revealed on her face like a brand. Nonetheless, at the nearest stoplight, she craned her head to look at herself in the rearview mirror.

The light turned green before she could imagine whether there was a new wisdom in her eyes or not.

Chapter Sixteen

"Hey, Aunt Amy, I've got one."

At Mike's exuberant call, Amy snagged her net, leaned over the rail of the dock behind her house, and scooped up the crab dangling from the end of Mike's baited string. "It's a keeper," she said.

"How many does that make now?" Bethany asked.

Amy carefully kept her fingers out of pincer range as she maneuvered the crab into the holding basket. As best she could, she counted the number of crabs squirming around and over each other. "Eighteen, twenty?"

"Is that enough for dinner?" Mike wanted to know, checking the knot that secured his line to the rail.

"Depends on how hungry you are."

Bethany squatted down for a closer look at the basket. "Do you think Mom will want some?"

"Probably. She loves crabs."

"How come she isn't here with us, then?" Mike tossed the question out as nonchalantly as he fingered the day-old chicken neck he was using as bait.

"She had things to do," Amy explained.

"She's had things to do all week," Beth groused. "All she's done is work."

"Oh, yeah?"

Bethany went back to her own line. "Yeah. We ordered pizza three times this week for dinner."

"I love pizza," Mike declared. "Except with anchovies."

Rolling her eyes at her brother, Beth sneered, "No one likes anchovies, Michael. You're such a dweeb."

He was unfazed. "You're just mad because you had to unload the dishwasher this week."

"Well, it isn't fair. I always get stuck with the rotten chores."

Amy tried to smooth her niece's ruffled feathers. "It's only been for a week, Beth. There are times when adults have to work extra."

"Yeah, but on Saturday?"

"That comes with having a job. Your mom needs your help."

"I think it sucks."

Michael laughed even as he taunted, "I'm gonna tell Mom you used that word."

"So? I didn't swear." She turned to Amy. "Was that swearing, Aunt Amy?"

"Not exactly, but it isn't the nicest of words either."

"See," Beth challenged to Mike. "I didn't swear." She turned a dismissing shoulder his way, every inch of her posture proclaiming she was very much the wise, older woman who had no use for anything as lowly as an eight-year-old brother.

Amy wanted to laugh, especially when Mike stuck

his grimy thumbs up his nose, waggled his fingers, and shook his butt from side to side—all of this directed at Beth's unsuspecting back.

Some things were timeless. She could remember resorting to similar ploys when she had been Mike's age. As the youngest, she had frequently been low man on the totem pole. Like Mike, she hadn't enjoyed it at all, and like Mike she had contended as best she could with siblings who assumed that a pecking order was the only right and natural course.

The memory made her sad.

"Hey, Aunt Amy, someone's here," Mike said.

She blinked herself back to the present, glad to be distracted before she could dwell on the family's problems. Her gladness escalated when she saw Seth approaching from the side of the house.

"Hi," she called out. "I thought you were working this afternoon."

"Change in plans." He slipped his hand around her waist and brushed a light kiss over her lips. "Thought I'd stop by."

Very aware that Mike and Bethany were watching them with enthusiastic curiosity, Amy sidled one step away to make the introductions.

"Is he your new boyfriend?" Beth wanted to know.

Before Amy could reply, Seth said, "Yes," giving her a look that said *deny it.*

"That is *so* romantic," Bethany sighed.

Mike grunted out a more masculine opinion. "I think it's gross. Kissing is gross."

"That's because you're stupid," Beth assured him.

Mike's eyes bugged out. "I'm really gonna tell

Mom this time." To Seth, he explained, "Mom doesn't let us use that word."

"Enough, you two," Amy intervened. "Why don't you go inside and get some sodas."

"But what about my line?" Mike asked. "What if I get a crab?"

"I'll watch your line for you," Seth promised.

Mike openly debated the wisdom of that before finally relenting, and then not before he gave Seth excruciatingly detailed instructions on how to draw in a crab.

"Think I can handle it?" Seth asked as soon as Mike ran off after his sister.

"I don't know. How good are you at brain surgery?"

"I hope the fate of the human race isn't hanging in the balance." Bracing his forearms on the rail, Seth let his fingers gently ride Mike's line, but his gaze followed Mike. "They're cute."

"I'm partial to them." As close as she was to Claire, it was only natural that she would view her children as special. More so recently, in that their youth and exuberance were blessed distractions.

"Where's your sister today?"

"Working overtime."

"So you're playing the babysitter-aunt."

"I don't mind. The older they get, the less I see of them."

"I know the feeling."

She took up a spot at his side, leaning back against the rail. "I talked with Melody a few days ago."

"She told me." He carefully drew the line up, hand over hand. "She said it was 'cool' with you if she came out this week."

"I told her I'd show her how to stretch a canvas."

Crossing her arms over her chest, she gave voice to a worry that had been nibbling at her. "Is Gail all right with this?"

"With what?"

"With your 'girlfriend' spending time with her daughter."

His head turned her way sharply, his gaze just as pointed. "Why wouldn't she be?"

"Because she doesn't know me."

"I know you. That's good enough."

"For you."

"Trust me, if Gail had a problem, she'd let me know."

"Ah."

"The shy type she isn't."

"I can't blame her, at least not with the welfare of her daughter. She has the right to be protective." When Seth didn't disagree, she relented to a teasing smile. "So, I'm your girlfriend, huh?"

"What did you think you were?" He drew the chicken neck out of the water only to find no crab attached.

"I hadn't labeled us."

"Don't you think it's about time you did?"

"I don't know."

"What do you tell people when you refer to us?"

On a shrug, she said, "I say we're seeing each other."

"That's a euphemism for we're sleeping with each other." He gave her his full attention again. "It's more than that, and you know it."

"I know," she whispered. Seth was more than her lover; he was rapidly becoming her best friend. But she was still a long way off from thinking in terms of marriage. "I have to get used to the idea. Give me time." Which was another euphemism,

this one for *let me come to terms with who I am; let me
settle the fiasco that was once my family*.

"I've never been the most patient of people,
Amy."

Willing to be charmed by his disgruntled confession, she slapped her hand to her forehead. "I
would have never guessed."

"Smartass."

"I was simply pointing out the obvious. You move
at warp speed."

"True, but I've never lied to you, Amy. You can
trust me."

Of late, her trust in people had been as abused
as her faith in marriage. The argument with Mark
had proven that in spades. It was depressing to
realize that the brother she thought she knew, the
man she believed was so selfless, was operating
under a load of delusions.

She slipped her arms about Seth's waist. At his
gentle questioning of her shift in mood, she told
him about the scene in Mark's office. Her anger
was long gone, having been replaced by a sense of
the inevitable. Nonetheless, it was nice to be able
to turn to Seth, to share, and in the sharing receive
the support not only of his arms but of the strength
of his will, and his unshakable commitment.

It amazed her, that devotion of his. He bestowed
it on her with seeming effortlessness. Instinctively
she wanted to give herself gleefully up to it, but
hope and doubt squared off. And that made her
angry at the forces that had forever changed her
life.

"Are you working Memorial Day?" she asked,
determined to have some of the normalcy of her
old life back.

"No, I lucked out."

"Do you have any plans?"

"No, why?"

"My relatives are getting together for a picnic. It's a yearly thing." An event she never missed, an event that annually reconfirmed bonds that had been established years ago. As never before, she held the tradition dear, needing it like a floundering ship needs an anchor. "I thought you might want to go."

He apparently didn't even have to think about it. "Sure, I'd love to."

"Really?" She tipped her head back to check out his expression.

"Really. It'll be fun."

And no doubt serve the purpose of fixing him in her family's mind as belonging at her side. She definitely knew how the man thought. "You're not very subtle, doctor."

"I never said I was." Behind his glasses, his eyes crinkled with his smile. "If I have to fight for a place in your life, I'll use whatever means are at my disposal. In this case, your family picnic."

"You're shameless."

"No, just very sure of how I feel and what I want."

"And when you want it."

"Yesterday, but I'll settle for the near future."

She drew a measure of strength from his assurance of what lay ahead. Considering the state of her past, her own confidence wasn't nearly as secure.

Wearing nothing but her pink terry-cloth robe, Claire stared out her kitchen window and deliberately refused to think of anything. The quiet in the house suited her satisfied mood and she didn't want to relinquish that. She folded her arms, sighed, watched a bunch of goldfinches fight over the seed in the feeder the kids had given her for Christmas.

The grass needed to be mowed. As soon as the thought intruded, she thrust it away and reminded herself to think of nothing. And for a few seconds longer she tried, honestly tried, to keep her mind blissfully empty, but it was a lost cause. John slipped up behind her, drew her back against him, and she was bombarded by a host of thoughts.

"I wondered where you'd gone off to," he whispered, his arms wrapped about her waist.

Oh, the thoughts the man inspired had her closing her eyes and tipping her head back against his shoulder. "You fell asleep. I was wide awake, so I came down here."

"You didn't have to do that."

"You were tired." She turned to slip her hands up his chest. He had put on his clothes, but his shirt was unbuttoned.

"*Zapped* is a better description." A lecherous grin made him look completely out of character, like some disreputable despoiler of virgins in a historical romance instead of the respected banking executive.

Flustered, still struggling with the novelty of an affair, she asked, "Are you hungry?"

He answered by raising one sandy brow, his grin turning speculative.

"Not that way," she choked out. "I meant do you want something to eat?" The instant the words were out, she realized her mistake. John burst into hearty laughter, hugging her tighter.

"God, Claire, you're a trip."

Silently she fumed, calling herself a naive little fool lacking the kind of sophistication that someone like John was no doubt accustomed to in grown women. Not knowing what else to do, she tried to squirm out of his arms, but he didn't let her go. He simply cupped her face in his hands and kissed her.

"This is a side of you I've never seen," he said. "I like it. Not that I don't like the professional Claire O'Riley. It's hard not to. She's so efficient and unflappable." His expression softened. "But this insecure side is kind of nice."

Mentally she rolled her eyes. He'd pegged her with that one. The problem was, she didn't want him—or anyone—to know just how deep her insecurities did run. That fear in itself had her worrying that if he ever did know, he would want nothing more to do with her.

"I'm a little bit new at this, John."

"Hey, am I complaining?"

"No, but—"

"But nothing. It's because you aren't the type to sleep around that I'm here with you."

"What do you mean?"

"I mean that I find your moral standards as attractive as the rest of you."

"Oh." She was at a loss. She had been prepared to defend herself against what she considered her own personal shortcomings. To find that John saw the flaws as strengths was a revelation. "Oh."

"But in answer to your original question," he commented lightly, his hands linking at the small of her back, "yes, I'm definitely in need of food." He nodded toward the refrigerator. "Got anything good in there?"

She grimaced. "Not really." Embarrassed, she thought better of telling him that since seeing him, she hadn't been to the store as regularly as she should have. "We could go out," she suggested, hope saturating her voice.

His expression closed up instantly. "I don't think that's a good idea, Claire."

Disappointment came hard on the tail end of his reply. "We could go over to Williamsburg."

"Judy DeMarcoff in accounting lives there." He eyed her meaningfully. "And so do your brother and sister-in-law."

She could have, and perhaps should have, let the issue drop, but she persisted. Despite logic and adult rationales, she needed to be reassured of herself as a person and not just one half of a secret sexual equation. "Okay, then, Norfolk. We're less likely to be spotted together in Norfolk than here on the Peninsula."

With visible hesitancy, he mulled the matter over. "What about your kids? Aren't you supposed to pick them up soon?"

His reluctance said it all. He found her physically and morally attractive, but not nearly as attractive as his career. Pushing out of his arms, she tugged on the sash of her robe, turning away to stare out the window again, forgetting the basic premise with which she'd begun the affair. "Of course. Sure."

"Claire," he breathed softly. "Don't be like that."

"Like what?" The smile she gave him over her shoulder dripped honey.

"All bent out of shape. You know how it's got to be."

She turned that syrupy smile to the ceiling. "Yes, I know. I forgot there for a minute. Stupid me." She had to remind herself that she had gone into this affair knowing full well that it had to remain extremely private. She knew it. Knowing, however, didn't assuage the feelings.

He cupped her shoulders from behind. "I'm sorry, Claire." When she said nothing, he stepped away. "Are you going to be able to handle this?"

"What?"

"Our seeing each other."

Screwing each other would have been a more apt phrase. In her resentment, bitchiness came easily. "Yes."

"I don't want you to get hurt."

Too late for that, but that was her own fault, not John's. He had not led her on; he'd made no promises. From the outset, he had been honest with her. That was one of the reasons she liked him as much as she did, why she couldn't stop wishing they could have more than sex.

She faced him as squarely, all the false hopes and needs shunted aside. "I can handle it." She topped the comment off with a confident setting of her jaw and the same professional smile she used in the office. "I'm a big girl."

Her show of what he had no doubt deemed maturity worked. His tension dissipated easily, to be replaced by a heightened sexual awareness. "You're that, all right."

She had come to know that particular look in his eyes. It broadcast clearly and loudly where his thoughts were headed.

"What time do you have to pick the kids up?"

"In about fifteen minutes."

"Do you think your sister will mind keeping them a while longer?"

It was more a question of whether she wanted to go back upstairs. Her answer was immediate. If that was the only place she was going to be able to enjoy John's company, she might as well make the most of it.

"I don't think Amy will mind. She hasn't in the past." But things were different now. The relationships she had always taken for granted were altered. There was no telling how Amy would respond.

To her relief, Amy's response was standard, typical Amy. "No problem."

"Are you sure, Ame? I hate to dump them on you like this, but I'm running late and I still have some errands I've got to take care of."

"I'm sure. The kids are still out on the dock. Tide's coming in, so they're hauling in crabs as fast as they can."

"Did you get many?"

"Enough for the four of us to have dinner."

"Four? Is Mom there with you?"

Amy's reply wasn't instant. "Uh, no, actually. I have a friend here."

"A friend?" Something in Amy's tone told Claire that the friend was not of the female persuasion. "You mean like a date?"

"No, not a date. He's just here, that's all."

Claire was shocked. It had been years since there had been a man in her sister's life. "Do I know him? Who is he?"

"Dr. Donovan."

"Dr.—" Claire literally pulled the receiver away from her ear and stared at it in amazement. "The doctor from the emergency room?"

"The same."

"I didn't know you were seeing him. When did this start?"

"Right after Mom was released from the hospital."

Claire looked to the calendar on the wall and

counted off more than five weeks. "You're kidding. You didn't say anything about this. Why didn't you tell me?"

"Things have been busy. You know that. The right moment never came up."

"Does Mom know?"

"I told her the other day."

A pang of hurt knotted itself in Claire's chest. "She didn't say anything to me."

"I asked her not to, Claire."

"Why?" The hurt was deepening, touching base with familiar feelings of being the odd man out, of being the flighty middle sister who couldn't be counted on or taken seriously.

"Because I wanted to be the one to tell you, and I wasn't ready until now."

Grudgingly she tried to accept Amy's reasons. They were sound. The past weeks had been pretty bad for her sister, and Amy was cautious to begin with when it came to men.

They hung up moments later to promises of sitting down for a long chat—a chat which, Claire knew, would be centered around the men in their lives, a chat that would be completely one-sided. There was no telling Amy about John.

A bulletproof V-8, 383-cubic-inch engine that delivered 480 horsepower at 6000 rpm, and a flatout speed of 195.2 mph: the car was one of a kind. Feeling the power beneath his hands and body, Mark was as close to orgasm without sex as he had ever been.

Running his palms over the leather cushioned steering wheel, he reveled in knowing the car was his, from the Bose CD system to the magnetic gas-cap holder. So what that it had cost him slightly over 120,000 dollars, and that was before interest on the loan. Driving this kind of machine was not the simple act of getting from point A to point B. It was a frame of mind, a lifestyle, an event that turned people's heads.

It was not a family car intended for juice packs and sticky fingers. It was not to be used to cart the kids to their soccer games or bags of groceries home from the shopping center. It was a man's car to be used for a man's purposes, and he'd been lucky to find it. He couldn't wait for Peggy to see it.

"You bought a new car?" she asked minutes later. Standing on the driveway, she viewed the sleek, black Firebird with gray eyes popped wide. "I didn't know we were thinking of buying a new car."

"We weren't, but this one came along and I couldn't pass it up. It's one of a kind, Peg, custom ordered, but the poor guy died four weeks before the car was delivered." He smiled like a little kid with his first bike. "What do you think?"

"I don't know what to say."

"Here, sit in the driver's seat." He held the door open and watched approvingly as she sat behind the wheel. "The seat practically surrounds you."

Peggy looked skeptical. "It certainly is comfortable." She scoped out the dash. "This looks like a cockpit."

"Exactly; that's what makes it so special."

"How much did it cost?"

"I got a good deal on it."

Giving him a smiling sideways glance, she repeated her question.

"Around a hundred grand," he told her.

Her smile vanished, her breath choked off. "A

hundred thousand? You paid a hundred thousand dollars for a car, without discussing it with me?"

"Peggy, we can afford the monthly payments."

"That's not the point." She shoved her way out of the car before whirling on him. "How could you have done this?"

"Done what?"

"Spent that much money without talking to me first."

"Peg, the deal was too good to pass up. I wanted to act on it before it was too late."

"A day would have been too late? Two hours? At the very least you could have picked up the phone, Mark."

She'd sucked the joy right out of his day. "Why, just so you could play Captain Bring-down?"

"I'm not saying I would have tried to talk you out of buying the car. I'm saying that I had the right to know you were going to spend that much of our money." Staring at the car again, she shook her head in blatant amazement. "God, Mark, this thing costs as much as some houses. I can't believe you did this."

He saw the hurt in her eyes, blended in with her awe, and suddenly, she made him feel like a jerk. "Well, what do you want me to do, take it back?"

That earned him a furious squeal. "Oh, no, you don't. You're not laying this on me. You're not going to get me to say 'take it back' just so you can blame me for the rest of your life."

"Well, you're the one who doesn't want the car."

"I'm the one who wanted to be consulted about the car. That's not the same thing at all. You've handed me a *fait accompli,* as if my input or opinion didn't matter."

That wasn't the way it had been. He had seen

the car and something in him had responded. Days ago, Rene Bellieux had implied that he was the best. Since then, he had been feeling better about himself than he had in months: powerful, clever, intelligent, as one-of-a-kind as the Firebird. He had acted on every one of those sensations, feeling like a man's man; independent, strong, capable. To ask Peggy's *permission* to buy what he wanted hadn't even entered his mind.

Turning away, he shoved his hands onto his waist and stared out across the yard. He resented her for second-guessing him, and for not supporting his decisions. In doing so, she threatened to make him feel inferior and inept, and as discontented as he had been for months.

"I suppose you want me to apologize," he snapped, refusing to give in to the once-plaguing dissatisfaction. "Say I'm sorry I bought the thing."

A heavy sigh preceded her words. "Oh, Mark, the car isn't the issue."

"Could have fooled me."

"It's the fact that you did this on your own."

He glared back at her over his shoulder. "Since when do I have to check out every little decision with you?"

"You don't, but this wasn't a little decision. This one cost a lot of money."

"My ability to make a sound judgement is not limited to some preconceived price fixed in your mind." He turned to face her squarely. "I know what I'm doing, and I'm more than an extension of you."

"This has nothing to do with your autonomy. It has to do with you respecting me."

"What about you respecting me? Why can't you accept what I've done?"

"Because it goes against everything we've ever had in our marriage." Without warning, her eyes filled with tears. "You didn't share this with me, Mark. You bought this car as if I didn't even exist."

He threw his hands into the air and walked away, frustrated that he couldn't get her to see reason. He could never forget that she existed—she was his wife—but she either refused or was unable to see his side, that he hadn't purposely set out to upset her, that he had simply done what he was goddamned entitled to do. He worked hard for the money he made. He could spend it any way he damn well pleased.

"I'm going to take a shower."

"Don't walk away, Mark. We need to finish discussing this."

"What is there to talk about?" He kept right on walking. "You've already made up your mind."

"So have you."

Again he responded with more silence, telling himself that if he said more, he was going to lose his temper, and he honestly didn't want to do that. Halfway through the kitchen he was met by Sarah and Tyler.

"Hi, Dad," Tyler exclaimed

"Hi, Daddy," Sarah echoed.

"Hey, you two." Damn, but he was glad to see them. He stooped to gather them for a group hug. "Where's your sister?"

"Taking a nap," Tyler said.

"That explains why she's inside on a Saturday afternoon, but why aren't you out playing?"

Sarah explained, "Jenny and Jimmy's mom is taking us all to the movies. We're waiting for her to pick us up."

Mark found comfort in the innocent joy underscoring his daughter's response, especially with Peggy's criticism making hash of his temper. "Have a good time," he told them, all the while envying the lack of complications in their lives. The extent of their worries went no further than how much homework they may have or which program to watch on TV. He wished his life could be so simple.

With an internal start, he realized he'd come close to achieving that wish that morning. As he had been signing papers for title and license, life had been very straightforward. He had wanted the car; he'd arranged to buy the car. He had felt good and confident. Peggy or Amy or his mother hadn't even entered his mind.

But Rene Bellieux had. She'd been there on the fringes of his awareness, smiling that thousand-watt smile, telling him all morning that he was the best of the best. And he'd loved every second of it.

Chapter Seventeen

The picnic was all Amy remembered it being from years past: a warm albeit muggy day; lots of food; cars lining the street in front of her Aunt Mary's house; and every cousin, aunt, uncle, and extended family member laughing and talking at the same time.

Viewing it all, Amy marveled that some things never changed. Great uncles still clustered together in an attempt to solve the country's economic problems; aunts sat huddled close, gossiping over the latest scandal; and kids still ran around with faces smeared with everything from cake to dirt.

The timelessness was comforting—one generation passing its traditions down to the next. Those traditions defined who they were, not only as a family but as individuals. That nearly fifty busy individuals chose to set Memorial Day aside for each other, year after year, was a statement of their commitment to the ideal of family. In that, it was easy for Amy to feel no different from the family member she had always been.

"How long does this last?" Seth asked her.

They were standing on the far side of the tables that had been set up in the backyard, close enough to enjoy the happy melee but far enough away to hear each other. "All day. The diehards will be here until midnight."

"Are you one of the diehards?"

"No. I turn into a pumpkin by ten. Besides, most years I take Mom home." But not this year. Claire had insisted on chauffeuring their mother to and from the picnic.

"She's looking well."

Amy followed Seth's line of vision to where Ellen sat with her sisters on the raised deck. "Physically, she's doing fine."

"What about emotionally?"

"I don't think she's having any fallout from the stroke, if that's what you mean."

"It isn't."

Her lips thinned with regret. "She's feeling guilty, and my brother isn't helping."

Seth craned his neck for a better view of the gathering. "Is he here yet?"

"No."

There was enough acerbity in the single word to cause Seth to smile. "And you don't care if ever shows or not."

"The ass. And I don't want to talk about him. It'll only ruin my day." Which she was determined not to allow to happen. She had had to remind herself lately that she was responsible for her own happiness. She could either let Mark continue to steal her joy or she could do her damnedest to protect herself. "Come on, let's get something to eat." Slipping her hand into his, she put forth her best grin. "Besides, my aunts will never forgive me if I don't give them a chance to check you out. How's your bedside manner today?''

Not that he needed it, she mused an hour later. His natural charm, wit, and intelligence had him fitting in with an ease Amy found very satisfying.

"This is so amazing," Claire said.

"What is?" Seated with her mother and sister, Amy looked up from her plate of food with her query.

"You dating Dr. Donovan."

"Why is it amazing?" She smiled at the way he had several of her second cousins hanging on to his every word.

"I don't know; maybe because of the way you met."

"A hospital is as good a place as any," Ellen claimed.

Amy did her best to keep her concern from showing. Her mother had been unusually quiet all afternoon. "Cousin Silva is undoubtedly glad we didn't meet in a bar." She paused to roll her eyes. "Although, she's probably in a snit about the fact that Seth is divorced."

"Silva is a bitch," Claire assured them.

"She's just old," Ellen said.

Amy scoffed. "She's younger than you, Mom."

"Doesn't make any difference. She's set in her ways."

Claire vented a snorting grunt. "That doesn't mean her ways are right. She needs to come down off that high horse of hers and be more accepting of others. Sort of like someone else we know."

Amy gave her sister an irate glare. "Claire, not now."

Shrugging with one shoulder, Claire returned,

"Why not? Mark brought this on himself. Where is he, by the way? He is coming, isn't he?"

"I guess," Amy replied, watching her mother wring her hands. "Mom, don't let him upset you."

"I can't help it." Her voice cracking, Ellen looked from one daughter to the other. "What if he says something?"

Claire insisted, "He wouldn't."

"He might," Ellen worried.

Amy took hold of her mother's hands. "I don't think he will, Mom, but if it makes you feel better, I'll talk to him."

"So will I," Claire added.

Ellen's gaze skimmed a small portion of the nearby faces. It was perfectly clear to Amy that her mother feared what the family would think if they ever knew the truth. Through divorces and emergencies, weddings and even illegitimate babies, unconditional support and acceptance were the standard. But adultery, committed by one of the family's more cherished members, might be stretching even this family's tolerance.

Amy supposed it was perfect timing for Peggy to show up right then. Tyler, Sarah, and Julia raced across the backyard to join the other youngsters. Amy held her breath, waiting for Mark to bring up the rear. Three seconds, eight; she inhaled, but her brother remained absent.

"Hi, everyone." Peggy's greeting was as bright as it was unruffled as she slowly made her way around relatives, exchanging hugs and kisses even though she carried an enormous platter of cookies.

"Doesn't look like Mark's with her," Claire whispered to Amy.

"I can't say that I'm sorry," Amy muttered back. By the time Peggy joined them, she had been relieved of the cookies and she had to straighten her sunglasses. "Whew, what a crowd."

"Where's Mark?" Claire didn't waste a second.

Neither did Peggy. Letting some of her anger show, she carelessly tossed her hair back off her forehead. "Home. Which is fine with me. I'm not talking to him so it's better that he's not here." Sitting, she confessed, "You won't believe what he's done."

To say that Amy was stunned would have been an understatement. "*A hundred thousand dollars for a car?*"

"Has he lost his mind?" Claire raised both hands. "I take that back. My brother doesn't have a mind."

Amy went on. "How could he have done that without discussing it with you?"

"Thank you," Peggy sighed. "I'm glad someone agrees with me." Her ire gave way to hurt. "I just don't understand him any more."

"It's all my fault," came Ellen's choked whisper.

Her movements in unison with Claire's and Peggy's, Amy looked to her mother. "Mom, don't say that."

"It's true."

"No, it isn't," Peggy vouched. "Mark's buying the car has nothing to do with you, or what you did thirty years ago. He's been like this for months."

Ellen looked skeptical. "He had been restless, but now he's angry. He's changed."

"That's his own problem," Claire scoffed. "We've all tried to reason with him, but he's set on playing God."

"Claire's right, Ellen." Peggy leaned forward to fold Ellen into a hug. "You're wrong to condemn yourself. If anyone is causing upset, it's Mark." Leaning back, her gaze turned soft. "I won't lie to you, Ellen. I was shocked when Mark told me the truth, but it was a long time ago. You had to have had your reasons. It isn't fair for me or Mark or anyone to judge you. Somehow, Mark has to find a way to come to terms with this."

Tears came to Ellen's eyes. "But what if he can't? What if he hates me forever?"

Amy offered her reply. "He won't, Mom. He's just being stubborn." With all her heart, she prayed she was right. It was bad enough that they were all having to redefine who they were, not only within themselves, but in relation to each other. Nothing would be solidified until Mark reached an understanding with himself. Right now it appeared he was more intent on satisfying some selfish need than on striving to adjust and accept.

Ellen rose and headed for the house. Amy came to her feet, intending to go after her, but Peggy stayed her.

"Let me. I haven't had a chance to talk to her yet."

Amy agreed by nodding.

Claire wasn't so silent. "I am sick to death of this."

"We all are."

"Yeah, well, if Mark doesn't get his act together, he can kiss this family good-bye."

"That's what I'm afraid of—that we'll never regain what we had."

Claire looked dubious. "Why would you want to? What was so great about what we had?"

"Well, to start with, we had each other to rely on."

Claire slouched deeper into her chair. "Yeah, well, I think all these personal interactions needed to be overhauled."

Amy was stunned. "Why?"

Careful to keep her voice low, Claire said, "Because I don't think any of us have been completely honest with each other."

"Yes, we have."

"Oh, come on, Amy. If you and I had been truthful, we would have told Mark a long time ago what we thought of him: that he's overbearing and sanctimonious."

"He doesn't mean to be."

"Are you defending him?"

"No, but—"

"But nothing. He overassumed the role of head of the family ever since Dad died, and we let him get away with it." She fussed with a cuticle on her thumb. "I'm more guilty of that than anyone."

"Why do you say that?"

"Because it's true." She left off her study of her nail. "I relied on him, and you and Mom, too, when I should have learned to cope with things on my own." She dragged her gaze away. "I've been such a wimp."

"No, you haven't. You've just had a tough time of things."

A rueful smile, strong and blatant, softened Claire's features. "See what I mean about our not being honest with each other? You're doing it right now, Ame, saying nice things to spare my feelings."

Amy was, and only in retrospect did she realize that it was a pattern of long standing between her and her sister.

"Go ahead," Claire prodded. "Say it. Say I've been whining and insecure all my life."

It was true, but Amy couldn't bring herself to be so openly critical. "I wouldn't say whining," she hedged.

"Now who's being a wuss?"

"I am not a wuss."

"Then be honest with me. Tell me that I've been a coward."

Rising to the challenge, Amy conceded, "All right, you've been a temperamental middle-child brat since forever."

The words should have been cause for outrage. Instead, Amy stared at Claire. Claire stared right back, and then together they choked on reluctant laughter that finally broke through.

"I don't believe I said that," Amy said.

"No, I'm glad you did."

Amy had to wonder why. This was so unlike the vulnerable Claire she knew. "Mark isn't the only person who's changed," she quietly observed of her older sister.

"Is that your way of telling me I've finally grown a backbone?"

"You're certainly more purposeful than I've ever known you to be."

"About time, don't you think?" Before Amy could respond, she reminded, "Be honest."

Again Amy was hit with her sister's newfound sense of conviction, and didn't know what to make of it, but she could see that Claire was proud of herself. "I think you've taken a huge step forward."

"You're such a diplomat," Claire sneered, softening the jab by leaning close for a hug. "I love you, Ame. If I haven't thanked you for all the years of coming to my rescue, I'm thanking you now."

Emotions collected in the back of Amy's throat, painful in their rush toward tears. "I love you, too, Claire."

"I'm glad. I'm glad that something good has come of all this mess."

Something had, Amy realized. Somehow through all the heartache and confusion, she and her sister were closer now than they had ever been, and on a level more genuine than anything Amy could have ever imagined.

Perhaps, then, Amy hoped, there was hope for Mark after all. And bringing the family back together. And her own floundering sense of self.

"You're awfully quiet," Seth said hours later on the ride back to his place.

"Just thinking."

"Good thoughts?"

She tipped her head from side to side. "More like interesting."

"Care to share them?"

With telling ease, she did. "I had a good talk with Claire this afternoon."

"I saw the two of you together. It looked pretty intense."

"We were baring our souls."

He threw a quick questioning glance her way.

"She was demanding honesty." Even now, she could hear the amazement in her voice.

"Obviously that surprises you."

"You have to know Claire. She's never been the strongest of people. We've always had to be careful of how we said things or what we did, because her feelings were so easily hurt. But today . . ." She let the words trail off as she gathered her thoughts. "I've never seen her as she was today. She was focused and brutally honest about herself."

"That's a good thing."

"I agree, but I didn't expect it from Claire."

"You never know how people are going to react to stressful situations."

"What do you mean?"

He had parked the car and they were making their way up the walkway to his front door. "You've all been handed a remarkable set of circumstances to deal with. Your sister seems to have reacted by finding an inner strength she didn't know she had."

"You know, I think you're right." She smiled at him in patent admiration for his insight.

"What can I say?" he chuckled. "I'm good."

"Modest, too."

"Now, your brother—"

She held up a hand on her way to the kitchen. She had filled Seth in on the details of Mark's new car. "I do not want to talk about him."

"You can't ignore him."

"Why not?"

"You know the answer to that as well as I do."

"Talking about him makes me angry. *Thinking* about him makes me angry."

"Then be angry, that's healthy, but you can't avoid him as an issue in your life."

She stopped at the sink to lean back and cross her arms over her chest, riled at the way he was goading her. "He's an issue, all right, one that I can't deal with."

"You don't have a choice. He's part of your life."

"So are taxes, but I avoid thinking of them whenever possible."

"Be serious."

"I am. I'm serious about giving up on Mark. I've done everything I can think of to bridge this gap between us, but there's no talking to him."

"Are you sure of that?"

"I've tried, believe me."

"Oh, I believe you, all right." Slipping his hands around her waist, he angled his hips to hers. For all the sexual possibilities of the pose, however, Amy was more comforted than aroused. "I just wanted to make sure that in your own mind you're convinced that there's nothing more you can do." His fingers flexed. "It's up to your brother now."

She eyed him suspiciously, wondering how he had maneuvered her so effortlessly into drawing the conclusion he'd been after, a conclusion she had not actively admitted to herself. A grain of guilt had been hovering somewhere in her psyche—guilt that her very existence was the cause for the antagonism between her and Mark. In riling her, Seth had made her admit that she had nothing to feel guilty about, especially not the fact that she was alive.

"You're slick, Dr. Donovan."

He responded with a smile of boyish delight. "I love it when you talk dirty."

"And brilliant." She rested her hands on his shoulders. "It's no wonder that I love you."

He stilled completely, his humor giving way to something that flicked through his eyes and touched Amy with its raw intensity. "You've never said it before."

"I know."

"Do you mean it?"

"Yes." It was the first time in weeks she had felt so certain about anything. It was a profound relief that she could be her normal, decisive self again, especially in regard to so monumental an issue.

Expelling his breath, he sighed, "It's about time. I was beginning to worry."

"It's been difficult for me. My instincts haven't been all they should be."

He dismissed her explanation with a shake of his head. "As long as you can say the words, it doesn't matter."

"I do love you, Seth." Words to back the senti-ment, which in the ensuing half hour was expressed upstairs in his bed. They made love as they never had, giving and taking in ways Amy sensed Seth had been desperate for. She, too, gloried in the sharing, far richer for the admission of love.

"I do like your bedside manner," she mur-mured, her body draped over his in the languid aftermath of release.

"Your own is pretty fantastic."

Pressing a kiss into the damp hair on his chest, she inhaled deeply. "I was inspired."

"Enough to marry me?"

She couldn't prevent the tensing of her muscles. "Seth," she began, only to have him cut her off by dragging her farther up his chest.

Eye to eye, he soothed, "Don't go all skittish on me. It isn't as though I haven't mentioned it before. You know how I feel, what I want."

"And you know how I feel."

"You say you love me."

"I do, but I'm not ready to get married, at least not right now. Give me more time to get used to the idea." His slow grin surprised her. "What are you smiling about?"

"Your progress." Wrapping his arms about her, he explained, "The last time I mentioned marriage you couldn't even consider the idea. Now you're at least open to it."

She mulled that over and, as usual, found him right. She had made progress, albeit slow. She still was not as confident of life as she once had been, but neither was she mired in emotional muck, unable to make a decision of any kind. As Seth said, she was making progress, and there was joy to be found in that.

Chapter Eighteen

It had been a very good week. In terms of Amy's internal palette, a burnished gold accented by touches of bronze and pewter would have described her days. She was, if not pleased, then at least relieved by the fact that she and Mark had survived without a single harsh word between them. To know that this was accomplished for the most part by avoiding each other was a bit demoralizing, but peace was peace and she would take it any way she could get it.

Tonight, peace came with a glazing of youth. Claire was once again working late, and Amy had agreed to sit with Bethany and Mike. At the moment, they were upstairs in their separate rooms, supposedly doing their homework. She couldn't be sure. The silence was encouraging, but that alone was no indication. She would give them another five minutes before she casually wandered up to oh-so-casually check on them.

In the meantime, she was putting the last touches on dinner. Spaghetti, salad, and garlic bread. Nutri-

tious and better yet, fast, which was an absolute
necessity. Seth had pulled the midnight shift at the
ER most of the week. His days had become her
nights, which meant she had lost enough sleep to
keep her constantly wishing for a nap.

She didn't mind, but still she was glad he would
be nine-to-fiving it again, if for no other reason
than that she could see him in broad daylight. A
normal sleeping routine would be nice, too. She
could have easily dropped off standing right there
at Claire's kitchen counter slicing cucumbers.

"I'm hungry, Aunt Amy." Mike made his an-
nouncement as he clamored his way into the
kitchen.

"You're always hungry, but not to worry, the
pasta's already cooking. Why don't you set the
table."

Forks, plates, and glasses were laid out in record
time; Bethany joined them and dinner was on.
Mike dug in with typical boyish disdain for manners. Bethany toyed with her salad as if it were
liver.

"What's wrong, Bethy?" Amy asked.

She looked up quickly. "Nothing."

"Are you feeling all right?"

"I suppose."

"Then why aren't you eating? Aren't you hungry?"

"When's Mom coming home?"

Without meaning to, Amy glanced to Mike. He
stopped chewing long enough for Amy to see the
question in his eyes as well. "She said she'd be
home by seven, sweetheart."

Beth checked the time on the wall clock before
making an attempt at eating. It wasn't long, however, before Amy noticed her niece's appetite wane
again.

In hopes of distracting Beth from missing her mother, she asked, "How was school today?"

"Good," Mike answered.

"How about you, Bethy?"

Her reply was a sullen one-shouldered shrug.

"Bethany got a D on her test in math," Mike tattled.

Bethany erupted. "Shut up, Michael."

Scrunching up his face, he sneered, "Mom's gonna be pissed when she finds out."

"I hate you!" she screamed.

Caught completely off guard, it took Amy a few seconds to get a handle on the situation. "Stop it, both of you."

"He started it," Bethany railed back.

"Well, neither one of you is going to finish it." She backed the command with every ounce of aunt-authority. Silently she prayed it would be sufficient. She rarely had to pull rank on them to this extent.

Thankfully, they settled down, sulked their way through the rest of the meal, and finally retreated to their rooms. Amy waited only long enough to set the dishwasher before going up to talk to Bethany. It was already going on seven-thirty.

"Can I come in?" Poised in the doorway, she waited for the invitation.

Bethany seemed to debate the matter. "Yeah," she finally relented. Sprawled out on her bed, surrounded by all seven of her Barbie dolls, she made room for Amy to sit. "Are you going to yell at me?"

"No. It's over and done with. Besides, that's a mom thing to do."

"I wish Mom would feel the same way." Utter helplessness filled Beth's expression. "I didn't mean to get a D on my test, Aunt Amy."

"I'm sure you didn't. No one sets out to get a D."

"Mom's gonna be mad, but it wasn't my fault."

"Did you try your best?"

"Yeah, but I didn't understand what we were doing."

"Why didn't you ask your teacher to explain it again?"

"I did. I still didn't get it. Mom said she would help me over the weekend, but I guess she forgot or something. I asked her again last night, but she didn't have time. She never has time for us any more, Aunt Amy."

There was little doubt that Claire's work schedule had been grueling lately. Poor Bethany had gotten caught in the backlash. "I'm not the greatest at math, but do you want me to see if I can help?"

For the first time that night, there was animation in Beth's eyes. "Could you?"

Fractions and decimals were conquered by sheer grit, diagrams, graphs, even sketched-out pies, but in the end, Beth understood the concept of .50 being equal to one half. Amy was proud of them both: Beth for overcoming a sense of defeat, and herself for so stoically contending with such a hideously left-brained function as mathematical conversions.

If it hadn't been eight forty-five, Amy would have treated Bethany to a bowl of celebration ice cream from the freezer. Practicality prevailed and the best she could do was get her niece and nephew ready for bed.

"I thought Mom was going to be here by seven," Mike complained, covers drawn to his chin.

"She must have gotten tied up. I'm sure she'll be home soon."

"Then can I stay up until she gets home?"

"Nice try."

"Please?" He stretched the word out to comical lengths.

Amy laughed. "No way. Now go to sleep before you get us both in trouble." And that was that.

Bethany didn't relent as easily. She had withdrawn again, Amy noticed, her mood as troubled as it had been at dinner.

"Are you still worried about what your Mom is going to say about your test?"

"I guess."

Smoothing Beth's hair back from her face, Amy promised, "I told you I'd explain everything to her."

"I know."

"Maybe she can even talk to your teacher and explain what happened. Maybe your teacher will give you a retest."

"Maybe."

Amy had hit a stone wall. Something else was obviously bothering Beth. "Sweetheart, what is it?" Without thinking, she laid her hand on Beth's forehead to check for fever.

As she had done so frequently all night, Beth gave one of her one-shouldered shrugs. "Does Mom love us?"

Stunned, she sat back, a crooked, disbelieving grin curling her lips. "Of course she does. Oh, Bethy, how can you even ask that?"

"I don't know."

"She loves you and Mike more than anyone or anything on earth." She searched Beth's face, saw the sadness, and simply reacted. "Oh, Beth," she sighed, offering a hug she hoped would suffice. Thankfully, Beth reciprocated. "I know this has been hard on you, honey, but just because your mom's work is taking her time away from you doesn't mean she doesn't love you. She would much rather be with you than at the bank, but she doesn't have a choice. Can you understand?''

But Amy knew it didn't matter. Beth could understand the situation until the cows came home, but beneath any acceptance she might feel, she was vulnerable. And it didn't take a genius to figure out the reasons. Bethany had already lost her father. It was only natural that emotionally she would be more dependent on her mother. Until now, Claire had been a constant with no deviation, focusing most of her energies, and time, on her children. Her job had suddenly altered that status.

As she settled down in the living room to wait for her sister, Amy thought of how best to explain all this to Claire. True, her sister had been unusually self-confident lately, but Beth's troubles were sure to strike at the heart of Claire, as a mother and a woman. Amy was fully prepared for Claire to become defensive. It was, after all, what Claire did best.

By ten, Amy was still waiting, although not on the sofa in front of the TV. Concern had her pacing from the front windows to the kitchen in a restless attempt to calm her fears. It wasn't like Claire to be late, and three hours at that. After a long debate, she finally relented and called the bank.

Fifteen rings later she hung up, more worried than ever. Her imagination, never lacking in any situation, took full flight. It was while she was in the middle of picturing her sister being wheeled into Seth's ER that she heard Claire's car pull in the driveway.

Amy didn't know whether to be relieved or angry.

She was feeling mega doses of each, so much so that Claire's breathless entry into the house didn't faze her in the least.

"Where have you been?" She started right in, ignoring the fact that she sounded much as their mother had years ago when they'd been kids, ignoring the fact that fear had put a hard edge on her voice.

"I'm sorry I'm late," Claire breathed around an apologetic smile. "I got caught up."

"You're over three hours late. I was worried. I didn't know what happened to you."

"Nothing happened. I told you, I was working."

"Then why didn't you answer the phone?"

For a prolonged moment, Claire looked as if she had been caught red-handed in some illegal activity. "What?"

"I called the bank," Amy repeated, shoving a hand through her hair. "You said you'd be home by seven. By ten o'clock, I got so worried I called the bank."

"Oh." Claire sidled away to loop her purse over the newel at the bottom of the stairway.

" 'Oh'? That's all you have to say?"

"What number did you call?"

"Your number, at your desk, but you didn't answer."

Claire's laugh was as brittle as it was patently forced. "I wasn't at my desk." Arms wrapped about her middle, she turned back with a weak smile. "I . . . I wasn't . . . we weren't at my desk, so I didn't hear the phone."

Amy had never seen her sister look as uncomfortable as she was right then. "Are you sure you're all right?"

"I'm fine, really." Claire grimaced and seemed

to dig deep for composure. "I'm sorry, Amy." Her apology emerged slowly and was backed by obvious remorse. "I didn't mean to worry you."

There was no doubting Claire's sincerity. Amy accepted it, feeling deflated as the last of her anger dissolved. "Well, you're home now; you're safe; that's all that matters; but next time, call if you're going to be late."

Claire's answer was a nod and more nervous facial expressions: her lips pulled to one side, brows rising and lowering for no apparent reason. Finally, she made her way into the living room and leaned against the back of the sofa. "How are the kids?"

"Asleep."

"Were there any problems?"

"No, but you need to talk to Bethany." She explained about the math test.

"Oh, shit," Claire muttered, covering her eyes with a hand, her shoulders slumping. "I was supposed to have helped her."

"That's what she said."

"I've been so busy at . . ." Her words dried up before she dropped her hand away. "I . . . I've been short on time, especially around here."

"You don't have to explain to me."

"Was she upset?"

Carefully Amy broached the matter of Beth's real worries. "She wasn't happy, and math was the least of it."

"What do you mean?"

On a weighty sigh, she said, "She asked me if you still love her."

Claire's reaction was all that Amy's had been, only intensified a hundred-fold, Amy could tell, by true maternal instincts. "She thinks I don't love her?"

"Not exactly. She just needed to be reassured."

"But why? I don't understand."

"Claire, you're all she has. You haven't been around as much as she's used to, so she's feeling insecure."

Again Claire pressed her fingers to her forehead, shielding her eyes. "So this is all my fault." There was defeat and resentment in her voice.

Amy had been afraid of this. "I'm not blaming you, Claire."

Her head snapped up. "But you think I'm a lousy mother for forgetting to help her own daughter so she won't get a D on her math test."

"I didn't say that."

"No, but you're thinking it."

"What I'm thinking is that work has got you in a temporary stranglehold and you let a few things slide." She held up a hand to forestall Claire's response. "Not intentionally, Claire. No one is a better mother than you, but Beth obviously feels left out of your life right now."

"What life?" Claire sneered. "Until now, I haven't had a life. I went to work and I took care of my kids. End of story." She shoved off the sofa and pressed a fist to her chest. "But what about me, Amy? Don't I get a life of my own?"

"Of course."

"When? After I clean this house or help Beth with her math or take Mike to Little League or go grocery shopping or deal with half-assed customers at the bank?"

Amy couldn't imagine the pressures of being a single parent. "I don't have any answers for you, Claire. And I'm not going to tell you I understand, because I don't. I don't know what it's like to lose a husband you loved and suddenly find yourself in the middle of a life you never bargained for. I don't know how you've managed as well as you have all these years."

"That's just it. I've only *managed,* Amy, but I haven't lived." Claire crossed to the fireplace. "I've had to put my whole life on hold. People and places and doing all the fun things in life have passed me by." Pounding a fist on the mantle, she argued, "It wasn't supposed to be this way."

Amy's heart was truly caught by her sister's distress. "I didn't realize it was this hard on you."

"Yeah, well, it is."

"You can't let it get the best of you."

Claire glanced back over her shoulder. "Here comes the pep talk, right?"

"No. Here comes the truth."

"Please, don't."

"Why? Weren't you all gung ho for honesty last weekend?"

"I don't want to hear your criticism."

"You won't. I'm going to tell you that you have a lot to be grateful for."

Claire spun about, her face drawn with amazement. Flinging a hand wide, she asked, "What's so wonderful about what I have?"

"To start with, Bethany and Mike."

"Spoken like an aunt and not a mother. You get to be with them on your own terms—enjoy them for a while and then turn them and all the responsibilities back over to me."

"That's right, and I envy you."

"Oh, please."

"I do, Claire. I would love to have kids."

"Go talk to Seth."

"It's not that easy and you know it, especially now. I can't be completely sure of him because I can't be completely sure of myself these days. But it was different for you and Dan.''

''How?''

''You were secure in each other. Your identities were intact, as individuals and as a couple. Through the day-to-day grind, the loving, the fighting, having children, you were committed to each other fully, with no reservations or doubts.''

''But I don't have that anymore,'' Claire wailed softly, her eyes glazed with tears. ''I'm supposed to be grateful for that?''

''Yes. Don't you see?'' She closed in on her sister and took hold of her hands. ''Some people go all their lives without ever experiencing what you and Dan had. They'll never know the kind of love you were lucky enough to have. It's them I pity, not you.''

''I want it all again,'' Claire demanded, yanking her hands out of Amy's clasp.

''I know you do.''

''I'm entitled, aren't I?'' Anger and resentment carried her across the room.

''Yes.'' Amy thought to add, *As long as you don't hurt your children,* but left that unspoken. She wasn't about to cast judgement on her sister.

''I deserve to be happy.''

''You do.''

Amy's continued agreement seemed to exhaust the worst of Claire's temper. Traces lingered, however, as she blatantly fumed from within, obviously at war with herself. ''Then you don't hate me for what I did tonight?'' she finally asked with extreme caution.

''No, why would I hate you for being late?''

"But what if I was enjoying myself? Would you be mad at me for that? Would that make me any less of a good mother?"

"I don't see how." With a shake of her head, Amy turned to humor. "You're human, Claire, strange but human. How anyone can enjoy themselves working overtime at a bank is beyond me, but hey, if it makes you happy, so be it."

"I have been happy," Claire declared. "For the first time in years."

"That's nothing to feel guilty about."

"I feel guilty for neglecting the children."

"I can imagine, but it's not as if you were out robbing convenience stores or screwing another woman's husband. You've gotten caught up in your job; that's all." The look on Claire's face stopped her. "Hey, are you all right?"

Claire had gone white. The line of her mouth looked wobbly. "Yes."

"You don't look it."

"It's getting late." She headed for the front door. "The day has just crashed in on me."

"Are you sure you're all right?"

Wrapped up in her arms, Claire retorted, "Just go home, Amy."

Amy could not contain her amazement. Insulted as well as stunned, she stared openmouthed and wide-eyed at her sister's back before finally collecting her purse and jacket. All the while she wondered what screw was suddenly loose in her sister's head this time. Claire was known for her mood swings, but she was setting new records tonight.

"I was trying to help." She shoved an arm into a jacket sleeve.

"I don't need anyone's help," Claire sniped.

"Fine. Next time, call a sitter to take care of your kids." She was out the door. "And whenever you can spare the time to help Bethany with her spelling, look up the word *ingrate.*"

Chapter Nineteen

Mark decided he was getting sick and tired of the tension around the house. After a whole week, Peggy was still fuming silently. What little she had to say to him was of the chilly-stare variety. Or she talked around him, transmitting her messages via one of the kids. *Julia, tell your dad that dinner is ready*—when she knew damn good and well that he was within hearing distance. *Tyler, have you reminded your dad about Father-and-Son Night tomorrow?*

It was Peggy at her pissed-off worst. She had resorted to this type of behavior once or twice before, but never for such a length of time. Nor had she ever entrenched so deeply, ignoring him most of the time, making a single cup of coffee in the morning instead of a full pot, leaving him to his own defenses in the laundry room, and sleeping as far to her side of the bed as humanly possible. Sex had definitely gone the way of wishful thinking.

That in itself was another source of aggravation. He knew he wasn't going to get so much as a kiss until Peggy stopped being angry, and he didn't have a clue as to when that might be. From what he could tell, she had yet to resolve the issue of his buying the car. Logically, an open discussion seemed the way to go, but *she* wasn't talking to him.

Making his way into the kitchen, he decided that he could be just as stubborn as her.

"Hi, Daddy." Julia offered him an oatmeal smile. Sarah and Tyler added their greetings, their innocent acceptance like sunshine on a gloomy day.

"Good morning, everyone." His gaze swept them all, Peggy included. She avoided having to speak to him or even looking his way by making sure she sipped her coffee. He resigned himself to another frosty morning, which added further to the mountain of frustration and resentment that had been piling up.

For the sake of the kids, he maintained a relaxed, attentive facade. He drank his coffee and ate a piece of toast, not rising until the three were headed out the door for the school bus. Then, he dropped all pretenses.

"How much longer is this going to go on?" he demanded, taking a stance in the middle of the kitchen.

Peggy stacked up the breakfast dishes, not even glancing his way. "That's up to you."

"Me? You're the one who has refused to talk."

"What's there to say?" She shouldered past him on her way to the sink. "You're mister know-it-all. You have all the answers. You've made it perfectly clear that you don't need to talk to me about anything."

"Shit." He slammed his hands onto his waist, his pride shredding right before his eyes. He had been determined not to give an inch, and yet he was the one struggling for a compromise. "What do you want me to do? Say I'm sorry?"

"Not unless you mean it."

"Okay, I'm sorry."

"For what?"

He rolled his eyes. "For making you mad." But all he got for his apology was a pursing of lips and a snide arching of one brow. "What? Wasn't that good enough?"

"I'm sure you think it is," she returned as she loaded the dishwasher.

"You want me to apologize for buying the car."

"For the *way* you bought the car."

"I don't fuckin' believe this."

His language jerked her straight. "Don't you dare swear at me."

As amazed as he was angry, he turned for the den to get his jacket, only to pivot and face his wife again. "I'm not sorry I bought the car, Peg."

"That's not the issue."

"The hell it isn't."

"Then we have nothing to talk about."

He was back to square one. "You're not going to be satisfied until I take the damn thing back, are you?"

Glaring at him as if he were the dumbest man on earth, she scoffed, "I'm not going to be satisfied until you understand that what you did was completely selfish."

That did it. He did turn this time, stalking into the den on a wave of fury, slamming out of the house in a grand show of temper. He couldn't help it. He knew if he didn't release some of the rage, he would do something stupid. Or he would give himself a heart attack.

Careful not to take his anger out on the Firebird,

he drove to work, letting himself be soothed by the car's interior, and by the looks he occasionally drew from other drivers. It wasn't long before he could think clearly about his argument with Peggy.

He resented her calling him selfish. Unfortunately, he squirmed at the grain of truth underscoring her accusation. Maybe he had been thinking solely of himself when he had bought the car, but wasn't it about time he did something for himself? Hell, he worked hard for every penny he made, pennies that he either poured right back into the company or else spent on his family or home. He wasn't going to castigate himself for thinking and acting like an independent man for the first time in his entire marriage. Hell, he wasn't going to feel guilty over that.

He entered his office, with Peggy relegated as much as possible into a deep dark corner of his mind. Oh, she wasn't going anywhere. Her presence was very real, and he had no doubt that she would jump out at him at odd times during the day, but he'd be damned if he would allow her to control his every thought.

As it had been for days, work was his salvation. He concentrated fiercely, breezed his way through two separate meetings, reviewed a stack of contracts, took time for lunch, met with his attorneys, and made it back to his office in time to okay a presentation for one of the local malls. His mood was up when Cicily phoned him to tell him that Rene Bellieux was waiting to see him.

Surprise hit him first; they weren't scheduled for a meeting. Fascination came next; she had a profound effect on his ego.

She entered his office as she always did, long

legs gliding, her smile as lazy as her walk. "Is that your new car out there?" she asked.

Coming to his feet, he smiled in genuine warmth. "You mean the Firebird?"

"That sleek, black thing."

"As a matter of fact, it is mine."

"Nice." One of her dark brows flicked upward. "Very nice."

He was struck by that one simple gesture. Peggy had done much the same that morning, but instead of approval, the gesture had delivered contempt.

"Thanks, I'm enjoying it." He gestured for her to sit. "What brings you here, or did I forget an appointment?"

"No, nothing like that. I wanted to make a few changes in the copy for those ads we discussed. I just finished up with an appointment downtown so I decided to stop by." She tossed her purse onto his desk. "I didn't expect to find you free, but I'm glad you are."

Wondering if every word she said was destined to make him feel like a million bucks, he personally fetched the file for Bell Electronic Systems himself. The changes she wanted were certainly not complicated, but they did involve more than simple editing. The impromptu meeting soon included Amy and Barbara Chan. He made it absolutely clear to them that Rene was to get exactly what she wanted.

That was accomplished in under an hour. Mark had to give Amy credit for working her artistic magic on the layout designs. Rene was thoroughly pleased, and that pleased him. Behind closed doors once again, he savored the sense of satisfaction he felt.

"Any other problems?" he asked.

"Not a one. Thanks to you."

"That's what I'm here for."

"You make your job sound so easy."

"You're easy to work with, Rene." Other people, other problems should be so undemanding.

"You haven't talked with my father recently," she laughed, swinging one leg from where she sat with a hip perched on the edge of his desk. "He'd tell you a different story entirely."

He did his damnedest not to follow the leggy movement that shifted the skirt over her thigh. Standing at the far corner of his desk, it took a concerted effort. "Your father's a good business-man, just set in his ways."

"And you're incredibly tactful." She pinned him with a teasing stare that challenged him to disagree.

He couldn't disagree, or look away, or seem to get his breath. Everything inside him seemed to shift downward. Alarms sounded in his head, warn-ings to back out of this moment as fast as possible, but the truth was, he didn't want to any more than he wanted to give up the Firebird.

"Well," she prompted.

"Well, what?"

"Are you or are you not going to kiss me?" She tilted her head to one side. "You've been wanting to, and I confess, I've been curious."

Stating it so plainly should have dashed the cold water of reason in his face. "Curious about what?"

"About how long you were going to pretend we're not attracted to each other."

She came to her feet, but he closed the distance between them, giving himself no chance for con-science or ethics. He took her in his arms and did what he'd been fantasizing about doing for weeks. Adrenaline spewed. He was instantly hard. He deepened the kiss.

"My, my," she finally got out around a saucy grin. "From the feel of things, you're more than curious yourself."

He swallowed with great difficulty. He couldn't help himself. It had been sixteen years since he had kissed a woman other than Peggy, and it was as exhilarating as it was unpleasant. His conscience, so late to kick in, did so now with a vengeance, making him feel inept and foolish and dishonest when only seconds ago he had been the master of his universe.

The sensation sucked. And he wasn't going to tolerate it.

If the first kiss had been to satisfy her curiosity and his lust, the second was to prove to them both that he was in charge of his own life. Revenge, too, was mixed in with the sexuality, for all the crap he'd had to tolerate in his life lately: condemning wife, adulterous mother, sanctimonious sisters.

He heard Amy's voice and her knock at the door at the same time that it opened. He couldn't step back quickly enough, nor could he or Rene wipe the signs of passion from their faces.

"Oh, God," Amy whispered, her hand on the door, her face ashen. She stared at them as though she couldn't believe what she had seen, horror and accusation so obvious Mark wanted to curse.

Rene moved away, her lips rolled in over her teeth, her gaze focused on her shoes as she folded her arms over her chest. Amy finally seemed able to move—right out the door and down the hall.

"Shit." He shoved a hand through his hair, his stomach twisted into a knot the size of the national debt.

"Talk about bad timing," Rene returned. She

looked at him without lifting her head. "Is this going to cause problems for you?"

More than likely. "No. I'll handle it."

"I'm sorry, Mark."

"Don't be."

"I think it's time I left." Retrieving her purse, she stopped to lay a hand on his arm. "Let me know if there's anything I can do." She gave his arm a gentle squeeze. "Call me."

He didn't take the time to decode any messages there may or may not have been in her parting comment. He was too swamped by the situation in which he suddenly found himself. Like a guilty schoolboy who had been caught truant, he felt he had to make his explanations to a higher authority. Except that Amy was his sister, not his judge, and his private life was his own. He didn't have to tell her anything.

The guilt stayed with him, however, as well as the dread, both defying logic and adult rationalizations.

Amy could not get home soon enough. She left the office without shutting down her computer for the night, stopping only long enough to grab her backpack and then drive away. As numb as she felt, she couldn't summon the strength to worry about layout designs or even traffic for that matter.

God had to have been her copilot, because she was turning off Jefferson Avenue for Oyster Point before she realized where she was. With a shake of her head, she forced herself to concentrate on rush-hour traffic.

The snarl into Poquoson was typical, eight lanes that eventually narrowed to one in either direction.

Perversely, she enjoyed what was usually an annoyance, just as she didn't mind the ducks that noisily greeted her in her front yard, demanding corn for all they were worth.

She went through all the motions involved; changing clothes, spreading out the ducks' dinner, checking the messages on her machine. All the while, she kept her mind ruthlessly wiped free of what she had witnessed in Mark's office, absolutely refusing to allow herself to think about it now. She couldn't; she truly could not. If she did, she wasn't certain what she would do. Crying would be the very least of it. She sensed that innately.

It was with mixed feelings that she heard a car turn into the driveway, remembering only then that Seth was bringing Melody over for another painting lesson. At the moment, dealing with a thirteen-year-old, even one as great as Mel, felt daunting. At the same time, the prospect could be her salvation for the night.

"Hi." She put forth her best effort at being up.

Melody responded in kind before hurrying into the studio. Seth, with his doctor's observing, detective eyes, was less enthusiastic. Lingering over the kiss he gave her, he took the time to study her face.

"What's wrong?"

"Nothing," she answered too quickly, catching herself with both hands in her hair. It was a dead giveaway that her nerves were frayed. "I'll tell you later."

"Are you sure?"

"Yes."

He paused, weighing her responses with open intent. "We can postpone this for another time."

She wished he weren't so persistent, or that she

hadn't been so obvious. She had worried him and she hadn't wanted to do that. He didn't deserve to be caught up in her family's mess. And, too, he was reacting by being the concerned lover or the practiced physician, trying to make everything all right when she wasn't sure she wanted that. Not now, at any rate.

"I don't want to get into it now, Seth. Please." She splayed the fingers of both hands, jabbing him with a pleading look.

It had to have been the last that convinced him to let it alone, at least for the moment. "If that's what you want."

"It is." To soften the effect of her words, she touched her fingertips to his cheek and dredged up a smile. "Really. Mel and I have plenty to do." She shooed him toward the door. "Go do whatever it was you were going to do for the next two hours."

Obviously prepared to bide his time, he relented, but not before he promised, "We'll talk about this later."

Amy wasn't about to debate the relativity of when "later" might be. It went without saying that she and Seth had different timetables. His was bound to be far earlier than she was going to be prepared for. But for the next two hours, at least, and hopefully for tonight, she would be spared having to think about Mark.

"Is everything cool with Dad?" Melody asked as soon as Amy joined her.

"Oh, sure. He's just being a doctor."

Melody rolled her eyes. "He's so bad at that. It's worse than when he's like, you know, a father. It's like he has to be in charge and fix things. It's definitely not cool."

She was willing to be charmed by Mel's adolescence. In return, she expended every ounce of energy she possessed to immerse them both in painting. Seth was back before she checked the clock even once.

"Is it seven-thirty already?" Mel asked, a paint-brush in each hand.

Her father gave her a crooked grin. "Afraid so."

"And I was just getting to the good part."

Amy purposely stayed out of the conversation. The two hours of concentration had taken the edge from her nerves, but she was still feeling awkward with herself. Anything she said to Seth would more than likely come out sounding emotionally suspect. As keen and persistent as Seth was, he would push for explanations she wasn't ready to give.

She honestly thought she had bypassed the inevitable when he took Melody home. He didn't linger or promise to call. The kiss he gave her was abbreviated to the point of being nonexistent. Watching him drive away, she exhaled deeply and then surrendered to the pent-up need to take some kind of action by changing the paintings on the walls.

Canvases came out of her studio in groups. Landscapes were replaced by abstracts; portraits hung next to still lifes. As escapism went it was great therapy, which was unexpectedly cut short by Seth's return. Without knocking, he let himself in.

Sitting on her heels, surrounded by years of work, she silently stared up at him and told herself she should have known he wouldn't let her be. When he had said they would talk later, he had meant just that.

There wasn't any need for him to prompt her. She knew what he wanted to hear—the reasons for why she was one raw nerve. She had been running from this exact moment for hours and, if not for Seth, would have continued to do so for hours to come. But he hunkered down in front of her, slipped one hand around to the nape of her neck and she was lost, to the inevitable as well as the compassion beneath his touch.

"I caught Mark with another woman today." The shame wasn't hers, but she looked away.

His fingers ceased their gentle massage for an instant before resuming. "Damn. What happened?"

"Nothing original, I'm sure. I walked into his office without thinking and found him and one of our clients swapping spit, as Melody would say." The first of all the emotions she had purposely been avoiding hit home. She began to shake with anger. "How could he, Seth? Peggy loves him; she's the best thing that ever happened to him. How could he cheat on her?"

"I don't know, hon. And neither do you."

"What does that mean?"

"They were kissing. That doesn't mean they're having an affair."

"Minor point," she snapped. "That doesn't make it right."

"I agree."

"All this time he's been condemning Mom, and yet he's no better." She surged to her feet. "What a goddamned hypocrite."

"It would appear so."

"Appearances, my ass." Revulsion was joined by hurt. "How could he, Seth?" Her shaking increased, the tears rose. "How could he betray Peggy this way?"

He drew her close. "I don't know. I see it all the time, people who come into the ER with stories about how a wife or a husband cheated on them, but I've never understood it."

"Don't promises mean anything anymore?" she cried into his chest.

"They're supposed to."

"Not to Mark." She gripped his shirt with both hands, feeling betrayed all over again. Her faith in marriage and love had been rocked to its core. Still, she realized that some part of her had to have held a tiny spark of faith because of Mark and Peggy. Despite what had happened between her parents years ago, she had taken it for granted that Mark and Peggy were solid, with an honest marriage and an enduring love.

Was it nothing but lies? Were all her ideals hollow and meaningless? Naively, the answer was no, but reality had taken place in Mark's office.

She choked on a snide laugh. Through Seth, she had let herself begin to regain her faith. Now she felt like a fool—a child, ignorant and ridiculous. It was all a crock of shit: love and marriage, commitment, trust, honor.

Stepping back, she turned her back on Seth, and on her own naïveté. With hands on her hips, she stared at the ceiling and wished for this night to end. "Maybe it would best if you left."

"Nice try, Amy."

"I'm serious. I want to be alone."

"You're only going to brood."

"Then that's what I'll do, but I want to do it by myself." She looked back at him over her shoulder. "Please, Seth."

It was there in his expression, the I-don't-believe-this-crap look that prefaced a motherload of determination. There were also signs of hurt. "I thought we'd gotten past this, Amy."

"What?"

"Your retreating when you've got a problem instead of letting me help."

She turned to face him. "I just want you to leave me alone for a while."

"With anyone else that would be no problem, but you don't want to be left alone; you want a full withdrawal."

"That's not—"

"Sure it is. You've tried it before."

"And as I remember, you didn't listen to me then."

"I'm not going to now."

"Why?"

"Because I love you."

She wrapped up in her arms, her mouth pinched, her gaze directed at the floor halfway between them. She did not want to hear about love. "Then give me time."

His frustration evident in his voice, he maintained, "That's all I've ever given you. But this isn't about time, or having your personal space to get your head together. This is about you excluding me from your life."

He was right, and as volatile as she felt, her control was in serious doubt. She didn't want to hurt him, but she was afraid that was what she would do if he persisted. "Don't you understand? I am on the edge. Having this discussion now would not be wise."

"This discussion is long overdue."

"Don't badger me."

"I can't seem to get through that thick head of yours any other way." That earned him an infuriated glare. "That's right, thickheaded, stubborn, and too independent for your own good."

"Don't you dare try to tell me what's good for

me," she railed, all the anger and frustration finally seething up. "All my life, people have been telling me what's good for me, what's bad, what's right and wrong and honest and decent." She flung a hand wide. "But it's all been a lie. First with my parents, now Mark. You say you love me, but for all I know that's as meaningless as the rest."

"The hell it is," he yelled back, goaded at last. She finally pushed him too far. "So your brother's fucked up. That's his business. It has nothing to do with you."

"But I believed and trusted in him the same way I did with my parents."

"You forgave them. In time, you might feel the same way about your brother."

"You can't know that."

"You're right, but what are you going to do until then—put your whole life on hold, put *us* on hold? That's asinine. You've got to make up your own mind, decide for yourself what's real and what's not."

"Pardon me if the basis of my life has been trashed lately."

"Then build a new basis for yourself. If the one you were handed in life isn't perfect, then create one that you can depend on, that you can shape your life around."

"How am I supposed to do that?"

"With my help."

She had no answer for that, and even if she did, she was suddenly so drained it was hard to think logically. So much of what she had said had been pure knee-jerk reaction: he'd goaded; she'd retaliated. The venting had released her tension, but it also left her unable to figure out how to go on from here.

"Do you love me, Amy?"

"Seth," she whispered, feeling stretched beyond her tolerance.

"I want an answer."

She couldn't give him one, not one that was honest, not one that he deserved to hear.

What he heard was the silence, laden, she knew, with all she could not say. He straightened, seeming to retreat right there in front of her. When he spoke his voice was saturated with as much regret as accusation.

"You can't live your life according to your brother's standards or your sister's or your mother's. At some point, you're going to have to live true to yourself. Until then, you're playing at life."

With that he walked out, carefully avoiding the paintings that lined the floor all the way to the door.

Chapter Twenty

"Seth."

He turned at the sound of his name, not recognizing the voice until he could place it with a face: Amy's sister.

"Claire. Hi."

She rushed across the lobby of the hospital, out of breath. "I thought that was you."

"In the flesh."

"How are you?"

"Fine." A lie there. "And you?"

She took a swipe at the hair escaping the fastener at the nape of her neck. "Not too bad. I dropped Mom off next door at Dr. Jamal's office."

"Problems?"

"Oh, no," she was quick to assure him. "Just a checkup. While she's there, I needed to get with the hospital on Mom's bill."

Again he asked, "Problems?"

Again she assured him, "Nothing like that, but you know how things go with insurance companies."

The doctor in him was tempted to toss his hands into the air in disgust and jeer out his opinion on that subject. That same doctor exercised complete discretion and kept the opinion to himself. "If there's anything I can do, let me know."

"Don't tempt me," she laughed, appearing to settle in for an extended chat. She cast her weight onto one leg. "So are you coming or going?"

"Coming." His shift didn't start for another half hour, so he was early, but he had been too restless to stay at home any longer.

He hadn't been able to think of too much other than Amy all night. Consequently, what little sleep he had managed had not been restorative. This morning he had woken to a sensation of emptiness both internal and external. He had been alone in his bed, and very much alone in life.

"How about you?" he remembered to ask. "Are you finished up here?"

"Haven't even begun, which is why I took the whole day off from work. These things always take forever, but I'm determined, although Mom would say stubborn."

He wondered if it was a family trait. At the thought of Amy, his patience waned. Unable to help himself, he glanced at his watch.

"I didn't mean to keep you," Claire said.

"You didn't, but I should be on my way." As much for Claire's sake as his own. He wasn't fit company at the moment.

"Well, tell Amy I said hi." On a sly smile, she added, "Between her schedule and mine, you see her more than I do these days."

His response was an insipid curl of lip and as pleasant a parting comment as he could muster. Headed for the ER, he hoped he had contained any signs of the anger that had begun to churn again.

There was little use in his trying to center himself. He knew that as he shoved open the double doors leading into the department. In retrospect, arriving early didn't seem like such a good idea any longer. He had escaped having to face the emotional baggage at home only to have more than enough time to do so now, when he should be getting himself mentally focused.

Damned emotional bleed-through. This wasn't the first time Amy had done this to him, the first time he had allowed it—a true testament to how important she was to him. What a pisser that she didn't feel the same way. Until last night, he had believed she loved him. Now he didn't know what to think.

Taking a seat in the doctors' lounge behind the triage desk, he faced the inevitable with ill grace. The barrage of feelings came at him from all angles, picking away at his control until he seriously considered leaving. In his present state of mind, he wasn't going to be worth a damn to the patients. In his present state of mind, he wasn't good for anything other than trying to make Amy see reason.

It was out of the question, of course. There was no helping Amy with this one. He couldn't pull any magic tricks out of his medical bag and make this right. As frustrating as that was, he had to accept it just as he had to accept that he wasn't sure of exactly how things stood between them. He had walked out; she had let him go. Where in the hell did that leave them?

As definite as his personality was, he didn't do well with shades of gray. Needless to say, he had no choice in this instance. The cherished heirlooms of love and family he had suppressed for so long, life's riches he thought he'd realized in Amy, were in doubt.

Elbows resting on his spread knees, chin tucked into the crook of his steepled fingers, he found himself alone with a single emotion: sadness. Logic and reason had destroyed the anger; Amy needed time. Compassion and understanding had killed the resentment. He knew Amy's life had been pure hell lately. All that remained for him was the sadness.

"Dr. Donovan," Holly Grant interrupted, poking her head around the door she shoved open. "We need you in room two."

And medicine. He still had that. He hoped to God that his ideals about medicine would be satisfying enough to fill his life as they once had.

Claire felt as if her heart were lodged at the back of her throat. As she sped down the street toward home, she checked her watch for the umpteenth time, knowing she was late, knowing that the kids had gotten off the bus ten minutes ago and she hadn't been home. The fact that they had their keys was little comfort.

She scanned the front of the house as soon as it came into view, anxiously looking for signs that all was well. She barely had the car in park before she lugged two sacs of groceries out of the backseat and raced up the front walk. Mike was there to swing the door wide. His sweet little face was the best sight she had seen all day.

"Hi, honey. I'm sorry I'm late." She looked toward the stairs. "Where's your sister?"

"In her room."

"Bethy," she called out, catching the door with her heel to kick it shut. "Bethy, honey, I'm home."

It wasn't until she could hear the muted sound of her daughter's voice that she released a sigh of relief. This was the first time the kids had had to let themselves in, and she had yet to get comfortable with the idea. Other moms might be at ease with the latchkey notion, but she wasn't.

"Everything all right here?" she asked on her way to the kitchen.

Trailing beside her, Mike made a face. "Sure, except that Puke-face is being stupi—" He caught himself. "She's being dumb."

"Why?"

"I don't know. Girls are so weird. What's for dinner?"

"Tacos."

"Can I have a snack?"

She reached into one of the bags she placed on the counter, withdrew an apple, and tossed it his way. "Wash it first."

He made another face, this one bordering on disgust. "Can't I have cookies or something?"

"No."

Mumbling his way to the sink, he halfheartedly ran the water. "I had an apple with lunch."

"And now you're going to have one for a snack."

"It isn't fair."

His sullen complaint stopped her for a second. "Don't start, Michael. I've had a long day." Thankfully, he didn't press the issue and retreated to the living room. In no time, she could hear the sounds of Nintendo. "Do you have homework to do?" she called out.

"Just a little," he called back.

Which could mean anything, coming from an

eight-year-old. Bags emptied, she rescued her son from Mario world. "Upstairs, kiddo."

His protest was loud and pouty.

"You know the rules," she told him.

In a rare fit of temper, he slammed the controller down. "I think the rule sucks."

Claire didn't know who was more surprised by the outburst. She was definitely shocked, but Mike looked as if his eyes were going to pop out of his head. He stared at her without speaking, obviously waiting for her to explode.

She felt the anger. It erupted at once, yet was tempered by restraint. Not sure why she wasn't yelling, she gave him her most daunting stare. "Don't you ever take that tone of voice with me again."

Eyes still wide and uncertain, he nodded.

"Now go upstairs and do your homework."

He all but slunk out of the room, his shoulders slumped, his head lowered in dejection. Claire shook her head, wondering what in the world had come over him. Sassing back was not his usual style. He was too even-tempered, but even on those few occasions when he did get angry, he had never resorted to disrespect. That was more in keeping with Bethany, in age as well as temperament.

She went upstairs to check on her eldest. As had become the case more frequently lately, Beth's door was shut. She entered without knocking to find Beth lying back on her bed, hands stretched toward the ceiling, holding a book. Claire assumed this was a new mode of studying, one of great intensity since Beth didn't acknowledge her in any way.

"Hey, sweetheart." She interpreted the straining

of Beth's chin as a greeting of sorts. "What are you reading?"

After several seconds, the offhanded answer was, "Science."

It had always amazed Claire how much could be said by not saying anything at all. Body language spoke volumes, and Bethany got her message across with the negligent lift of an eyebrow and the thinning of lips.

Claire sat before patiently lowering the book, snaring Beth's hands as well as her attention. "All right, what's this about?"

Beth regarded her with a sullenness reminiscent of Mike's. "Nothing."

"Something's bothering you."

"No, there isn't."

"Then why didn't you come down to say hi when I got home?" She didn't wait for an answer. "Why are you trying to ignore me?"

Beth's response was another of her silent shrugs.

"Come on, Bethy," she coaxed, tired of having to assuage a ten-year-old's displeasure. "I can't fix what's wrong if you don't tell me what it is."

"I'm fine."

She was tempted to give up, and if she hadn't remembered Amy's take on the situation, she would have left her daughter to sulk. But what Amy had said days ago could not be ignored, and neither could Beth's resentment.

"Are you mad at me for coming home late?"

Beth said, "No," but her expression was more eloquent, asking in return, *What do you think?*

"It couldn't be helped, sweetheart. I had to take Grandma to the doctor and help her out with a few things at the hospital."

All the signs of concern tugged at Beth's brow. "Is Grandma sick again?"

Smoothing a hand over Beth's head, she said, "No, she's fine. The doctor needed to check her out."

Obviously relieved, Beth assumed her frosty manner again, her gaze lowering to her hands resting on her chest. Claire knew when she was being shut out. Again, the urge to walk off in irritation, to tell Beth she wasn't going to play this little game of punishment, hit hard. The voice of reason, underscored with self-doubt, prevailed, and a ton of what-ifs hit home. What if she had somehow screwed up Beth's life? What if Beth was really troubled?

"I know you're mad at me."

Beth's glance flicked to her, darted off briefly, returned and stayed, full of suspicion.

"Things haven't been easy lately, Bethy. I hope you can understand that."

"Because of Grandma?"

"In part."

"You're never home any more."

The accusation stung, more so for the resulting guilt Claire would have given anything not to feel. And she resented not only the sensation, but her own daughter for inspiring it.

"I'm home as much as I can be."

"Which is never."

"That's not true."

"Yes, it is." Beth reared up, pushing back in the same move so that her back was against the headboard. "Mike was scared when you weren't home today."

Guilt was joined by remorse. "I told you, it couldn't be helped. I was running late and then had to stop at the store."

"Why couldn't you go to the store later? Or yesterday? Why didn't you go then?"

The answer was because she had been with John after work yesterday when she should have been taking care of much-needed chores. On a surge of defensiveness, she came to her feet. "I do the best that I can. You should try to be more understanding and help out around here instead of complaining and making life more difficult than it already is."

"You don't love us any more," Beth cried.

She dug deep for composure, but between the guilt and the growing anger, she could not scrape up even an ounce of self-restraint. "You're right," she yelled, angry that she had been goaded to this point. "I don't love you. Or your brother. That's why I make sure you get to school on time and have enough food to eat and check to see if you're feeling all right. That's why I go to all the parent-teacher meetings and have a job that allows me to work my schedule around yours. That's why I see to it that you go to church every Sunday and have some kind of an allowance. That's why I still get up in the middle of the night and check on you to make sure you're breathing . . . because I don't love you."

Tears slipped over Beth's cheeks; her bottom lip trembled. Claire was shaken and mortified by her outburst, but she was too angry to relent to softer emotions. She turned to find Mike standing in the doorway, plainly having heard it all.

"Go to your room," she told him on her way to her own bedroom. She slammed the door for all she was worth, fuming at how badly she had screwed up. There was little doubt that she had. She shouldn't have gotten angry, and having failed at that, she shouldn't have resorted to such lethal sarcasm. But she hadn't been able to help herself. Beth had called her on her own negligence, and it was as if something inside of her had snapped.

Flopping onto the bed, she hunched over in a position of defeat, one elbow on her knee, her forehead supported in her palm. As never before, she missed Dan.

Her tears brought with them pain and heartache. She had loved him so much, but he wasn't here for her. Or the kids. They needed him as much as she did, perhaps even more. They were so young— resilient, yes, but still vulnerable—and her loss of temper today hadn't helped.

The old insecurities threatened making her feel foolish and ignorant. She thought she had gotten past all of that. Apparently not; apparently she was still a victim to herself.

The ringing of the phone was intrusive. Four rings passed before she made herself answer. Amy's voice sounded worried. "You finally made it home."

Claire tried not to be insulted. "Of course I'm here. How did you know I was late?"

"I called earlier to see how things went with Mom, and Mike said they had to let themselves in."

Hearing it stated so bluntly intensified the guilt. "I was running late," she said, wondering why she was explaining. Was there some unwritten law that said she had to justify her every move?

"You sound terrible. Are you crying?"

"Yes."

"Why?"

She actually started to tell Amy, then stopped. Angry with herself now, she snapped, "I don't want to talk about it. Leave me alone."

"Well, excuse me for worrying," came Amy's indignant response.

"I didn't ask you to. I'm not a baby whose every move has to be watched. Stop treating me like an incompetent twit."

"I'm not."

"What do you want?"

"I called to check on the kids."

As defensive as she had become, Claire took that in its worst possible light, that she wasn't mother enough to her children. In excruciatingly exact tones, she said, "Mike and Bethany do not need you or anyone else to check up on them. I take good care of my children." Her control broke, and she lashed out. "I'm a great mother. You haven't got any right to judge me."

"I'm not judging you."

"Yes, you are. You did it the other night, too, when you told me about Bethy's test. It was there in your voice, like you know all there is to know about parenting. Well, you're not a mother. You don't have kids of your own, so where do you get off thinking you can offer advice?"

"Good-bye," Amy choked out. "I'm not talking to you when you're like this."

"Like what?" She was truly wound tight now, unable to stop the flow of words, the release of bitterness. "Like what, Amy? What exactly am I?"

"You're cracked. I don't know why I bother."

"Because you're Saint Amy, always the good one, the cute one, the talented one. I'm sick of it, and I'm sick of you."

The phone went dead in her hand seconds before Claire realized Amy had hung up. In retaliation, she slammed the receiver down with as much fury as she had slammed her door. Little was gained. Fury was still blazing away so fiercely, she started to cry again.

Shaking, she paced her room, muttering out all the things she hadn't told Amy: hostility and anger and, yes, guilt, coloring her convictions that Amy had been way out of line.

The ordinary finally came to her rescue, channeling her emotions and taming them to a tolerable level. Good mother that she was, she had children to feed. She browned ground beef as if national security depended on it, diced tomatoes and onions with all the intensity of a brain surgeon operating on gray cells. And then, without thinking, reached for the phone on the kitchen wall and dialed John's private number at work.

"Hi." She forced a determined cheerfulness into her voice. "It's me."

"What's up?"

"Not much. I was thinking of you; that's all." They chatted easily for a few minutes, giving her just enough time to consider the wisdom of her actions. Annoyed with her doubts, she blurted out, "Would you like to come over for dinner tonight?" He hesitated. She ignored the pause and rushed on. "It'll just be us, here at the house."

"You mean with the kids?"

"Sure, why not?"

"I don't know, Claire. That's not a very good idea."

"Who's going to know?"

"Claire." Her name emerged on a drawn-out sigh. "We've had this discussion before. It wouldn't be wise."

It was on the tip of her tongue to argue back that her children weren't going to jeopardize either of their jobs. Reality argued that she and John shared, by mutual consent, a very defined relationship that excluded the more mundane aspects of life.

And that was what she wanted from him, she realized—why she had called. Because she was standing there in her kitchen surrounded by nothing but the smell of chili, because she was suddenly, frighteningly alone, alienated from everyone who had once formed the core of her life. Her children resented her. Mark wanted nothing to do with her. Amy was probably so angry they would never speak again. Even Mom had withdrawn.

She had called because she wanted the everyday routine with John: the support, the sharing not only of bodies but of hearts and trust, sorrows and good times. Liking him as she did, it was little wonder she wanted more. He was a man worth liking. Unfortunately, she sensed that he was also a man who was giving her as much as he intended to.

Chapter Twenty-One

It wasn't often that Amy felt uncomfortable at the thought of being with Peggy, but as she sat in the local deli, waiting for her sister-in-law to show up, she had to consciously squelch the unease twisting in her stomach.

Peggy had called early that morning asking if they could meet for lunch. Amy's reflexive response had been yes, and only after she had hung up and was on her way to work had she begun to have second and third thoughts. Peggy wasn't the formal, let's-have-lunch kind of person. She was more direct and spontaneous, preferring to drop by the house or the office in order to discuss something she thought was important.

Surprise birthday parties and Christmas gifts were as serious as anything they normally ever talked about. But Amy sensed that, as difficult as Mark had been lately, Peggy wasn't going to want to have a little chat about Mom's secret wish list.

Fingering the straw stuck in her glass of iced tea, she considered how best to go on. She didn't lie worth a damn. How was she supposed to pretend that she didn't know that Mark was, if not having an outright affair, seriously tempted? Time for answers ran out as Peggy quickly approached.

"Sorry I'm late, Amy."

"No, I was early."

"Did you have any problem getting away?" Peggy slid into the other side of the booth. "I know I called at the last minute."

Amy fixed what she hoped passed for a relaxed smile on her face. "No, lunch hour is my own. I can pretty much take it when and if I want." She tried for humor. "Besides, you saved me from a really boring layout."

Under normal circumstances, Amy knew Peggy would have had a snappy comeback. Her sister-in-law merely gave an unconvincing smile, the first proof that their meeting was most definitely not the norm. Amy's discomfort level increased, making her want to squirm in her seat.

"What's wrong, Peg?" She blurted the words out, unable to bear the tension. As stretched as her nerves were becoming, eating was out of the question. There was no reason to sit there as if all was right in their worlds and prolong the agony.

For Amy, that misery was compounded by Claire. Yesterday's argument still had the power to haul her toward tears as effortlessly as it could shove her up against a wall of anger. Claire's angry attack had been unexpected and unwarranted, the more so given how close they had become lately. Between the roiling indignation and the hurt Amy was feeling, she was short on patience.

Peggy's face mirrored Amy's feelings. "You know, that's one of the reasons I wanted to talk to you. You're so damned honest and bottom-line about things."

Amy would have traded both those qualities for an ounce of the strength she felt she needed. "You rarely call and want to do the lunch thing. I figured something was bothering you." She toyed with the straw in her glass again. "I assume it has to do with Mark."

"Of course it does," came Peggy's irritated reply. At Amy's quick glance, Peggy visibly collected herself. "I'm sorry. He's got me so angry and tense . . . I have no right to take it out on you."

"Don't apologize. I understand fully."

"Do you?" The plea in Peggy's voice was overshadowed by the sheer vulnerability in her eyes. "Do you know what's going on with him? I feel like I don't know him any longer."

"Neither do I."

"But you're his sister."

"So?" She thought of Claire and was hurt all over again. "As I've learned once again, being a sister doesn't count for much."

"You've known him since you were kids. I was hoping you could give me some insight into what's wrong with him, and I don't mean this thing with your mother. That's just an excuse for him, the catalyst that set him off. He hasn't been himself for months."

This was the very instant Amy had been dreading. No matter which way she turned, she was caught. She didn't feel right about interfering and possibly causing more problems. On the other hand, she hated lying. Peggy didn't deserve that.

Glad to be able to tell a portion of the truth, she said, "I didn't notice anything different about him before all this happened with Mom."

"Nothing?"

She shook her head. "Not really. He's always been demanding at work. I've always ignored him."

"I wish I could do the same," Peggy sighed. "But I can't. I'm his wife." Lacing her fingers together, she ran the very tip of her tongue over her upper lip. "I'm scared, Amy."

The confession shocked Amy past her anxieties. "Why?"

"I don't know what to do." In desperation, she reached for Amy's hand. In utter hopelessness, she told it all.

Or so Amy assumed, and wished with a touch of Peg's desperation to have been any place other than right there. She didn't want to hear about the arguments between Mark and Peggy, or that they hadn't talked to each other in weeks, or that— Jesus, God—they hadn't had sex in longer than that. This was her brother about whom she was forced to listen. They had once been close, but their private lives had always been exactly that, private.

She felt like an intruder, and when Peggy's eyes filled with tears and she whispered, "I've begun to think he might be having an affair," *hypocrite* was the nicest thing Amy could call herself.

Shutting her eyes, she discounted Mark entirely and focused instead on Peggy. "Oh, Peg, I'm so sorry."

"It isn't your fault. I'm the one who's at fault."

"No, you aren't. You can't blame yourself."

"Why not?"

"Because Mark's responsible. He's alienated all of us, not just you."

"That's recently, and only part of the whole. This has been coming for months."

"Have you tried to talk to him about it, about how you feel?"

On a jeering laugh, Peggy said, "When we were still talking, he didn't want to listen. Now . . . We can't go on like this. The kids know something's wrong, but I don't know how to fix it. Mark thinks the car is the only problem, but that's least of it."

"What about counseling?"

"I don't know. At one time, I would have said sure, but I don't know how he thinks any longer."

"I'm as lost as you. I'm sorry. I know you wanted my help, but I don't know what to tell you."

"Tell me this is a phase, or a mid-life crisis— that it's all going to blow over and he's going to come to his senses."

"It's a phase, a mid-life—" But she couldn't finish. She didn't believe the excuses any more than Peggy did, probably even less. Peggy had doubts and suspicions. Amy carried with her the damning images of her brother and Rene Bellieux.

Those images combined with Peggy's depression made a farce out of their attempt at lunch. By the time the waitress showed up to take their orders, Amy was feeling nauseated. Peggy looked no better. They parted company in the parking lot, Amy with a gut full of anger and Peggy with tears that Amy found pitiful. If she hadn't had a deadline, she wouldn't have returned to the office at all.

She slumped into her chair at her desk, unable to work, and realized that Peggy had been more right than she knew on one very crucial point: this could not go on, not for any of them. Peggy had been referring to her own situation, but Amy admitted it was just as true for herself. She hadn't talked to Seth in two days, and it was her own fault. She had demanded time, and he was giving it to her.

He had been right to accuse her of putting her life on hold. But she didn't see how it was possible to forge a new personal foundation in a matter of days, or even weeks. To rely on Seth for help, as he wanted, required a trust of which she felt incapable. And that wasn't his fault. He hadn't done one damn thing to betray her. The deficiency was within her.

She couldn't blame him for walking out. He had been more than patient, tolerating a lunacy no sane man should have to. He had given and given, accepting her and all the reasons for her reluctance to commit fully. In return, she had given him sex and love restricted by a whole set of conditions.

That was so unlike her, and she was appalled. She may not love often or freely, but when she did, it was totally and absolutely.

"Can we talk?" Mark interrupted from the doorway, hands shoved into his pockets.

Her insides sank right along with her strength. Her day had gone completely colorless. "Can it wait?" She had had enough soul-searching for one afternoon.

"No."

She was too tired to stand her ground. "Then we might as well get this over with." He was careful to shut the door, she noted. "Smart move. We wouldn't want the rest of the staff to hear this particular discussion."

"Then you know what I want to talk to you about."

"I think I can figure that one out." The sarcasm rolled up out of the mélange of emotions making hash of her already tattered nerves. Mark didn't take to it kindly.

"Lay off, Amy. You don't know the half of it."

"I know more than you think." Giving him a nasty smile, she sneered, "I had lunch with Peggy."

His face paled. "What did she want?"

"Not that I owe you any answers, but she wanted to know if you're having an affair."

His reaction was more than she could have hoped for. She was infinitely glad to see his jaw slacken and lines of desperation crease his face, his body tense with an unmistakable air of dread. "What did you say?"

"Why should I tell you?" She hadn't consciously been seeking revenge, but it was hers now and she savored it, knowing full well she was sinking to levels she normally disdained in others.

Even though Mark wasn't wholly to blame for the upheaval in her life, he had contributed his share, and in that, he was an easy target. If taking advantage of that made her less of a person, so be it. At the moment, she didn't care. The Amy she had been two months ago would have surrendered to her conscience, but that woman was dead. She didn't know who she was now, other than someone who needed to strike back.

"Why should I tell you anything, Mark?"

"I have a right to know."

"Right?" She actually laughed. "You gave up your rights to everything the minute you kissed—"

"Shut up," he demanded.

"That doesn't work any more. We're not kids; I'm not the low man on the totem pole, little kid sister. If we want to get picky about it, I'm not really your sister at all. It's half-sister, a fact you've gone out of your way to shove in my face at every turn."

"I'm not having an affair with Rene."

"Well, whoopey-doo. Am I supposed to be impressed?"

"You could be a little more understanding."

His gall was setting new records. She came out of her chair on a burst of energy. "You self-righteous bastard. You don't deserve understanding."

"I'm trying to explain. Things with me have been messed up for months."

"Get a life."

"This was a one-time thing with Rene."

"Like I care? It's Peggy you should be worrying about."

"I am."

"Oh, you really looked worried with Rene's lipstick all over your mouth." Remembering the image fueled her anger. "You turned me into a liar today. I could have told Peggy the truth, but I kept my mouth shut." He closed his eyes and exhaled in blatant relief. "Not for you. I didn't want to hurt Peggy any more than you already have."

"I'm not having an affair," he vowed, grinding each word into chopped-up pieces.

"Why bother explaining it to me?" Her voice was suddenly loud enough to carry past the closed door.

His tone matched hers. "I didn't want you getting the wrong impression."

"Since when do you care about me—or anyone else, for that matter? You're just trying to save your own ass. You don't care what I think; you just want to make sure I don't tell anyone else about—"

The door opened on the tail end of her words, breaking the argument, and jerking Mark around to face Claire.

"I could hear the two of you halfway down the hall."

Mark looked ready to implode. "Shit."

"What's going on?" Claire asked, closing the door once more.

Amy eyed her brother before sneering, "Why don't you tell her, Mark?"

He returned her glare. "Don't."

"Don't what?" Claire wanted to know. "Come on, you two, Amy, what's happened?"

"We're having another of our family discussions," Amy scoffed, not anywhere near ready to forgive her sister.

"It doesn't involve you, Claire," Mark insisted.

From the look of her, Claire took the insult square in her insecurities. "You're discussing family business and it doesn't concern me?" She turned to Amy. "Why am I being excluded?"

Amy fought for composure and lost. "Nice going, Mark."

"What a fuckin' mess," he muttered. Pivoting, he made for the door, but Claire stood with her back to the panel, blocking his exit.

"Oh, no. You can't leave without—"

"Get out of the way, Claire."

Amy gave in to the headache pounding in her temples and took her seat. From behind the hand she pressed to her forehead, she could see Claire priming herself for a battle of wills.

"I want to know what's going on. I have a right to know."

Without thinking, Amy blurted out, "She has rights, Mark."

He rounded on her with a visible return of fury. "Now who's being self-righteous?"

"And who's being holier than thou?"

"You're both acting like a couple of babies," Claire accused.

That they had been reduced to name-calling was

pitiful enough to make Amy shut her eyes and bow
her head. She heard Mark say, "I give up," and
Claire charge right back: "That's typical. Whenever
you don't get your way, you just give up."

"You don't know what the hell you're talking
about."

"Yes, I do. You were the same when we were
kids. If we didn't play by your rules, you'd walk
off."

Score one for Claire, Amy thought.

"And you still do it now."

"How? When?"

"All the time. You take charge of every situation,
every discussion so that they go exactly as you want
them to. If they don't, you walk away or refuse to
have any more input."

"I will not discuss this."

"See what I mean?"

Score two.

"You're pulling at straws, Claire."

"No, I'm not. You have to have life exactly as
you want or we all pay the price."

"Like hell."

"You've been doing it for months. You can't
stand what Mom did, so you're punishing all of
us."

Score three. Amy opened her eyes, knowing
Claire had hit home with that one.

Mark drew himself up. "I'm not going to listen
to any more of this crap."

"See?" Claire raged, flicking a glance to Amy
for confirmation. "That's exactly what I'm talking
about. You ignore what you don't like." Shoving
off the door, she insisted, "How can you ignore
your own mother? Do you realize how much you've
hurt her?

"She hurt us all. She's a lying, scheming—"

Amy surged to her feet, refusing to let him finish. "Stop it!"

"You've ruined everything, Mark," Claire yelled. "Mom's a mess, you've upset Peggy; we're at each other's throats."

"You can't blame this on me."

"You've ruined the family."

Amy gripped her hair and shouted, "We don't have a family."

She stared through her tears, seeing Claire's awe and Mark's resentment, seeing a truth she had been running from for months. "We don't have a family," she repeated in a whisper, and felt an intrinsic part of her die. What they had were memories but no foundation, relationships but no real connection.

The intercom on her desk buzzed. Cicily's hushed voice resounded through the silence. "Amy, you better pick up on line one. It's Commonwealth Hospital. Your mom's had another stroke."

Chapter Twenty-Two

Rushing into the emergency room of the hospital, Amy battled the nightmare sense of déjà vu. The knowing should have eased her fears in some aspects, but the fact that her mother was here again precluded relief or comfort.

She reached the nurses' desk, Claire right beside her. They had driven over separately; she didn't know where Mark was. Again, the sensation of having lived this moment once before swamped her as she gave her name.

"Our mother, Ellen Chandler, has been brought in," she told the nurse.

The woman checked through her forms and files, her face impassive. Logically, that was for the best, how hospital personnel were supposed to act, but for Amy it was cold and inadequate. "Dr. Eldridge is with her now." With a polite tilt of her head, the nurse indicated the waiting room. "Why don't you have a seat. Someone will be with you as soon as possible."

To have expected anything more would have

been absurd. That didn't stop her, however, from chafing at the delay.

"Do you think Seth is here?" Claire asked, obviously feeling the same frustrations and fears. "Do you think he could find out something for us?"

Amy hesitated briefly, not wanting to drag Seth into more of the "same-old same-old." But desperation overrode her qualms.

The nurse's response was that Dr. Donovan was with another patient, but that she would pass along the message as soon as he was finished. Amy had no alternative but to wait.

Claire sat two chairs away, more composed than Amy would have thought possible. Her sister neither paced nor cried, but instead displayed more of the same unusual grit with which she'd faced Mark at the office.

Thinking of her brother, she sent repeated glances to the double glass doors, expecting to see him at any moment. At the same time, she questioned why she should believe he would be there. His presence belonged to another time, another man. He was different now; they all were. Months ago, they had clung to each other, taking and giving what strength they could. Now, they were as distant as strangers.

Claire jumping to her feet broke Amy's train of thought. She followed Claire's line of vision to see Seth approaching. Dressed in green surgical scrubs, he was a grounding sight, a stabilizing force in her sinking world. Instinctively she started to rise, but checked herself, unable to trust her instincts any longer. She watched him, though, never once looking away as he neared and then squatted down directly in front of her.

"I was told at the desk about your mother." With transparent restraint, he laid a hand on her knee.

She rested her fist on top of his hand. "They wouldn't tell us anything."

Claire asked, "Can you find out, Seth?"

That he had heard her was obvious, yet his gaze remained fixed on Amy. Turning his palm up to gently squeeze her clenched fingers, he promised, "I'll see what I can do."

He didn't have the time. They were joined by a doctor who introduced himself as Eldridge. Introductions were made with somber nods.

"She's had a bad stroke," he began.

"How bad?" Claire whispered. "Worse than the last?"

"I'm afraid so."

"Oh, my God."

"She's still alive, but she doesn't seem able to move the right side of her body. She's alert, breathing well. She's trying to speak, but can't."

Amy listened, trying not to anticipate the worst. "Can we see her?"

"For a few minutes. We're getting ready to take her upstairs for a CAT scan. I want to warn you, though: when you see her, please don't be frightened. She's hooked up to a host of monitors. She's on oxygen and we've inserted a catheter because she can't control her bladder. There's an IV in her left arm. Her right arm and leg are flaccid."

Definitely worse than before, Amy thought and tried to prepare herself, but nothing could have readied her for reality as she maneuvered around the attending nurse. She neared her mother's side and was indeed frightened, not by the array of medical paraphernalia running in and out of her mother,

but by the physical shock of seeing her mother
reduced to such a basic human level.

Drool ran from the corner of her mouth. Lips
that should have been pink were eggplant purple;
half of the body that had always been so vibrant
lay paralyzed. Face sunken and flushed, only the
eyes remained the same, saying everything that her
brain refused to allow her mouth to utter.

Amy saw the frustration and alarm and carefully
took her mother's left hand in her own. "Mom."

Claire laid her hand on Ellen's arm. "We're here,
Mom."

Still speaking silently, Ellen's eyes darted about
the curtained-off cubicle, searching, asking, and
finally accepting. She closed her eyes.

"You'll be fine, Mom." What she really wanted
to say, to do, was scream in rage at Mark for putting
that defeated look in their mother's eyes, for
deserting them all, for not being there when the
orderlies wheeled Ellen away for tests.

Seth was there, though. Through her tears, Amy
found him waiting near the nurses' desk. He neither advanced nor retreated, doing, she admitted,
precisely what she had asked: he was leaving her
alone.

"Try not to worry," he told them in his best
compassionately impersonal doctor's voice.

"Will she be all right?"

"I don't know. Regardless, she'll go into ICU to
be monitored for possible heart attack."

Claire burst into tears. Without thinking, forgetting the animosity she had been feeling toward
Claire, Amy slipped an arm around her sister's
shoulders.

"Leave me alone," Claire demanded, her voice
bitter and choked.

Caught off guard as much by the rage in Claire's voice as by the order itself, Amy watched her walk off. Shock instantly gave way to a renewal of ire.

As never before, the changes that had occurred in all of them, the distance that had been growing between them, was driven home. Each was a separate entity. Mark was with himself, wherever that might be. Claire chose to huddle by herself in the waiting room. Amy was left standing there, alone. She found it apropos that Seth was called off for another emergency, completing once and for all her sense of isolation.

Amy discovered that intensive-care units were worlds unto themselves: self-contained, heavily staffed, fully provisioned, and equipped with possibly the world's most uncomfortable chairs in the waiting area. After seven hours, she gave up trying to get comfortable and resorted to standing, then idly walking about, and finally sitting cross-legged on the floor with her back resting against the wall. No one else in the long, narrow room seemed to notice, but then there were only a few others present and they were too immersed in their own private traumas to give her a second thought.

Claire was not among the few. She had gone home to Bethany and Mike hours ago, and Amy was glad for that, glad she didn't have to constantly wonder or worry about what Claire might or might not do. She had not reacted well to the news that Mom had had to have surgery.

Dr. Jamal had arrived to decipher all the information from the tests, and reported that Ellen's stroke had been caused by a burst artery; surgery to the left frontal lobe was necessary to "evacuate the clot" and "repair the damage."

Amy's initial response had been like taking a fist to the chest, but she had maintained her composure, taking heart from Dr. Jamal's open optimism. Claire, however, had withered into an inconsolable, unapproachable heap, rousing herself only when they had been allowed into ICU after surgery to see their mother at short, regular intervals.

Again, Claire had not been able to handle the situation. She had taken one look at their unconscious mother, head swathed in layers of gauze, tubes and wires running in and out of her body, and had left.

And once again, Amy had found herself alone, truly alone for the first time in her life. She had placed the necessary calls to aunts and uncles, and to Peggy. But now at a little after midnight, sitting on the floor with her back to the wall, she was still alone.

It was going on two in the morning when she woke up, realizing a little after the fact that she had dropped off right there on the floor. Her second coherent thought was for her mother. The third, admitted with a sense of defeat, was that it was time for her to go home. She had remained because to do otherwise had felt impossible, but staying would accomplish nothing.

She left after making sure the ICU staff had her number. The nurses's reassurances that Mom would be fine were her only company for the drive through the night.

Mark hesitated before stepping out of the elevator on the second floor of the hospital. All around him was silence—not the pristine kind found deep in the forest, but the eerie kind that felt unnatural. Why he noticed it he didn't know, not any more than he knew why he had come here at three in the morning.

He couldn't pinpoint what his motivation was. All the old feelings that would have prompted him no longer seemed to fit. He had outgrown them or they had altered themselves in the last few months, morphing until they were not recognizable as emotions at all.

Guilt was there as he made his way to ICU. So were anger and resentment, confusion and dread. Perhaps hope, but not intensely enough for him to distinguish it from a sense of duty. He wished like hell that he could blame his being there on obligation, but something inside him wouldn't let him accept that. The situation was too complex and underscored with the unavoidable fact that the person lying in ICU was his mother.

There was no escaping that, although God knows he had tried, all to no end. He was right back where he had been nearly three months ago, giving the nurse his name, listening to her directions, then finally standing at the foot of his mother's hospital bed.

He tried to remain unaffected. It wasn't possible given the sheer volume of equipment surrounding her: monitors, machines, wires and tubes, and the odor of antiseptic, medications, and sick bodies. And too, there was the heavy bandaging around her skull. Swallowing with difficulty, he reasoned it would have been impossible for any person to see all that and not be shaken.

Feeling justified in his reaction, he breathed deeply, hands firmly planted in his pockets, and experienced much the same social discomfort one does when attending a wake. With her lying unconscious and unmoving, the similarities in this instance were too close.

"Shit," he muttered. He should have never come. He should have gone home, or found another hotel lounge when the one he'd been in had closed. Why in the hell was he putting himself through this? Her being his mother should no longer have been reason enough, but he was very much afraid that it was.

Resentment boiled up, spiking his anger. He wanted to hate her—he thought he did. Then what explanation was there for the helpless sense of concern that suddenly had him in a stranglehold? He didn't want to care, or worry, or goddamn it, love her, but he did.

Dear God, he did love her. And he *did* hate her. He couldn't separate the two and that was a hideous way to feel. Restricted by the edicts of each, he was firmly mired in the inability to act. All he could do was react.

Tears pooled up in his eyes, weak, useless, pitiful. They seemed to epitomize what he had been reduced to: a man no longer in charge of his own life. And in that, he didn't know who he was any longer. The sense that he was someone's son, which had once been so strong, had been bastardized. *Husband,* in its most encompassing terms of lover, companion, and best friend, had been stretched past all endurance—maybe even beyond repair. *Brother* and *conscientious parent* no longer seemed to apply, and *savvy businessman who knew better than to cross professional lines* was highly doubtful.

His identity was gone. He had lost it somehow, or given it away; or worse, it had been stolen. Staring at his mother, he could easily blame the latter on her and thus absolve himself of all responsibility. But believing that would be admitting he had been too weak and ineffectual to retain what was his, and he couldn't admit that. Even if it meant he had been wholly in the wrong for condemning his mother all these weeks, he couldn't admit that he had been so horribly fragile as to let someone else steal his sense of self. Whoever the hell *that* was. God help him; he didn't know.

It was all her fault. Again and again, Claire blamed herself for her mother's stroke. If she had been a better daughter and a better mother, none of this would have happened. Her mother would be safely asleep in her own bed.

What was that saying—what goes around comes around? Huddled into the corner of the sofa, she rued that the saying was true. She had been selfish, putting her own wants and needs above everyone else's—her children's especially—and in return, God was punishing her by giving Mom another stroke.

She wallowed in the misery of that until her tears finally dwindled away. Then she made a conscious effort to be more rational. The effort may have been useless. She hadn't been to bed; she was too tired and stressed to think very clearly. The best she was capable of was little truths, one at a time.

She hurt, physically and mentally. Her shoulders ached as much as her head.

She wished she could sleep. That way she wouldn't have to worry about Mom.

She loved her children with all her heart and soul. The tears came again when she thought of how rotten she had allowed things to become for them.

She loved her mother. And Amy, too. They had had their moments lately, but the love was still there.

She hated Mark. She wasn't going to dwell on him.

She missed Dan. Dear God, she would for the rest of her life.

She missed her father. Deep inside her, a sad yearning bloomed. It had been a long time since she had thought of him. In the turmoil of past months, he had slipped from her memory.

"Oh, Daddy, I'm sorry. I wish you were here." She would have sucked up his hugs and steady presence like a dried-up old sponge. "Mom's in trouble, but I guess you know that." She imagined that was the least of what he knew, and mentally she squirmed. She knew exactly what he would think of her affair. In her mind's eye, she pictured that disapproving frown of his, the one that had creased the bridge of his nose, and she smiled.

Odd that in the midst of such a terrible night she could find a touch of soul-deep pleasure. Compared to the transient quality of any recent pleasures, it was rich and enduring. More important, it was real.

Not much in her life was lately. She had always struggled with a sense of fraudulence, but at least she had been honest in her struggle. For that, she hadn't been a fake, but rather an uncertain woman tying to do her best. Strange that in having given herself permission to be strong, to do as she pleased, she had truly become the false woman.

For someone too tired to think straight, she congratulated herself for having reached that conclusion, although she didn't know what to make of it. Truths at four in the morning were enigmatic enough. Mom's being in the hospital clouded the issue all the more.

She fell asleep before she could get up and call the hospital again.

Chapter Twenty-Three

Amy didn't know whether to be surprised or not when she looked up from her mother's side and saw Claire. Neither did she know what to say. As wiped out as she was this morning, she couldn't play the benevolent sister, could not muster the energy needed to ignore her abused feelings. Forgiveness was buried somewhere beneath the memory of Claire's unwarranted hostilities of late, and a headache brought on by stress.

"How is she?" Claire asked, taking up a stance on the other side of the bed.

Amy was careful to keep her voice very neutral. "She's been awake on and off."

Claire's gaze roamed her mother's face, peaceful in sleep. "Has Dr. Jamal checked on her?"

On a waspish impulse, Amy was tempted to come back with "What am I, your personal information center? You couldn't think to ask at the desk?" Calmly she said, "Earlier." There her tolerance ran out and she made her way back to the waiting area. She took a seat at the window, turned sideways to prop her elbow on the chair back, and stared down at the parking lot. When Claire joined her minutes later, she didn't react at all.

"Have you been here all night?"

She didn't so much as glance Claire's way. "I went home around two this morning."

"Have you had breakfast?"

The sound of concern was intolerable. She swiveled her head around to jab a hard look at her sister. "Oh, please, Claire. If you can drag yourself out of your self-indulgence long enough to notice anyone other than yourself, you'd see that I'm mad at you."

Claire blinked repeatedly. Her brows arched. "I'm sorry."

Tiredly, she scoffed, "Give it a rest." And for a while, she thought Claire would.

"You're absolutely right," Claire finally whispered, sounding as if the words had to be dragged from her. "I have been selfish lately. I haven't been fair to you." She fingered the denim covering one thigh. "To anyone."

"Saying 'I'm sorry' doesn't make the hurt go away, Claire."

"I know."

"And the way you've treated me hurts. I expected it from Mark, but not you. Never you."

"I'm sorry."

"I don't want to hear it."

"Are you going to be able to forgive me?"

It was too soon for Amy to answer honestly. "Ask me some other time. Right now, the best we can do is keep our personal feelings to ourselves for Mom's sake."

"What do you mean?"

"What I mean," she returned, exhaustion adding a hint of sarcasm to her tone, "is that we have to make some decisions about Mom. She's going to need special care, in a rehab center. You and I have to be, at the very least, civil to each other. We can't afford to give in to my hurt and your regret."

Blinking rapidly again, Claire nodded. "You're right. Of course." After a moment's pause, she asked, "What about Mark?"

Amy gave her a look that said, "What about him?"

"Have you seen him?"

"No, but the night nurse said that he'd been in to see Mom right after I left." Which still amazed her. When he hadn't shown up in the ER, or later when Mom had been in surgery, she had accepted the fact that he wasn't going to be there at all. He had made his feelings perfectly clear. And she had damned him. "Between you and me, I'm surprised he even bothered."

"After the way he's treated Mom, it does seem hypocritical of him."

Amy let the comment stand. She could neither dispute it nor add anything to it. And from all outward appearances, Claire felt the same and said nothing more.

They each retreated to a silence that was all-encompassing, preferring to take turns at their mother's side rather than be in each other's company for any length of time. The arrangement was awkward, but Amy tolerated it as best she could.

Aunts and uncles began to arrive just before noon; Barbara Chan and Cicily came by on their lunch hour; friends filtered in and out in a constant stream—so it took Amy a long count of five to realize that Mark had joined them. She instantly condemned his timing, then thought better of it.

Perhaps it was best that the three of them not be alone together. They would more than likely go at one another again, and here was not the place and now was not the time.

If there truly was a "right time" for such a thing. She didn't think so, but Mark apparently was of a different mind. Curious, she watched him approach Claire before making his way to her. "Can we talk?"

Had he asked her hours ago, she would have been in his face. The support she had received from friends and relatives, however, had shaved the fine edge from her temper. She relented, although warily.

They found a quiet spot at the end of the long hall on the far end of the second floor. The only seats were a wide window ledge. Amy sat. Claire, it seemed, preferred to stand, her arms crossed defensively over her chest, facing Mark. He leaned back against the wall.

"All right," Claire started right in. "You wanted to talk. Talk."

Amy eyed him carefully. He looked as tired as she felt, a bit resigned, but other than that, she couldn't define his mood.

"I spoke with Dr. Jamal an hour ago." He waited with patent expectation for them to reply. What he thought they had to say was a mystery to Amy. She silently stared right back; Claire followed suit, the silence lengthening until he got the message. "We discussed Mom's recovery."

As if she couldn't help herself, Claire asked, "Why do you care?"

After a moment's pause, he slowly admitted, "I deserved that."

"Yes, you did," Amy quietly agreed. "But we're

not going to get into an argument, Mark. For Mom's sake, Claire and I have already tabled our differences, at least for now. We expect the same from you."

"No argument there," he said.

"Well, that's a first," Claire sniped, then held up a single hand. "Sorry. I shouldn't have said that." She lowered the hand to her lips and rubbed her thumb over her cheek.

"Thank you for that much," Mark said to her.

Over her fingers, Claire's eyes accepted the gratitude, but offered nothing in return.

"I realize I've been a . . . been a, uh, a—"

"An asshole," Amy supplied for him.

Scrubbing his palms together, he was temporarily at a loss. "That's one way of putting it."

"I can try another if you like."

"No. No, it isn't necessary."

Amy reserved opinion on that.

Mark stumbled on in uncharacteristic hesitancy. "I was here early this morning. I, uh, I was in to see her."

"Are you waiting for a medal?" Amy wanted to know. "I'm not criticizing." Although she knew she was. "But why are you telling us this?"

"Because it's obvious we have to think about what happens next."

Claire spoke up. "We already have. We know Mom has to go into rehab."

"That's what Dr. Jamal told me," Mark said. "So I thought we better discuss it, decide on a facility, make arrangements."

Amy had to give him credit, although she questioned where his latent concern came from. Part of her resented his involvement, but that was a purely selfish reaction on her part. "You're right; there's a lot we have to decide on."

"But not today," Claire insisted. "I want to talk to Dr. Jamal first and see what she thinks would be best for Mom."

"All right," Mark agreed. Once again he scrubbed his palms together, then shoved his hands into his pockets. "Will you call me and let me know what she has to say?"

Not "Call me," or "I'll do it," Amy was quick to note. There was no order involved, no taking charge as he had once done. In this matter he was willing to let Claire, of all people, take charge.

"I'll call you and Amy. This is a group decision."

That they all realized this was encouraging. They were willing to set aside their differences and agree to agree.

"Is that it?" Amy asked, coming to her feet. She hoped so. She wasn't anxious to test the limits of their fragile detente, and she wanted to get back to Mom.

"Yeah." His expression said otherwise.

Amy lingered while he decided whether or not to say what was obviously on his mind.

After another prolonged silence, he nodded and mumbled, "Thanks." He gave them each a look of poignant intensity. "Both of you." With that, he turned and left.

He didn't get farther than the bank of elevators at the other end of the hall. One of the doors slid open and Peggy stepped out. He was surprised.

"Hi," he said for lack of anything better to say. The remoteness that had chilled her expression for weeks was intact and in place.

She rolled her lips in over her teeth before asking, "How's Mom?"

"Pretty good, considering."

Like casual acquaintances, they went through the standard array of polite questions peculiar to instances like these and the typical, equally polite answers. It was all said in under thirty seconds.

"I'll go in and see her," Peggy concluded.

She was five feet away before he could think to call out to her. "Peg?"

She turned back, like Claire, giving nothing except painfully restrained condemnation.

"Before you go in, can we—" He gestured to nowhere in particular. "Can we, uh, talk?"

"I don't know. Can we?"

He had thought dealing with his sisters had been bad. It was nothing compared to what he knew he would face with Peggy. "I'd like to try." If she was still willing to listen. There was no guarantee that she would—or have anything to do with him, for that matter. And he couldn't blame her.

Thankfully, she nodded and they eventually ended up in a corner booth of the hospital's cafeteria. It wasn't as private as he would have liked, but it was the best available at the moment, and he didn't want to put this off any longer. And yet, he didn't know how to start.

"I don't know where to start. This is pretty hard for me."

"The only thing I've ever known to be hard for you, Mark, is admitting you're wrong. Is that what this is about?"

Claire and Amy had restrained the worst of their feelings. Not so Peg. Her voice may have been hushed, but it was underscored with wrath.

"It's about a lot of things."

"I can well imagine." She leaned back, her head tilted to an intrinsically defensive angle. "Why don't I make this easier on you? I think you should move out."

His breath literally stopped in his lungs. "What?"

"I know this is the worst time to tell you, but I want you to move out of the house." Her eyelids flinched. "It would be best for the kids."

"What about us?" The words were instant and involuntary, and he regretted them at once. Shoving his elbows onto the table he gripped his head in both hands. "Don't say it, please." He didn't think he could bear to hear her recount every reason why there was no *us*.

"What would you have me say, then?"

"I don't know." Dropping his hands to the table, he repeated, "I honest to God don't know, Peg. I realize I've messed up—badly—but I don't know how to fix things." He felt like a stranger to himself: alien, rudderless. The past seemed like a lie; the future, a frightening unknown. The sense of emptiness was devastating. No identity, no direction. No family. He had nothing. He was nothing.

Everything of any worth left within him crumbled, and he broke into silent sobs. He didn't even think to care that he was in a public place, with people coming and going. It just didn't matter. With head bowed, hands lying limply on the table, he cried like a little boy, alone in a grief of his own making.

"Mark." Peg's whisper was accompanied by the touch of her hand slipping into his. He grasped the slender fingers with frantic need, so desperately grateful for that simple contact, the tears came harder. It was the single most humbling experience of his life.

Odd that at that moment he should be able to recognize rock bottom for what it was. Odder still was that it was strangely cathartic, as if now that he had reached this point, he wouldn't have to fear it again. Maybe knowing this was what gave him the strength to lift his head and face Peg squarely.

Her expression was a revelation. He had expected the same distant chill, and yes, it was there, but so were sympathy and concern, mixed right in with the tears in her eyes.

"Is it all gone, Peg?"

Raising one shoulder, she shook her head. "I don't know. It's up to you."

It was. He alone was responsible for putting his life, and hers, back together. "I, uh, I have a lot of problems I need to work out."

"I know. And it's been more than your mother's affair."

"How did you know?" He had only come to that realization in the early hours of the morning, while he stood at the foot of his mother's hospital bed.

"I've seen it coming for months. You haven't been happy."

For some reason, it was tough to admit that. In the end, he forced himself to. "You're right; I haven't been happy. And I've taken it out on you."

"And your mother and sisters."

"Yeah."

"Which is another reason you should move out." At his questioning look, she explained gently, "If you can't be happy with yourself, Mark, you'll never be happy with anyone else." Her fingers tightened on his. "You need counseling."

Defeat lay in that admission—a sense that he wasn't capable enough or strong enough to help himself. He ground his eyes shut, wishing like hell that his stay at rock bottom would end.

Lifting his eyes to hers, he nodded. "Okay. You're right."

Peggy smiled. For the first time in so long he couldn't remember, she actually smiled at him with genuine pleasure.

"What should we tell the kids?" he asked.

"The truth: that you have some problems you need to work on and you have to do that by yourself."

"It'll be hard on them."

"Of course it will." The acerbity was back in her voice. "But so have these last months. Do you think your behavior hasn't affected them? I won't let them live like that any longer." Her tone gentled. "They'll understand, Mark. And I'll help you in any way I can."

Which was more than he deserved. Cautiously he said, "I know I've hurt you." He watched her expression close up, her gaze drop to their clasped hands, then slowly rise to meet his once more. "I'll understand if you can't forgive me."

She took the time to breathe deeply before saying, "It's going to take time." Another pause. "I can't be sure that we'll ever have what we had before, that our marriage will be the same. I don't see how it can be, but that might be for the best. What we had obviously wasn't strong enough to survive. We'll just have to work it out."

She said *we*. So simple a word, and yet it gave him everything that mattered; it gave him hope.

Chapter Twenty-Four

"Got a minute?" Claire stood in the doorway of John's office, comfortable in her professional persona.

"Claire, what are you doing here at this hour?"

The bank wasn't due to open for another forty minutes. She had purposely arrived early. "I wanted to talk to you, in private if we could."

He settled back in his chair behind his desk. "Sure." He glanced to the lobby behind her.

"We're alone." Her smile was touched by sadness. "Don't worry," she added, taking a seat opposite him.

"How's your mother?"

It was nice of him to ask. But then, there had never been any doubt that John was a nice man. "She's making a great recovery from surgery. The damage from the stroke will take more time, but we're all hopeful. She'll be released into rehab at the end of the week."

She had talked to Dr. Jamal as she'd intended. Armed with the doctor's advice, she had discussed the matter of a nursing facility with Amy and Mark. And it had been a true discussion. Mark hadn't pulled rank; Amy had contributed her opinions; but most important, Claire had felt like an equal, confident as she had been so few times in her life.

"Amy's handling all the details." Which pleased Claire immensely. The responsibilities were balanced and shared. Better yet was that she didn't feel threatened by Mark's or Amy's involvement.

She honestly didn't feel threatened by much these days. It dawned on her that she had gotten a backbone somewhere in the past few months— not a false sense of strength born of rebellion, but a true sense of purpose.

"I don't know if there's a right or wrong way to say what I have to say," she began, adjusting her shoulders into a more comfortable position. "So if I mess up, bear with me."

"This sounds serious." John's sandy brows angled severely. "Don't tell me you're thinking of quitting. I don't want to hear that, Claire."

"No, this has nothing to do with my job, although you might want to fire me after you hear what I have to say." Pausing for a steadying breath, she said, "I think it might . . ." Stopping, she collected her thoughts, rephrasing her words in order for them to sound exactly as she wished. "It would be best if we didn't see each other any more."

The news stopped him for a few seconds; his face gave him away. "Why?"

"Because," she sighed, gently drawing the word out, "I want more from a relationship than you're willing to give." Until now, she had been content with scraps of affection and sex, but she needed more. She *deserved* more.

What a revelation that was. Sometime in the middle of the night, she had lain in bed knowing she was going to end her affair, and why. But justification had come as a complete surprise. All her life, she had lived with a feeling that she wasn't as good or as strong and, therefore, less deserving. What a shock to suddenly realize she didn't have to settle for less in life.

"I'm sorry, Claire."

She had to smile. He was looking extremely uncomfortable. "There's no need. I knew what I was getting into from the start. I thought I could be happy with what we had." A superficial relationship. "But I'm not." Yes, she wanted the sex, and the friendship and laughter, but she wanted the commitment, too, the kind she had had with Dan. The kind her parents had had. "This isn't your fault. Or mine either. We just want different things."

"Have I done anything to upset you?"

"No." He had disappointed her, and he wasn't to blame. He had always been honest with her. "Please, don't think that. You've been wonderful." All that he was capable of being with her. It simply wasn't enough. Again, that wasn't his fault.

"So have you." He gave her one of his gentle smiles, one she wished could have been underscored with love. "You really have been wonderful."

"Am I supposed to say thank you?" she laughed.

"I don't know."

Still clinging to her smile, she said, "I'll understand if you want to fire me."

"Why would I want to do that?" He had all the appearance of an astonished man.

"Well, I just dumped you. You could be mad at me."

"I could." He openly contemplated the choice with narrowed eyes. "I won't say my pride and ego aren't dented, but I'm not going to let my personal feelings interfere with a business decision. You're damn good at what you do around here. I would hate like hell to lose you." His tone mellowed. "Besides, I like you."

"I like you, too," she returned, glad she wouldn't have to find another job, even gladder that she and John could remain friends.

"Is this going to get maudlin?"

"No. I promise." She stood, feeling good about what she was doing, about herself, and gave him a parting smile that reflected an inner peace. The feeling was too new for her to ignore.

Her life wasn't perfect. She had as many problems as the next person—a sick mother, fences to mend with her brother and sister, children to reassure and raise into adulthood, a job that at times was aggravating—but it was her life and she was going to rely on herself to make the most of it.

Even if she wanted to go back to the old Claire, which she didn't, the family structure on which she had so heavily relied was gone. She didn't know what it was now, or what it would be in the future. Regardless, she was prepared to welcome its presence, but it was from herself alone that she would draw the strength to live.

Getting Mom settled in Merryview Rehabilitation Center was relatively painless, or as free of hitches, Amy thought, as any move could be. She and Mark saw to getting Mom discharged from the hospital. Claire met up with them at Merryview.

The facility was on the James River in a quiet section of Newport News. Carefully tended green lawns and paved pathways led down to the river. Artistic landscaping would insure shade through the rest of the summer, colorful leaves in the fall, and lots of blooms next spring. If Mom was here that long. Dr. Jamal had given them a timetable for recovery, but it was by no means set in stone. A great deal depended on Mom.

Turning away from the scene out the window, Amy gave her full attention to her mother as a nurse and an orderly went about getting Mom fully situated in her bed. It had been more than two weeks since her stroke. She still looked frail, lying immobile, her face drawn, a smaller bandage covering the incision high on her forehead. For all of that, though, her eyes were free of the fear and hopelessness that had glazed them weeks ago.

Determination glinted from those beloved eyes now. Mom certainly was not pleased to be where she was, but she would tolerate it because she understood that she had no other choice if she was going to be herself again. She was a fighter; she wasn't one to let a stroke, or anything else, defeat her.

In only one matter could Amy refute that: Mark's rejection. That had brought their mother as close to giving up as Amy had ever thought to see. She was glad mother and son had made peace with each other.

Oh, there had been no grand proclamation on Mark's part. He had not arranged for a special time in which he could be alone with his mother so that he could apologize or bare his soul. In fact, to Amy's knowledge, he never visited Mom by

himself. Someone was always with him: either her,
Claire, or Peggy, or even his children.

Obviously, he thought he needed a buffer. Amy
could live with that because, little by little, day by
day, his quiet, steady presence had accomplished
what an outright apology would have: it had
bridged the gulf between mother and son.

That wasn't to say that Mom and Mark were as
close as they had once been. Amy couldn't put her
finger on precisely where the relationship stood.
It wasn't strained, but neither was it as open and
relaxed as before, and Mom's inability to speak
had nothing to do with it. Amy was amazed how
well their mother could make herself understood
with a single harsh look or a tender squeeze of her
left hand.

No, wherever her brother and mother were in
regard to each other, it was definitely different,
but, Amy sensed, more honest. With nothing to
hide from each other, they were forging a new
bond. A work in progress, Amy liked to think, much
like what was going on between her and Mark and
Claire.

She shifted her gaze to her sister. If Amy had to
assign colors to the state of affairs between her
and Claire, she would have chosen beige with an
occasional accent of blue. No bright lights of anger,
no blazing highs and lows that made her think
of resentments or jealousies, no temperamental
flashes of crimson. Just a steady flow of a pleasing
neutral that every now and then edged toward comfort.

Definitely another work in progress, and an original to boot. They were friends as well as sisters,
but that friendship had always been underscored
with tension and sometimes strife. This sense of

satisfaction was unique for them, and Amy liked it even though she didn't know where it would take them.

Bittersweet green, on the other hand, typified things for her and Mark. She sighed as she looked to him, seated facing their mother's bed, and added a jarring shade of orange to the color scheme. He was in such transition that on most days he struggled to be at peace with himself, let alone with her.

He had moved out of his house, which saddened her. Peggy had pushed for it, and to Amy's surprise, Mark had defended Peggy's decision. As he put it, he "needed to find out who the hell he was." For too long, he had thought he was their father, and that wasn't healthy for him, or fair to those who loved him.

He hadn't said as much, but Amy suspected he was seeing a therapist. It would certainly account for his regular absences from the office three afternoons a week. And for the outward signs of growth. His willingness to let her and Claire arrange for Mom's rehab was just one of many.

There was no way to pick colors for Claire and Mark. Neither had chosen to confide all the nitty-gritty details to Amy as they once would have, so she couldn't assign colors with any accuracy. She would have been blind, though, not to see that black and white had been blended into a fine shade of gray.

The good thing about gray, she mused, was that it was so easily adaptable. It accepted the harmony of blue as easily as the discord of red. And pushed far enough, it could leave its neutrality behind and emerge as a color all its own, one that didn't exist on any spectrum but was real nonetheless.

With the nurse and orderly gone, Amy sat on the foot of the bed and embraced all the colors that comprised the Chandlers. The mélange was muddy right now, but in time and with effort, the colors would sort themselves out into a fresh and enduring painting. She would have to wait patiently for the end result.

Not so easy to abide was her own personal sense of transparency. No colors, no contrasts, no depths—nothing. It had been like that until a few days ago, when she had begun to feel the scarlets and cobalts begin to seep in again.

Reaching out, she laid a hand on her mother's foot. "Mom, I need to get going."

Ellen gave her best attempt at a one-sided smile. "Mark and Claire will be here with you for a while longer." Habit braced her for a barrage of questions from her siblings, but the intrusive queries, routine a few months ago, remained unspoken. It took her a second or two to realize that this was more of the new Chandler family interaction. They didn't have to know each other's every move. They didn't have the right to expect constant, absolute, self-sacrificing devotion from each other. They were a family unit, but they were individuals who were each entitled to lives independent of each other.

As healthy as she knew the outlook to be, however, she still struggled within herself. Old habits were hard to break. She had to remind herself that she had been at Mom's side since seven that morning and it was now going on two. She wasn't abandoning anyone.

Mark did ask, "Will I see you later in the office?"

He could have been checking up on her. She chose not to think so. "Probably not. Why?"

"There's a new account that I want you to look at."

"Will tomorrow morning be all right?"

"Do I have a choice?"

"No."

Shrugging, he accepted the inevitable with good grace. "All right."

"We'll be fine," Claire said.

That it should be Claire offering reassurance struck Amy with humor. "I know."

She walked into the ER at Commonwealth feeling so nervous, she could have easily been admitted for high blood pressure. Not only had she never come here to see Seth for personal reasons; she was very much afraid of what her reception might be.

"Is Dr. Donovan available?" she asked the nurse at the triage desk.

"He's with a patient right now. Can I help you?"

"No. I'm a friend of his and I need to speak to him."

She was directed to wait, and assured that Dr. Donovan would be told she wished to see him.

More waiting. Biding her time had never been her strong suit. In the last months, she had been forced to pause and linger and, in some ways, come to a complete stop. She had tolerated it because it had been necessary, and in that she had grown as a person, but frankly she was sick to death of putting her life on hold. And she was bitterly sorry that she had forced Seth to do the same.

"Amy."

She looked up from the magazine lying closed in her lap, nervous all over again at the sight of him in surgical greens. "Hi." She tossed the magazine onto the end table. "I'm sorry to bother you here, but I needed to talk to you." She glanced left and right and then swept the area behind him. "Is this a bad time?"

"No. Come on."

He led her past the nurses station to the doctor's lounge behind, and shut the door. "Is everything all right with your mom?"

"Oh, yes, she's settled in." Standing in the middle of the room, she had to consciously keep from twisting her fingers together. Quietly, slowly, she said, "I didn't come here to talk about her. I came to talk about us. If you'd rather not discuss this here, I understand. We can arrange to meet later."

She couldn't read his face; he was wearing his doctor's facade. "Why don't you sit down," he suggested, indicating one of the chairs.

"No, I don't think I can." On a sick smile she explained, "I think I'm too nervous to sit."

"Why are you nervous?" His tone was doctor-to-patient.

Abruptly, she decided to sit, and shoved her hands in between her tightly clasped knees. "I haven't been fair to you. I've made your life difficult. You have every right to be angry with me."

"Who says I've been angry?"

He was giving nothing away while she had her guts spilled all over the room. "You have been, Seth; we both know it, and I don't blame you at all. I hurt you." And she deeply regretted that. "I'm so sorry."

All he did was nod, then rub at one eye behind the lens of his glasses. That done, he braced his hands on his waist and silently stared at her. She felt like a bug under a microscope.

She came to her feet, hitching her purse strap over her shoulder. "Maybe this wasn't such a good idea. Maybe we can talk on the phone or something."

For the first time, there was a flicker of emotion in his expression. "Calm down, Amy."

"I can't. I . . . I feel so awful about what I've done, and there's so much I need to say." And she could feel herself falling apart.

"Then say what you have to say."

With a gallant effort, she collected herself. "It isn't that easy. I don't know how you feel about me."

"What would you have me say?"

Unable to control the nervous laughter, she answered, "That you still love me." Laughter died; tears rose. "That you forgive me for screwing up our relationship, that you still want to marry me. Then I'd be able to tell you that I love you, that I finally have my life together, that I would marry you right now if you still wanted me."

What little she could see through her tears was a blur, but it was enough for her to see him close the distance between them. "It's about damn time," he muttered before wrapping her in his arms.

She hung on with all her might, up on tiptoe, her arms clinging to his shoulders. The urge to laugh and cry at the same time was overwhelming, and she would have surrendered to both had it not been for the exquisite feeling of having just found her way home. "I've missed you," she mumbled into his shirt.

"Good."

Laughter won out.

"You've put me through hell," he told her, his

doctor's hands reacquainting themselves with the lines and curves of her back.

"I know and I'm sorry. It's all been such a mess." The doctor's hands became those of a lover and cupped her behind. "As long as you love me and want to marry me, that's all that matters."

Chapter Twenty-Five

"It's the funniest thing I've ever seen," Melody laughed. "Dad's a nervous wreck."

Amy looked up from where she sat in front of the vanity mirror, ignoring the bustle of activity going on around her in the small room at the far end of the church. "Your father never gets nervous."

"That's because he doesn't like, you know, get married every day."

"True."

"It's so cool to see him pacing."

"He's pacing?" Amy couldn't picture that. Seth was the most composed, unruffled person she had ever met. He thrived on stress and emergencies. She smiled in gleeful humor, finding it wonderfully endearing that after impatiently chafing for ten months for this wedding to occur, Seth was suddenly hit with a case of nerves.

Ten months. The time had slipped by in what now felt like a whirl.

"Hey, here come the flowers," Melody announced.

Amy watched her soon-to-be stepdaughter dance her way across the room to intercept the florist. In her navy blue bridesmaid gown, she looked beautiful.

"I'll see if I can keep a lid on her," Barbara laughed. In a gown to match Melody's, she looked striking.

"It's about time the flowers got here," Claire said, slipping up to fool with the back of Amy's veil. "I was beginning to get worried."

Amy reached up to pat her sister's hand, knowing that if Claire didn't have one thing to worry about, it would be another. Last night at the rehearsal dinner it had been over who was going to bring their mother to the wedding. One of Mom's sisters had gladly volunteered, not in the least bit fazed that Ellen wasn't nearly as mobile as she had once been.

After ten months of rehab, Ellen was at home again, managing with the help of assisted-living nursing care. She had full use of her voice and arm, but her leg would most likely never regain complete mobility. She walked with difficulty and with the aid of a cane. Driving was out.

Still, Amy was thankful for the remarkable recovery. "Have Bethany and Mike already staked out their pew?" she asked.

Claire met her gaze in the mirror. "No, actually, they're not here yet."

That surprised her. "Who's bringing them?"

Claire's gaze slipped away before returning. "A friend of mine."

Something in Claire's tone made Amy tilt her head to one side in speculation. She didn't say anything, though, didn't pry as she once would have. And Claire didn't offer much other than, "His name is Allen. I hope you don't mind me asking him to the wedding. It was all very last-minute, very casual."

"No, that's fine with me." However, she didn't believe that Claire's decision was all that "casual." Claire had to feel extremely comfortable with someone before she would ever entrust her children to that person. As restrained as Claire was when it came to men, she had to have been seeing this Allen for some time. And she had kept quiet about it. This was the first hint Amy had that there was a man in Claire's life.

"Do the kids like him?" she asked, her voice low and filled with quiet understanding.

Again Claire met her gaze in the mirror. "He's good for them."

And for Claire, too, no doubt. She seemed more at peace with herself and certainly more confident, to the extent that she had forged a new relationship on her own, without the support of the very people on whom she had once relied so heavily.

"Here are your flowers." Melody delivered words and bouquet to Claire at the same time, then paused for a dramatic sigh. "I love your dress. It's so cool."

Claire laughed. "I've never been a matron of honor before."

"Well, you definitely look cool."

"You both do," Amy said, liking the blend of Melody's navy with Claire's sapphire. No wimpy pastels for this wedding. She had decided on colors as vibrant as those of her internal palette.

Not a day went by that she didn't send up a prayer of thanks that the colors of life had been restored to her. Perhaps some of the hues were gone now, erased by the changes in her life. But in their places were new colors, just as powerful, just as meaningful.

The photographer stepped near. "We need to get a family shot."

"We can't do that yet," Claire explained. "Our brother isn't here."

"Yes, he is," Barbara said, joining the group.

"Yeah," Melody confirmed. "I poked my head out the door a minute ago and I saw him come in with Mrs. Chandler."

Amy exchanged a quick look with Claire. "His wife or our mother?"

"Oh, his wife, definitely. I think it's so cool that old people still hold hands."

Amy could not contain her surprise. It had been a long, tough road for Mark and Peggy. There had been days when he was barely approachable, and times when Amy had been sure Peggy was ready to throw in the towel. They had struggled through the holidays for the sake of their children, but to Amy's thinking, it had been an uncomfortable, strained disaster whose effects had been felt by all.

He was still living in an apartment, still in private counseling as well as marriage counseling with Peggy. Amy had to give him credit for doing his utmost to salvage his marriage. His efforts, apparently, were paying off if he was indeed holding hands with Peggy once again.

"Oh, there's the music!" Melody trilled in excitement. "Is that our cue to get ready?"

It was. Melody was first in line, Barbara next, and Claire behind her. Mark was at her side to escort her down the aisle. That was the way it ought to be, Amy thought, the way she wanted it to be: the blending of new and old family members.

Waiting for her at the altar was Seth, waiting to begin their life together, to forge a bond through love and marriage and the creation of their own personal family.

Hiding her secret smile, she placed a hand low on her belly. She and Seth had been spontaneous once too often. She couldn't be happier. In fact she found it quite lovely that this baby, only six weeks along in the making, should be present on the day its new family was being created.

She carried her happiness down the aisle, like a treasured heirloom to be carefully tended now and for all the years to come.